T0130163

SILENCED IN SEQUINS

Another cold gust of wind hit Kelly, and she muttered a curse. It was freaking cold, and she was trying to get an audience with Diana Delacourte rather than being inside her boutique where it was nice and warm.

She found the website. She stopped walking and tapped on the menu. A passing bird overhead caught Kelly's attention, and she looked up. The bird flew out of sight into a thicket of trees. But a glimmer of silver in the snow caught her eye. She took a few steps to get a closer look. It was fabric.

A scarf?

She propelled herself forward and realized it was a wrap. The same wrap she saw Diana with last night at the party.

What was it doing outside?

She reached forward to snatch up the fabric when she noticed a lone silver stiletto shoe.

She fretted her lower lip and craned her neck forward as if to get a sneak peek of what lay ahead. God, she hoped she would find the silvery sequined dress. Maybe Diana had done a striptease out in the cold, snowy night. Kind of like those people who belonged to a polar bear club and dove into freezing ocean water.

That was it. Diana was a polar bear stripper.

Kelly's gaze swept the landscape, and when it settled on what she'd hope not to find, her body shivered, and not because of the cold. It was because she'd just discovered Diana wasn't a polar bear stripper.

No, Diana Delacourte was dead . . .

Also by Debra Sennefelder

Silenced in Sequins

Debra Sennefelder

LYRICAL UNDERGROUND
Kensington Publishing Corp.
www.kensingtonbooks.com

LYRICAL UNDERGROUND BOOKS are published by

Kensington Publishing Corp.
119 West 40th Street
New York, NY 10018

All Kensington titles, imprints, and distributed lines are available at special quantity discounts for bulk purchases for sales promotion, premiums, fundraising, educational, or institutional use.

Special book excerpts or customized printings can also be created to fit specific needs. For details, write or phone the office of the Kensington Sales Manager: Kensington Publishing Corp., 119 West 40th Street, New York, NY 10018. Attn. Sales Department. Phone: 1-800-221-2647.

Lyrical Underground and Lyrical Underground logo Reg. US Pat. & TM Off.

First Electronic Edition: January 2020
ISBN-13: 978-1-5161-0894-7 (ebook)
ISBN-10: 1-5161-0894-9 (ebook)

First Print Edition: January 2020
ISBN-13: 978-1-5161-0897-8
ISBN-10: 1-5161-0897-3

Printed in the United States of America

For my niece Jennifer Confield, whose grace and strength are inspiring.

Chapter One

It's so beautiful.

It wasn't every day a gal from Lucky Cove, New York, was in the presence of a Gucci dress.

When Kelly Quinn first laid eyes on the halter-neckline black cocktail dress, her breath caught. The body-conscious garment was expertly constructed, and its faux tortoiseshell ring at the back of the neck was elegant.

She swiped the dress one last time with a lint roller to prepare for its photo session. She then gave the dress a gentle tug, and it draped perfectly on the mannequin.

Exquisite.

Of course it was. It was an authentic Gucci cocktail dress that would've cost her a month's rent back in New York City. Now it was consigned to her boutique, the Lucky Cove Resale Boutique, for sale.

She set the lint roller down and picked up her camera and snapped a flurry of photographs. She wanted shots from all angles of the dress, including a close-up of the MADE IN ITALY label.

The windfall of the Gucci dress, plus seven other designer garments consigned last week, prompted her to give herself a crash course in not only photography but also how to set up an account on MineNowYours. com, a mega resale website where she could sell the dresses and earn a decent commission.

The "oh my god, finally a designer dress" moment she'd been dreaming of since taking over the business had come to a grinding halt when she checked the label. The dress was a size two. All the dresses were a size two. In the two months she'd been running the boutique, she'd learned the number of customers who frequented the store that were a size two were few.

She did her best to hide her disappointment. She seriously couldn't believe she was looking at a Gucci and feeling disappointed. It made no sense to her. The consignor, Wendy Johnson, couldn't help if she was a svelte size two, thanks to her excessive exercising, constant dieting, and many trips to New York's premier plastic surgeon.

Kelly didn't know such intimate details of the lives of her other consignment clients. But every week her new employee, Breena Collins, gave her updates on Wendy's life, thanks to the latest episode of *Long Island Ladies*.

In some office building in midtown Manhattan, a group of television people got together and whipped up a reality show about a half-dozen spoiled, pampered, and wealthy housewives on Long Island.

How could it not be a hit?

Long Island had it all—mansions, expensive toys like yachts, endless stretches of beach, and the biggest playground for the most wealthy, the Hamptons.

Lucky Cove was tucked along the coast and attracted weary summer weekenders from the city looking for a charming main street, quiet roads, and a stretch of undisturbed beach. The quaintness of the town was what Long Island getaways used to be for city dwellers. Before the rise of cell phone videos, selfies gone wild, and reality television.

Kelly had enough drama in her life, thank you very much. So when the fashion gods gave her the designer dresses she'd been praying for, she needed to laser focus and decide how she'd sell the garments for the best price. She couldn't get sidetracked by Wendy's detailed description of each dress.

Yes, it was lovely that Wendy's personal shopper at Bergdorf Goodman knew her tastes. It was spectacular that her husband made reservations at the most exclusive restaurant on the island. And how grand it was that she wore one of the dresses the night she tossed a drink into the face of a fellow Long Island Lady.

None of which affected the price of the dress. The labels dictated the price, followed by the condition of the garment. Hence, Kelly's eagle eye as she inspected each one.

Kelly knew designer fashions, thanks to her previous job as an assistant fashion buyer. What she didn't know was how to authenticate designer items, and if she wanted to pursue designer fashions and accessories, she needed to learn how to spot the fakes. She couldn't hope to consign and sell a Hermès bag if she couldn't prove beyond any doubt that it was the real deal.

Not too many designer items were coming into the boutique at the moment, but she hoped to change that, and with these new acquisitions, she could be actively consigning luxury items soon.

Kelly set down her camera. She turned the mannequin to get photographs of the back of the dress. She smoothed the dress one more time and picked up her camera.

She yawned.

Between setting up the Mine Now Yours account and sending out newsletters, there was Thanksgiving, and last night she'd stayed way too late at her sister's house and eaten way too much. She yawned again. It seemed the turkey coma carried over to the next day.

Up an hour earlier than normal, she wanted to photograph all the cocktail dresses before she opened the boutique. Black Friday for brick-and-mortar stores wasn't what it used to be, but she had no idea of what the day looked like for a consignment shop.

As her granny used to say, "You live and learn."

The advice wasn't very reassuring, but it was all she had at the moment.

She bought advertising in local newspapers; pulled out every visual display trick she'd learned in fashion school and at Bishop's and dressed up the window; and e-mailed her anemic mailing list. She then said a prayer to the fashion gods.

Kelly adjusted the elastic waistband of her leggings—her best fashion friend after a day of indulging turkey and all the trimmings. She smoothed her plum-colored sweater tunic—more camouflage—and another yawn escaped her lips.

"Hey, what are you doing?" Breena Collins appeared in the doorway holding a tray of coffees and pastries from Doug's Variety Store, where she also worked part-time.

Kelly lowered her camera and turned toward Breena's voice, then stared at the sight of her friend and coworker. She was still getting used to her former high-school classmate's bright new hair color.

The petite redhead bustled into the photography studio. It sounded so much more professional than it was.

On a tight budget, Kelly had purchased three umbrella lights online and a vintage floor vinyl backdrop to make the photos look as good as possible. Yes, the dresses were designer, and while they didn't carry their four-figure price tags any longer, they wouldn't be cheap either.

"I wish I could afford one of her dresses. It would be so cool to own a dress from Wendy Johnson."

Kelly arched an eyebrow. She wondered just how much weight Wendy's named carried. While she couldn't reveal the consignor when she put the items up for sale, maybe someone would recognize the floral, sleeveless Zac Posen dress from the infamous drink-toss-in-the-face episode of *LIL*, everyone's shorthand for *Long Island Ladies*.

"Too bad we don't have a layaway plan, huh?" Kelly set her camera down on the small round table, where she had collected a basket of tools of the trade—lint roller, binder clips, seam ripper, and small scissors. She took a coffee from the tray.

Breena nodded. "How was your Thanksgiving?"

"Good. Caroline's fiancé was there with his family." It was the first holiday Kelly had spent with her estranged sister in years. After a tragic accident ten years earlier, Kelly and her sister had drifted apart. The divide between them got wider and deeper, to the point where they eventually just became little more than acquaintances. The bright side to Kelly's unforeseen inheritance was the chance to rebuild her relationship with Caroline.

"Good to hear. My parents had a houseful too. I'd like to know when my adult brothers will grow up." Breena set the tray on the table and then drifted to the rolling rack, where the rest of Wendy Johnson's consigned dresses hung.

"I don't think they ever grow up." Kelly took a drink of coffee. Unofficially, the autumn season was over, and all things were turning festive. Doug's Variety Store now served its annual Holly Jolly coffee brew. The aroma was robust, and hints of cinnamon and nutmeg mingled together in every sip.

Breena pulled a sequined gown from the rack and dashed over to the narrow full-length mirror. She held it up against herself and gazed at her reflection.

"Va va boom!" She had the full bust to work the deep V-neck of the gown. In fact, she had all the right curves to work the dress. What Breena didn't have was the height. Wendy Johnson was at least five-feet-seven, give an inch or two.

"I don't remember her wearing this dress on the show." Breena spun around, still holding the dress against her body, and faced Kelly. "I love it. I can see me entering the party now; all eyes turn on me as I strut in, leaving all the guys drooling."

"Yes, they would be." Kelly walked to Breena and held out her hand. "How about envisioning yourself straightening up the displays?"

Breena frowned. "Buzzkill." She handed the dress to Kelly, swooped up the tray of coffee and pastries, and dashed out of the photography studio. Kelly extended her arm to look at the dress. It wasn't designer like the other dresses. Actually, it looked more prom than posh. While it wouldn't fetch a high three-figure price, it would sell fast if she priced it right. She gathered the other hanging dresses, along with the silver-sequined gown, and hauled them out to the sales counter, where she attached price tags. She'd come back for the Gucci dress. She still had to figure out its price.

Kelly carried an armful of Wendy's dresses out of the photo studio. Pepper Donovan, not only a longtime employee of the boutique but also Kelly's grandmother's best friend, stood behind the counter, reviewing the weekend's marketing plan.

Kelly realized putting together an official marketing plan was a bit fussy for a small consignment shop, but the document helped her stay organized and focused. She had a lot to juggle. She was gaining inventory, tackling minor remodeling in the upstairs apartment where she now lived, working the sales floor, and writing articles for the fashion website BudgetChic.com.

As she approached the counter, Pepper lifted her chin and, over her reading glasses, gave Kelly the "Pepper glare." Kelly had been on the receiving end of that look since the day she took over the business and implemented her changes.

One change Kelly made had her butting heads with Pepper for days. When Kelly's granny converted the first floor of her colonial-style house into a retail shop, she was working on a shoestring budget, so she didn't have money to take down walls, resulting in a choppy layout for her shop. Over time, she got the funds for an addition to sell home accents, which Kelly liquidated, due to the low turnover of the merchandise, expanding the accessory and shoe inventory into that space. Pepper had fought to keep the home accents but eventually saw Kelly's vision.

Her acceptance of the changes wasn't limited to the shop. She'd given herself a makeover a few weeks earlier. Pepper's color-treated, shoulder-length blond hair was styled in soft waves, and she'd expertly applied a smoky eye and added just the right amount of rose-colored gloss to her thinning lips. For what would hopefully be a busy day, she chose a pair of olive-colored velvet pants and a white button-down shirt topped with a cream pullover sweater. Peeking out from under the collar of the shirt was a sparkly necklace. Pepper managed to make all the right fashion choices for a woman in her mid-sixties. She looked neither too young nor too desperate to hang onto her youth. She just looked great.

Except for the Pepper glare.

"What? It's only one page." Kelly dropped the dresses onto the counter. The mini snowmen lined up along the counter didn't escape her notice. On Wednesday afternoon, there had been mini pumpkins. She was impressed with how quickly Pepper had changed out the decorations and how serious she was about holiday themes.

"Seems a little formal, don't you think?" Pepper sorted through the dresses. "Are these in the computer?"

Kelly nodded. One of her first tasks was to update the inventory system. Granny and Pepper had been manually tracking inventory. Over the past few years, the system had become too chaotic to manage, and it left Kelly with a big mess. She sourced a new inventory system and had it installed in time for the kickoff of the busiest shopping season of the year.

Well, she hoped it was the busiest shopping season for consignment stores because she needed an infusion of cash to keep the business afloat.

"Yes, they've been added to the inventory. Can you print out the price tags and put these dresses out on the floor? I think this silvery sequin dress should be on a mannequin. There's a pair of shoes and clutch I think will look great with the dress."

"Okay. I'll take care of that now while you unlock the door. It's time to open." Pepper shifted over to the new computer that had been added to the sales counter area and proceeded to print out the price tags.

Kelly passed Breena, who was busy refolding a stack of sweaters. Her stride to the front door was purposeful. She'd been looking forward to Black Friday for weeks. Back in the city, the day was a blur of activity. She'd spent as much time as she could on the sales floor at Bishop's to help out the staff.

She unlocked the door and flipped the CLOSED sign to OPEN while wondering if she'd get the same rush of excitement from her own clothing boutique this Black Friday.

She pulled open the door and greeted the woman standing out in the cold. Their first customer of the day.

"Good morning. Welcome to the Lucky Cove Resale Boutique." Kelly stepped aside, and the customer entered.

Throughout the day, business was steady, but not the retail frenzy she was accustomed to. With both Breena and Pepper working, she could duck into the staff room, a combination kitchen, break room, and office, and work on a new article for Budget Chic. Her editor had assigned her the topic of holiday looks under a hundred dollars. The article was due in less than a week. No pressure.

The first draft of the article was complete, with three inspirational outfits and links to budget-friendly websites when Liv Moretti appeared at the back door with lunch.

"How's business?" Liv set the tray of sandwiches and chips on the counter by the sink. She'd texted earlier and said she'd stop by because she needed a break from her family's bakery. Kelly had asked if she'd pick up some food at the deli. She wanted to treat Pepper and Breena to lunch since they'd worked hard getting the boutique ready for Black Friday.

Kelly couldn't believe it was lunchtime already. Where had the morning gone?

"Steady." Kelly eyed the bag of chips. Given her overeating yesterday and her need to wear leggings because of their elastic waistband, maybe she should pass on the chips. "How's it going at the bakery?"

Kelly stretched. After a week of moving all the merchandise and displays in what used to be the dining room in order to paint, sitting too long hunched over her laptop made her feel stiff. She'd love to go to a Pilates session; it always worked out her kinks, but the only studio in town was owned by her uncle's third wife, Summer. So she'd keep her kinks.

"Quiet, which is a good thing after the craziness of Wednesday. I'm officially sick of pumpkin pie." Liv picked up a wrapped sandwich and a bag of chips and walked to Kelly's desk. Her lip twitched. "Not really. I love pumpkin pie. It's just that we baked so many of them. Now it's on to Christmas cookies."

Kelly took her sandwich and chips. "Thank you."

"No problem. It's nice to get out for a bit. Are you working on your article for Budget Chic?"

Before Kelly could respond, the door to the staff room swung open, and Breena burst in.

"Oh. My. God. You won't believe who just bought a dress! She was right here! And me too! I was here when she was here!" Breena's words were rushed, and her arms flailed.

"Wow. Calm down." Kelly stood and walked over to her employee. "Who was here?"

"Yeah, who has you so flustered?" Liv moved back to the counter. "When you get a grip, your lunch is here."

Liv plucked out her sandwich and a bag of chips, which earned her a sideways look from Kelly. Liv worked in a bakery and had enjoyed a large Italian Thanksgiving the day before and thought nothing of eating chips. More proof that life wasn't fair.

"Diana Delacourte!" Breena shared after taking a deep breath.

Kelly and Liv shared a look and both asked, "Who?"

Breena rolled her eyes. "You two really don't watch *Long Island Ladies*? She's one of them. Or she was. The show fired her."

Kelly didn't care if Diana Delacourte was on television. What she cared about was the fact that she had purchased a dress and might have clothing to consign.

"What dress did she buy?" Liv asked, but before Breena could answer, Pepper appeared at the doorway.

"Great. Lunch is here. I'm starving. But it'll have to wait. A bunch of customers just came through the front door. I need some help out there." With that, Pepper disappeared.

Kelly's mood brightened. Maybe her marketing blitz was paying off.

"Do you mind putting our sandwiches in the fridge?' she asked Liv.

"No. Go on. I'll finish my lunch before heading back to the bakery. I see you have a new magazine here." She patted the glossy edition.

"Enjoy. And thanks again." Kelly walked out of the staff room with Breena.

"Don't forget, I'm picking you up tomorrow night for the party," Liv called out.

And just as fast as Kelly's mood had brightened, it dimmed.

Her uncle Ralph's annual holiday party was always held on the first Saturday after Thanksgiving, and since she was back in Lucky Cove, she had no good excuse not to attend.

"Fancy schmancy," Breena cooed.

"Not really." As Kelly urged Breena forward, she glanced over her shoulder at Liv.

"I know what you're thinking, Kell, and no, you can't get out of the party. You've already RSVP'd, and do you really want to deal with Summer? You know how she gets." Liv smiled and then picked up the magazine, flipped it open, and munched on a chip.

Kelly hated it when her best friend was right. If she bailed on the party, Summer would never let her hear the end of it. She stepped into the main sales area of the boutique and accepted the cold, hard fact that, while coming back home had its share of bright spots, there were also her uncle and aunt.

She glanced at the cocktail dresses Pepper had hung up earlier. Maybe there was a bright side to the party. She had a shimmering gold dress she'd gotten at a sample sale before losing her job at Bishop's, and it would be perfect to wear to her uncle's party.

Anyone who was anyone would attend the party, and those "anyones" had closets she'd love to get inside. She could fit a stack of business cards into her clutch.

Her mood brightened again.

The party could be fun. She'd have a little champagne and a few appetizers and network with the posh society of Lucky Cove. What could go wrong?

Chapter Two

Liv was right. Kelly deserved a little fun. She'd been working nonstop for months—everything from looking for a new job after being fired from Bishop's to taking over the boutique to freshening up her new apartment. The first downtime she'd had was Thanksgiving at Caroline's. Dinner with her sister was nice, but she still felt like she was on pins and needles. She didn't want to say or do anything to jeopardize the new relationship they were building.

"Quit fussing. You look great." Liv tugged on Kelly's arm to get her to move more quickly. The party had already started. The house was bathed in light and festive decorations.

Kelly tucked a lock of hair behind her ear. "I guess you're right."

She smiled. Since her best friend was driving, she could indulge in a drink or two, but she'd have to take it easy on the food. Her shapewear was doing double duty—holding her belly in and reminding her not to indulge too much. So worth the hundred bucks it cost.

She glanced at Liv, and a twinge of envy pricked her. Her friend wasn't bound and tortured by shapewear. Liv's one-shoulder navy crêpe gown was a showstopper. Its simplicity was striking, and its complex V-neckline with a cold shoulder-cap sleeve was intriguing. Liv had added stud earrings and run some product through her dark auburn pixie cut for a cool, messy vibe that complemented the minimalist tone of her gown.

"Where did you buy your dress?" Kelly asked.

"A small boutique in Chelsea, when I was there last month with my sisters. It cost way too much, but I had to have it. I figured I'd have an event to wear it to someday."

Kelly laughed. "Buy it and the invite will arrive."

"Exactly. Come on. Let's get inside." Liv started toward the paved walkway that led to the front door of the two-story, shingle-style house. Its asymmetrical façade, gambrel roofline, and welcoming covered entry gave the home a classic yet informal feel, and no doubt had cost her uncle a pretty penny.

A formally attired butler greeted them at the front door.

"Fancy," Kelly whispered as she entered the center hall of the house. Classical music drifted from the living room, and the din of conversation filled the space as guests gathered into small circles or threaded through to the other rooms open for the party.

"Does your uncle always hire a butler for the party?" Liv took a flute of champagne from a passing waiter and handed it to Kelly, then took a glass for herself.

Kelly shrugged. "I don't know. He wasn't hosting them before he married Summer."

"Well, then, I guess we can thank her for us rubbing elbows with the upper class of Long Island." Liv chuckled as she lifted her glass for a toast.

"Do we have to?" Ralph's third wife, a former model turned trophy wife and Pilates studio owner, rubbed Kelly the wrong way. Liv gave Kelly a look, and Kelly lifted her glass and tapped Liv's glass. "To Summer."

"Kelly, dear, you've finally arrived."

Kelly winced at Summer's voice. She gulped her champagne, and Liv's eyes bulged. The waiter passed by again, and Kelly swiftly traded out her empty glass for another full one. Before she could take a drink, Summer was behind her and squeezed her shoulders.

"Trying to be fashionably late?" Summer came into full view of Kelly.

Summer's silk crêpe georgette gown had bows on each shoulder and a slit so high up her lower body that it bordered on not-so-tasteful. The gown was both chic and effortless, and Summer looked stunning in it, with her blond hair gathered up into a sleek bun. At the base of her neck, a simple diamond pendant dangled and caught the light from the chandelier hanging above. She wore matching stud earrings and had blinged out both hands.

"You look amazing." Kelly meant it.

While she and her aunt didn't see eye to eye on many things, they both appreciated fashion. You'd think they could have built a bond based on their love for clothing and accessories.

"So do you." Summer appraised Kelly's dress and then leaned in. "Please tell me the dress didn't come from your thrift shop."

And there was the reason why, even with their shared love of fashion and encyclopedic knowledge of every major fashion designer in the industry, they couldn't bond.

"No, it didn't come from my boutique. I purchased it at a sample sale months ago." Kelly didn't owe Summer an explanation, and she should've said yes, the dress was secondhand and that her aunt needed to loosen up her bun.

"Kelly's right. Your dress is to die for, Summer," Liv interjected into the awkward silence that fell upon them.

Summer's gaze drifted over to Liv, and she smiled . . . well, as much as her injectables allowed. "Thank you, Liv. Your dress is beautiful."

Liv smiled and murmured a thank-you.

"I'm glad you both could make it." Summer shifted her attention back to her niece. It was odd being Summer's niece since they were so close in age. "Kelly, there's someone here tonight I'd like to introduce you to."

"There is?" Kelly took a drink of her champagne.

"His name is Tyler Madison, and he's a successful architect, and he's single." Summer's eyes twinkled with matchmaking, and she reached out to squeeze Kelly's arm. "He's a catch."

Kelly gulped the rest of her champagne and ignored Liv's warning look not to drink so much so fast.

"I told Tyler you own a boutique, not a thrift store," Summer said.

"It is a boutique," Kelly said.

Summer's head bobbed up and down. "See, you got it." Summer released her grip on Kelly's arm. "Oh, and please don't tell anyone you own a thrift store. Nobody wants to talk about used clothing at a party like this."

She took in a sweeping glance of the center hall, which was filled with guests in very festive moods.

Kelly frowned. She had a clutch full of business cards to hand out. Yes, at some level, she knew someone could consider it tacky, but she wanted to be ready to promote her struggling business if the topic came up.

Liv's neck craned as her gaze traveled into the living room. "Summer, is that Wendy Johnson from *Long Island Ladies*?"

Summer's eyes lit up, and she clapped her hands together. "Yes. Not only is Wendy here tonight, but so is Hugh McNeil, the show's producer, and his wife, Tracy."

"You're a fan of the show?" Kelly asked.

"Fan? I am. But . . ." Summer's glossy, plump lips pressed together, and her eyes widened. She looked like she was about to burst. "I'm going to remain calm." She took a deep breath. "I'm being considered for the open spot on the show. Me! I can't believe it."

"Really? You want to have a camera follow you around all day and record your every move and word?" Kelly asked.

"Yes, of course. Do you have any idea how much publicity it would bring my Pilates studio?" Summer's head turned toward the dining room. "Excuse me. I must get back to mingling. I'll introduce you to Tyler soon." Summer dashed away and inserted herself into a huddle of coiffed and bejeweled trophy wives. Her people.

Liv stepped closer to Kelly. "Wow. I don't think I've ever seen Summer so excited. Well, not since she had Juniper."

"I know. She seems to really want to be on the show. Hey, do you know Tyler what's his name?"

"No. But keep an open mind. You haven't been on a date since Mark. He's nice, you know."

"Yes, he is. There just wasn't any chemistry." Kelly turned her head quickly to avoid Liv seeing right through her lie. There had been a whole lot of chemistry between her and the hot lawyer, and it scared the daylights out of her. She had too much going on. Her life was still in upheaval, and the last thing she needed was a relationship. Especially a serious relationship with the brother of the police detective who had arrested Kelly last month. Had she known they were siblings, she wouldn't have gone out on the date. No, she needed to forget about Smokin' McHottie Lawyer. "Let's check out the appetizers."

"You're such a liar. I saw how you looked at him."

"This isn't up for discussion."

"Fine. Just remember that good guys are few and far between."

"Like Gabe?" Kelly challenged. A month ago, she'd realized her friend had a crush on Pepper's son and then noticed he had one on her too. "Maybe you should lead by example."

"I . . . I don't know what you're talking about." Liv spun around and walked into the living room.

"Yeah, right." Kelly followed, only to stop in her tracks. Her mouth gaped open. The room was decorated beyond belief. It looked as if the elves from the North Pole had been let loose with no supervision. From the towering Christmas trees to the life-size nutcrackers to freshly cut greenery fashioned into wreaths and swags, the house was beyond tricked out for the holiday.

Kelly grinned when her cousin came into view. The dress code was black tie, which meant a tuxedo and black tie for the male guests. Leave it to Frankie to put his own unique spin on the dress code. The shawl-collared tuxedo jacket was a slim fit that he wore effortlessly, and his black tuxedo pants had tapered legs. Where he added his own flair was ditching the boring tie and classic tuxedo shirt for a white crew-neck T-shirt. Kelly was confident Summer had freaked out at the sight of her stepson wearing a plain old T-shirt with his tuxedo. Her grin spread into a full-on smile, and that was when she caught his eye.

Frankie made his way through the guests to reach his cousin and Liv. After a round of hugs, they settled into people watching, and Kelly kept an eye out for food.

"You ladies look lovely tonight," Frankie said. "You know, my dad always goes overboard on this party, but this year he's taking it to a whole new level. He's trying to impress television producer Hugh McNeil and his wife, Tracy Sachs."

"They produce *Long Island Ladies*, and Summer is up for a spot on the show." Liv took a drink of her champagne.

Frankie pouted. "How do you know?"

"Sorry. Summer told us when we arrived." Kelly knew her cousin liked to be the one to share all the good gossip first, and Liv had just knocked the wind out of his sail.

Frankie sighed. "Well, did you know Tracy is looking to move her production company out here to the island so she doesn't have to commute from her Southampton home into the city?"

"Let me guess. All this over-the-top decorating and the butler has to do with landing a development deal with Tracy more than it is getting Summer on the show." Kelly's uncle had a long history of never doing something that didn't benefit him. That was the reason her grandmother, Ralph's mother, decided to leave her business and building to Kelly rather than to her son. However, she didn't leave him out of the will. She was one smart cookie. She made him executor, which meant he had a lot of work to do for the estate with little financial reward. While it probably amused Martha to do this to her son, it was a source of irritation for Kelly because she had to continually deal with Ralph.

"My wife hates staying in the city." A man had approached them and inserted himself into the conversation. "Me? I love the hustle. There are too many malls here, and let's face it, the nightlife isn't as exciting as it is in the city."

Kelly, Liv, and Frankie exchanged looks. Not only had the person interrupted a private conversation, but he had also insulted their hometown of Long Island. Not cool.

"Where are my manners? I'm Hugh McNeil. Producer of *Long Island Ladies*. There are things about the island I don't appreciate, but the bat-crazy rich women you've got out here . . .amazing." He gulped his champagne and then dropped his glass onto a passing tray and stopped the waiter. "How can a guy get more of those jalapeño-stuffed mushrooms?" The waiter nodded, murmuring something Kelly couldn't hear, and then walked away.

"They're the best. Just the right amount of spice. Then again, there can never be too much spice." He ogled Kelly from head to stiletto, giving her the willies. Mister Producer might have had too much champagne.

"I believe I saw a waiter with mushrooms over there," Frankie pointed into the study, where heavy wooden sliding doors had been opened for guests to mingle in the comfort of floor-to-ceiling bookcases and deep-cushioned sofas.

Hugh gave a nod and headed off in search of his food obsession.

Kelly smiled her appreciation to her cousin as a waiter approached them with a tray of mini quiches. Each of them reached for a quiche just as raised voices caught their attention from the other end of the living room beside the grand piano. Their heads swiveled to the commotion.

"Catfight?" Frankie asked with too much excitement.

"Frankie!" Kelly admonished.

"No, I think he's right, Kell. Do you know who those two women are? The one in the silver dress is Diana Delacourte, and the other is Wendy Johnson."

Kelly studied the woman. Liv was right. Wendy Johnson looked different from the day she'd come into the boutique with her dresses for consignment. Her chestnut brown hair was swept up into an elegant chignon, and instead of active wear, she was wearing a matte gown with ruffled self-tie sleeves in a festive emerald-green color.

Kelly's gaze moved to Diana, who wore a silvery sequin . . . prom gown . . . oh, no, no, no. That was one of the dresses Wendy had consigned at the boutique. Kelly's stomach lurched. Wendy had to have recognized her dress.

"What kind of relationship do they have on the show?" Kelly dreaded the answer.

"Not a good one. I heard Wendy got Diana kicked off the show." Liv didn't look away from the two ladies.

"Didn't Wendy post photos of Diana at a nightclub having a meltdown?" Frankie asked.

"She did. She made Diana out to be a lush of a housewife on the prowl for younger men. Then the next thing you know, topless photos of Diana are popping up."

Kelly cringed.

"You look lovely in *my* old dress. A cast-off wearing a cast-off. How fitting," Wendy said in a louder tone, resulting in Diana squaring her shoulders and lifting her chin.

"Forget quiche. We need popcorn." Frankie popped the last bite of his appetizer into his mouth and chewed.

"What I find remarkable is you're able to fit into my dress." Wendy gave a haughty laugh before taking a sip of her champagne.

"I've made the conscious decision to live an environmentally friendly lifestyle. Recycling clothing is one of many things we can do to help save our planet. And it's the basis of my upcoming book." Diana adjusted the wrap around her shoulders and then propped her hands on her hips. Her ashy blond hair was pulled back into a messy ponytail, and fringed bangs swept her elegantly shaped brows.

"Ha! The only lifestyle you're living is that of a pauper!"

Diana's face reddened, and her lips twisted. "I don't have to take this from you, a sad drunk who's still hanging onto a sham of a marriage for ratings." Diana dropped her hands from her hips and stormed past Wendy, heading toward Kelly.

Oh, boy.

Diana moved at warp speed but came to a screeching halt when she arrived in front of Kelly. A flicker of recognition flashed in her angry, green eyes, and her nostrils flared.

"I know who you are! Your photo was in the newspaper. You own the consignment shop where I bought this!" Diana gestured to the gown she wore. While it looked less posh the other day on a hanger, on the former reality TV star it looked expensive and sexy.

Kelly fumbled for words. The local newspaper had done a feature on Kelly and the boutique a week earlier to promote the changes to the business and encourage shoppers to stop in. "I . . . I do own the Lucky Cove Resale Boutique."

"How on earth could your salesgirl sell me this dress knowing it came from her?" Diana made a grand gesture of turning and pointing at Wendy before she turned back to Kelly but didn't keep her voice down. "What kind of business are you running? It doesn't matter because, mark my word, you will regret what you did. Mark. My. Words." Diana breezed past Kelly, and the sound of her heels clicking on the entry hall's marble floor quickened and then soon disappeared.

"Wow!" Frankie grabbed a shrimp from a passing tray.

"I can't believe that just happened. Are you okay?" Liv asked.

"Not sure." Kelly wanted to crawl under a rock and stay there. All the eyes that had watched the blowup between Wendy and Diana were now focused on her, and she heard whispers. So much for handing out business cards.

"Brace yourself," Liv warned.

"What? Why? Oh . . ." Kelly saw the reason for Liv's warning. Summer was making a beeline for her.

"I can explain," Kelly said to her aunt as she hardened herself for an onslaught of wrath.

Summer clasped her hands together and smiled. "Thank you! Thank you!" She reached out and pulled Kelly in for a hug.

"What?" Kelly, Liv, and Frankie said in unison.

Summer let go of her niece and kept her voice low. "Hugh is going to eat all of this up. I couldn't have asked for a better turn of events. I'm going to be a shoo-in. And it's all because of your little thrift store." Summer squealed before grabbing Kelly into another hug.

Over Summer's shoulder, Kelly gave Liv and Frankie a confused look. She wasn't used to gratitude from Summer and didn't understand how a hostess could be happy about a loud argument in the middle of her party.

"I'm happy to help," Kelly said absently as her mind raced with the threat Diana had leveled on her and her business. Was the woman really capable of dragging Kelly and the boutique through the mud? The boutique was still too fragile to weather another storm like it had last month. Kelly was able to keep the store open, but she wasn't sure if she could do it again because money was even tighter now after the upgrades she'd made to the boutique and the upstairs apartment.

Summer released Kelly and ran a hand over her dress to smooth it. "I have to find Hugh." She spun around and dashed off in search of the producer.

Kelly looked at her cousin and her friend. "You heard what Diana said. Do you think I should be worried?"

"Probably not. She was embarrassed and humiliated and blowing off steam." Liv set her empty glass on a passing tray. "I wouldn't worry too much."

"Yeah, she's right. This will all blow over. Come on, let's find the buffet and get some real food." Frankie turned and headed toward the dining room.

Liv linked arms with Kelly. "Don't fret. Look, everyone has gone back to enjoying themselves. And we should too."

Kelly allowed Liv to lead her to the dining room, though she didn't have much of an appetite. Would there ever come a day when she wasn't worrying about the financial survival of the boutique?

Chapter Three

Sunday morning began like every other Sunday morning since Kelly had resettled back in Lucky Cove, except for two things. First, Kelly woke an hour earlier, and second, she headed out for a run. She'd wanted to start her Sundays like that since her move back home. But she'd never gotten around to it. Instead, she slept in and started her day in a leisurely fashion because the boutique didn't open until noon.

If she had gotten herself out of bed early in the previous weeks, then she wouldn't have had to struggle to get herself out of her shapewear last night. On her way out of the bedroom, she eyed the torture device that had kept all her jiggly parts right and tight in her dress.

She also knew that stepping away from pastries also kept all her parts from becoming jiggly. Her new plan was to indulge less and run more.

After filling Howard's bowl, she gave him a quick pat on the head. He didn't have to worry about his figure. He gave a soft meow and then chowed down. She'd inherited the orange cat along with the boutique and apartment. A package deal, apparently. The cat was slow to warm up to her, but they'd made progress since her first day in her new home. Now he slept on the bed with her and even curled up to her on the sofa. With Howard fed and his water bowl refreshed, she dashed out to the cold morning for her first run in weeks. She set the GPS on her smartwatch and took off for a two-mile run. She eventually wanted to do three miles but was starting off conservatively.

On the loop back home, she popped into Doug's Variety Store for a large Holly Jolly coffee with low-fat milk. She frowned when she passed on the cream, but her sadness was quickly replaced with an image of a leopard-print pencil skirt she had hanging in her closet. It was more than a little tight at the moment. Visualization was a strong motivating tool. Or at least she'd been told.

Standing at the counter waiting for her coffee, she heard snippets of conversation. The topic was last night's party and, in particular, the scene between Wendy and Diana that had played out in front of everyone. There was that much fascination with the glamorous housewives?

"Morning, Kell." Gabe Donovan approached from the front door. Off duty, Gabe was dressed in his distressed leather jacket and baggy jeans. That was how she was used to seeing Pepper's son. She was still adjusting to his police uniform, which made him look so grown up and responsible, far from the goofball she'd grown up with. "I guess I missed quite a show last night."

Kelly's head tilted sideways. "Not you too? Is everyone talking about the argument between what's her name and the other what's her name?"

"Wendy Johnson and Diana Delacourte."

Kelly's mouth gaped open. "How do you know their names? You're a closet *LIL* watcher, aren't you?"

A hint of redness tinged Gabe's full cheeks, and his gaze cast downward for a nanosecond. "I've heard people say their names."

Kelly nodded. "Ah ha, and like a good cop, you remembered the names."

"Exactly."

"What a load of baloney!" She slapped him on the shoulder.

"Assaulting an officer?"

"You're not on duty. Besides, I've known you since we were in preschool, and I'm exempt from whatever law you're referring to." She took a drink of her coffee, and it slid down her throat, warming her and giving her a little kick start of the energy her run had drained out of her. Pulling the cup from her lips, she glanced at the wall clock. Shoot. She had to get back to her apartment to shower and dress for work.

"Be sure to fill my mom in on every detail. She loves the show."

"Like mother, like son?"

"Don't you have to open the store soon?"

"Yes, I do, and I'm heading back now. Are you working today?"

"Yes, ma'am."

Kelly feigned insult. "Never call me ma'am again, or I'll have no choice but to share that photo of you on April Fool's Day. Remember?"

"Not cool, Kell."

"Neither is calling me ma'am."

"I thought you destroyed it."

Kelly half-shrugged. "Maybe. Maybe not. Want to risk it?" She smiled triumphantly and spun around to leave the store. She probably shouldn't have brought up the photo of a very awkward thirteen-year-old Gabe, but she couldn't resist. She knew it would eat at him all day. She sipped her coffee. Yeah, it was a little cruel, but wasn't that what lifetime friends were for? A little torture?

Lost in her thoughts, she didn't see the woman approaching and bumped right into her. After brief muttering from both of them, Kelly pulled back and recognized the woman she'd crashed into. Tracy Sachs, the powerhouse behind *LIL*.

New York women were known for their love of black clothes, and Tracy Sachs was no different. From her newsboy hat to her cropped silvery-gray hair to the scarf tucked into the neckline of her wool wrap coat to the trousers that grazed her sleek boots, she was dressed all in black. It was a stark contrast to her porcelain-skinned, heart-shaped face, which at the moment was touched with a little redness from the fierce cold wind; and her frowning, mulberry-colored lips.

"I'm sorry. I wasn't paying attention to where I was going."

"No, you weren't." Tracy's frown deepened into a scowl as she inspected her coat for any damage from Kelly's coffee.

Kelly checked her coffee cup's lid. All secure.

Tracy lifted her head, and recognition flashed in her pale blue eyes. "I know you. You were at Ralph's party. You're his niece who owns the consignment shop." Tracy's scowl turned into a smile as she shifted her Celine bag in her hands.

Kelly's heart did a little pitter-patter at the sight of the statement bag. What she'd give to get one of those on consignment.

"I wish I'd had cameras there last night because that scene between Wendy and Diana was awesome. Then Diana's run-in with you. Talk about good TV."

"I guess. I heard Wendy wrote a nasty blog about Diana, and then some photos of Diana appeared. Why would Wendy do that?" Kelly had reservations about Summer getting caught up in the den of barracudas who seemed to take pleasure in bringing women down just so they could get an extra fifteen minutes of fame. Was that the role model Summer wanted to show Juniper?

Tracy gave a throaty laugh. "Reality TV isn't pretty. But its ratings are amazing." She pulled out her cell phone from her coat pocket and checked for messages or e-mails. Kelly wasn't sure what she was doing with the device; what she was certain of was that their conversation was less important than the phone. Tracy shoved the phone back in her pocket as concern clouded her eyes.

"Is everything okay?" Kelly asked.

"I've been trying to get ahold of Diana since she stormed out of the party last night, and she hasn't gotten back to me. It's not like her to ignore my calls, especially since she's now desperate to get back on the show."

"Do you think she's in trouble? She was angry when she left Uncle Ralph's party."

Tracy shrugged. "I don't know why I'm stressing about this. Diana is probably sleeping off her hangover. I'm sure she consoled herself with a bottle of her favorite alcohol. Not sure what she's drinking these days."

"That's terrible." Even though Diana had lashed out at Kelly the night before, she felt sorry for the woman.

From what she'd heard, Diana had been in a bad marriage, was betrayed by her husband, was humiliated by a friend, and was then tossed off the show. It seemed like Diana's world had come crashing down around her very much like Kelly's world had a few months ago. The difference was that Kelly had a close-knit group of friends to help her regain her footing. It sounded like Diana didn't have a safety net.

Tracy shook her head. "No, what's terrible is what will happen to you when Diana finally sobers up. If you think the blog post Wendy wrote was nasty, wait until you see what Diana does to you and your little shop after being embarrassed like she was last night."

"I didn't do anything!"

"You sold her Wendy's old dress. So, knowing Diana as I do, what happened last night was all *your* fault. You know the old saying about any publicity is good publicity? Well, it won't be like that for you when Diana is finished with you. She will drag you and your shop through the mud."

Kelly's stomach rolled, and she got a little light-headed. Her business, her financial survival was fragile to begin with, and after the fiasco with psychics and rumors of haunted merchandise just weeks before Halloween, she didn't think the Lucky Cove Resale Boutique could weather another assault.

"Is there anything I can do to appease Diana? Maybe if I talk to her," Kelly said.

Tracy pursed her lips as she shook her head. "Not a good idea."

"Surely I can make her see there was no intention to embarrass her. We had no idea she'd be wearing the dress to a party where Wendy was also in attendance."

"You are so naïve, aren't you? Refreshing, really. Look, Diana only cares about herself and how she looks to her fans."

"She can't be all that bad. I'm sure I can persuade her." Kelly had worked with some of the most aggressive, ambitious women Seventh Avenue had to offer, from interns right up to the corporate floor. She could handle Diana. However, she hadn't been able to handle the all-powerful Serena Dawson when she'd fired Kelly in front of all of her coworkers after a series of events that Serena blamed her for but that had been out of Kelly's hands.

"Suit yourself. It's your funeral. If you'll excuse me, I really need a coffee and to get going into the city." Tracy stepped forward, her attention focused on the counter, where Doug took coffee orders.

"Wait, Tracy, I need something."

Tracy gave a cool look over her shoulder that showed she wasn't interested in giving Kelly anything. "What?"

"Diana's address." Kelly chewed on her lower lip.

"I don't think it's a good idea to go see her. You'll only make things worse."

"Well, then it'll be on me. But I have to try to reason with her. My business is at stake. You can understand, right?"

In one quick motion, Tracy sighed, rolled her eyes, and whipped out her cell phone. "Don't say I didn't warn you."

"Thank you!"

Tracy stopped scrolling on her phone. "If I give you Diana's address, I will need something in return."

"Like what? I don't have money."

"I don't need money. What I need is information. Besides Diana and Wendy, do you have any other Long Island Ladies pawning their designer clothes on the side?"

"No. Only them."

Tracy looked disappointed. "Too bad. However, in exchange for me giving you this address, I expect you will let me know if anyone else from my show comes into your shop."

"Why?"

Tracy laughed as she returned to scrolling through her contacts. "Oh, you are so naïve. It's actually sweet."

Kelly left Doug's Variety with Diana's address. She had some time to spare before the boutique opened. Though, just to be safe, she texted Breena that she might be late. She got a thumbs-up emoji from her employee.

The former reality star lived in Lucky Cove on a road tucked away, far from the center of town and with no water view. Settled in behind the wheel of her borrowed Jeep Cherokee, Kelly typed the address where she was heading into the vehicle's GPS system, and off she went.

The roads off the main thoroughfare were narrower than usual, thanks to snowfalls over the past few weeks. Town plow trucks had pushed the six-plus inches of snow to the sides of the road. Winter had made an early appearance and seemed to have settled in for a long stay. They were bracing for another storm on the horizon.

A canopy of bare trees covered Butternut Lane, a quiet stretch of road dotted with traditional Cape Cod homes built during the big boom of development in the 1950s as city families sought suburban living. While they sought space for their growing families, they weren't interested in originality. House after house she drove by looked identical. Even after all those years, not much had changed to those original homesteads of the burgeoning neighborhoods.

Up ahead, Kelly caught sight of the sign for Glendale Road and took the right turn. Glendale was unpaved, and her Jeep bounced over the ruts as it cruised along the heavily forested road. She slowed down as she searched for Diana's house.

On her left, she spotted the first house since turning onto the road. A small cottage with shingles and shuttered windows. Standing on the front lawn was an elderly man as weathered as his home, walking with a small, white dog. The two were bundled up in plaid jackets and didn't seem to mind the cold. The man's shaggy white hair peeked out from beneath his black wool cap. He looked up as Kelly drove by but didn't wave.

Her GPS alerted her that her destination was coming up ahead. The space between the cottage and Diana's house was another long stretch of trees and brush. She guessed all the empty acreage was waiting for development. That thought made her sad. While she hadn't called Lucky Cove home in several years, she still didn't want it to lose its small-town charm and become overrun with mega houses and fancy cars. So far, the small hamlet had found a balance between attracting vacationers and summer residents and maintaining the quality of life for lifelong residents.

Could that balance be kept in check?

She shifted her Jeep into PARK and grabbed her key fob and cell phone. Closing the Jeep's door, she said a silent prayer that Diana would accept her apology. Walking along the driveway up to the brick path, she tried to rationalize what she was planning to do. She really didn't owe Diana an apology since she had no idea how things would've turned out; yet if an apology kept Diana from trashing the boutique, then Kelly would offer the most heartfelt apology the former reality star had ever heard. Maybe she should have asked Breena for some acting tips.

Kelly climbed the steps up to the porch of the new-construction Dutch Colonial house and pressed the doorbell. Thanks to her inner conflict, she hadn't realized how cold it was. Now she wished she'd gone back to her apartment for a heavier coat before driving over to the house. She shoved her phone and key fob into her pocket and zipped it closed, then wrapped her arms around her body and gave herself a hug. And waited.

Nobody was home?

Kelly's teeth chattered as footsteps approached from the other side of the door. Finally. If she stood out here any longer, she'd be a Popsicle.

The door opened, and she was greeted by a grim-looking woman in her mid-sixties. "We're not interested in buying anything."

Kelly plastered on her best smile and evoked her most perky voice. "No, no, I'm not here to sell anything. I'm here to speak with Ms. Delacourte. My name is Kelly Quinn. I own the Lucky Cove Resale Boutique."

Grim Lady didn't seem impressed, nor was she budging from the small space between the open door and the doorjamb.

"I really need to speak to Ms. Delacourte."

"She can't be disturbed. You can e-mail her through her website." Grim Lady stepped back and closed the door.

"Really?" Offense and cold and worry swirled inside Kelly, giving her the courage to press the doorbell again. She might have left her finger pressing on the bell longer than need be. She had come to talk to Diana, and talk to the reality star she would. There had to be a way past Grim Lady.

The door opened again. Grim Lady looked even grimmer. Clearly, Kelly was testing the woman's patience.

"I've told you, Ms. Delacourte can't be disturbed. Now please leave." The woman's thin brows arched, and her lips pursed.

The wind gusted again, permeating Kelly's running jacket. Its soft panels of proprietary insulation weren't working very well as she stood there on the porch. "It's really important."

"I doubt that. Now go away."

The door closed again, and Kelly huffed. She resisted pressing the doorbell one more time. Instead, she turned and walked down the porch steps. Maybe she should e-mail Diana. She unzipped her jacket pocket and pulled out her cell phone. She typed in a search for the website as she walked back to her vehicle.

Another cold gust of wind hit Kelly, and she muttered a curse. It was freaking cold, and she was trying to get an audience with Diana Delacourte rather than being inside her boutique where it was nice and warm. She found the website. She stopped walking and tapped on the menu. A passing bird overhead caught Kelly's attention, and she looked up. The bird flew out of sight into a thicket of trees. But a glimmer of silver in the snow caught her eye. She took a few steps to get a closer look. It was fabric.

A scarf?

She propelled herself forward and realized it was a wrap. The same wrap she saw Diana with last night at the party.

What was it doing outside?

Kelly guessed anything was possible if Diana had been drinking late into the night like Tracy had suggested.

Even if Diana had discarded the accessory, Kelly couldn't leave it out in the wet snow. It looked vintage. And it was possibly a way she could get past the Grim Lady. She shoved the phone back into her pocket and went to the wrap. The snow was deeper as she stepped off the walkway, and a shot of cold went up her legs.

She reached forward to snatch up the fabric when she noticed a lone silver stiletto shoe.

Her spidey senses were screaming at her to turn on the heels of her over-priced, high-performance trainers and run . . . run fast, but she kept slogging through the snow as her heart beat so hard it was a miracle it was still in her chest.

She fretted her lower lip and craned her neck forward as if to get a sneak peek of what lay ahead. God, she hoped she would find the silvery sequined dress. Maybe Diana had done a striptease out in the cold, snowy night. Kind of like those people who belonged to a polar bear club and dove into freezing ocean water.

That was it. Diana was a polar bear stripper.

Kelly's gaze swept the landscape, and when it settled on what she'd hope not to find, her body shivered, and not because of the cold. It was because she'd just discovered Diana wasn't a polar stripper.

No, Diana Delacourte was dead.

Sprawled out and tucked in by the snow, still dressed in her silver dress, Diana's eyes were wide open but lifeless. Blood soaked the bodice of the dress. Kelly's legs felt frozen, but she forced them to move because she was going to be sick.

She dashed off to the side, near a thick mass of bare vines, and heaved. She felt light-headed, like she was going to pass out.

"What are you doing?" The Grim Lady's voice called out from the porch.

Kelly straightened and dug into her other pocket for a tissue to wipe her mouth. She turned to the woman, whose stance was firm and uncompromising. "I've found Diana!"

Grim Lady stepped off of the porch, tugging a bulky sweater around herself. "What are you talking about?"

"She's there." Kelly pointed. As her hand fell back to her side, she wondered about the scene that had unfolded last night between Diana and Wendy and how far their feud had gone. "She's dead. Someone murdered her."

Chapter Four

"Did you touch anything when you found Ms. Delacourte?" Detective Marcy Wolman asked from the passenger seat of Kelly's Jeep. Wolman had arrived shortly after two Lucky Cove Police Department cruisers arrived on the scene. Grim Lady, who turned out to be Diana's housekeeper, Nanette Berger, refused to allow Kelly into the house. Wolman did her best to keep from snickering when Kelly explained why she was waiting in her Jeep for the police to arrive.

"No." Kelly had the engine running and the heat blasting, but she still was ice-cold. She guessed finding a body could do that to a gal. Her feet were frozen, thanks to plodding through the snow in her running shoes. Had she known she'd discover a frozen corpse, she'd have chosen more appropriate footwear. "Was Diana wearing the other shoe? I didn't notice."

"Why did you come here to see Ms. Delacourte?" Wolman jotted down some notes. She looked warm in her dark-gray, zipped coat. It wasn't designer since she was on a police detective's salary, but it was good quality. Kelly would've liked to see a colorful scarf to off-set the dreary color, but sensible Wolman had chosen a plain black scarf that matched her plain black hat. She'd slipped off her leather gloves to take notes.

Kelly shifted, hoping to get better contact with the heated seat. "I wanted to discuss what happened last night. Let her know I felt horrible about what went down."

A flicker of recognition flashed in Wolman's dark eyes. "I heard about some brush-up at your uncle's party. It was between Ms. Delacourte and who else?"

"Wendy Johnson. She consigned a bunch of cocktail dresses, and Diana bought one. Wendy recognized it, and well, you've heard what happened."

Wolman looked up from her notepad and cast a look at Kelly. "You somehow manage to find yourself involved in drama, don't you?" Kelly did everything she could to refrain from rolling her eyes. Exhibiting any signs of disrespect would only backfire on her. "It kind of happens. Besides her missing shoe, where's her coat? Why was she outside still dressed up without a coat in this weather?"

"You also ask a lot of questions that aren't any of your business. This is an official murder investigation, and I don't want you involved in any way. Am I making myself clear?" Wolman stared at Kelly, waiting for an answer.

"Yes, you are. I'm just curious." Morbidly curious, but nonetheless, curious. And the last time she'd inserted herself into a murder investigation, she'd almost become the next murder victim. No, she was only curious. Nothing more. "I found her body."

Wolman's eyes softened. "I know finding a murder victim isn't an easy thing, and your interest is understandable. From what we can tell at this point, it looks like a stabbing. We'll know more once the autopsy is complete."

Kelly nodded and turned her head in time to see the procession of officials—a uniformed officer and two county employees from the coroner's office—carry Diana's body to the van. Her stomach rolled again, and she squeezed her eyes shut.

"Are you okay to drive home, or would you like an officer to take you?" Wolman's uncharacteristically compassionate voice drew Kelly's face back to the detective.

"No, I'm okay to drive back to the boutique."

Wolman closed her notepad. "Good. Let's have a chat about a different topic. My brother. He's worked hard to get where he is with his practice, and I'd hate to see him distracted or his reputation damaged in any way."

Kelly blinked. "What are you saying?"

"I think it was a good idea for you not to have a second date with him." Wolman pushed open the passenger door and stepped out. "I may need to follow up with you as the investigation progresses."

Kelly wrapped her hands around the steering wheel. Her fingers gripped the wheel as she pushed down her irritation at the detective's unsolicited advice about her personal life. She wasn't about to discuss her dating life with Marcy for two reasons. One, it was none of her business. Two, Kelly was confused about her feelings for Mark and didn't want to discuss them.

"Doesn't it seem odd that the housekeeper didn't wonder where her employer was all night? When I asked to speak with Diana, she said Diana couldn't be disturbed."

"The housekeeper, what she knows or doesn't know, isn't any of your concern. Good-bye, Kelly." Wolman slipped on her gloves, closed the door, and walked away from the vehicle.

Kelly glanced back at the charming and very large Dutch Colonial that once had been the location for guilty-pleasure television—a socially acceptable way to be a voyeur into someone's life—and that now was the scene of a murder.

* * * *

Kelly dropped her running jacket on the back of the chair at her desk and peeled off her gloves. She needed to get upstairs to her apartment and stand under a hot shower to thaw out. She retrieved her phone from her jacket pocket and checked for messages. There were a few, along with some new e-mails from retail supply vendors. Since it was Sunday, they were most likely automated messages to her initial inquiries. She'd been looking into getting logo shopping bags for the boutique but considering the minimum order required, it didn't take a math genius to figure out that plan was way beyond her current budget. She'd have to learn to love the carton of white boring bags her granny had purchased last summer.

"There you are. What on earth happened?" Pepper entered the staff room and dispensed with pleasantries.

After she'd received Kelly's text about finding Diana's body, she'd sent back a sad face with tears. Kelly had never thought she and Pepper would be texting, let alone with emojis.

"Diana was stabbed sometime between leaving the party and me finding her. That's all I know right now. Wolman wasn't in the mood to share much." Except for advice on not dating her brother.

Kelly walked to the kitchenette section of the staff room, a bare-bones kitchen with a drafty window over the sink. The robust aroma of fresh-brewed coffee was a godsend to Kelly. She poured a cup and carried it back to her desk.

"I need a shower. I'm still frozen to the core." Thank goodness, the building's furnace was in good shape, and hot water wasn't a problem. Then again, maybe that simple thought just jinxed it.

"I haven't told Breena about what happened." Pepper pulled a chair from the small, round table where they ate lunch to the desk and sat. "I'm not sure how she'll react. She's a big fan of the show and those ladies." Kelly swallowed her first sip of the coffee. "I'll tell Breena."

"Tell me what?" Breena had entered the staff room. Her glossy red hair was styled in beachy waves, and she'd added a pop of deep pink gloss to her lips.

Kelly admired Breena's fun with fashion and makeup. Maybe it was from her drama days. She always got the lead parts in all of the high school plays and loved dressing in costume.

Breena had gone off to New York City, like Kelly had, to pursue her acting dream, but she returned home unemployed, broke, and with a little girl to support. Besides working two jobs now, she was taking night and weekend classes in marketing. As much as Kelly was struggling, she couldn't imagine what it would be like to be responsible for a child, another life. Inheriting Howard the cat was more responsibility than she'd bargained for.

Pepper gave Kelly a look. It wasn't her infamous Pepper glare, but it was a pointed look. Then Pepper stood and walked toward Breena. "You'd better sit down."

"Why? What's going on?" Confusion covered Breena's face as her brows furrowed.

Pepper disappeared out of the room, and Breena approached Kelly's desk with hesitation.

"Are you firing me?"

"No. Nothing like that. But I do have some bad news. Sit." Kelly gestured to Pepper's vacant chair. She reached for the box of tissues and slid it closer to the edge of the desk. "You know I went to see Diana Delacourte this morning."

"Yeah. How'd it go? Oh, I'm guessing, by the look on your face, that it didn't go well. I'm sorry, Kelly." Looking a little more relaxed, Breena leaned back and crossed her legs.

"No, it didn't go well. Not well at all." Kelly was stalling. She didn't know how to tell Breena what happened. Maybe it was better to blurt it out, like ripping off a Band-Aid. "I found Diana dead. Someone murdered her."

Breena's head tilted, and she stared at Kelly as if processing what she was just told.

"I know you're a big fan of the show and this news is unsettling."

Breena leaned forward and rested her arms on the desk.

Her eyes were wide with as much curiosity as Kelly had had earlier, though now she was just plain exhausted and in need of a thawing out. "Murdered? How? Why? Did you find her? Who killed her?" The rapid fire of questions dizzied Kelly. Breena's reaction wasn't what she'd expected. It looked like she wouldn't be needing the tissues. "Yes. Stabbed. Don't know. Yes. Don't know."

"Wow. Do you think Wendy Johnson killed her? Maybe she followed Diana back to her house and they continued to argue and then Wendy stabbed her." Breena leaned forward and flattened her hands out on the desk. Her eyes narrowed as she waited for Kelly to respond.

"I guess it's possible. You know, I need a hot shower." Kelly stood and grabbed her phone and coffee mug. While she'd love to toss around theories with Breena, she wanted to get warmed up and put on some fresh clothes and not relive the awful moments of staring down at Diana's body.

"Right. I should get back out to the sales floor. I'm here for a couple more hours, then I need to leave. Mom is watching Tori and has to leave to visit Grandpa at the nursing home."

"How is Tori feeling? Any better?"

"Yeah. It's one of those twenty-four-hour bugs. I think I'll keep her home tomorrow, just to be safe." Breena stood and left the staff room, and moments later, Kelly did the same. She headed upstairs to her apartment.

Kelly padded into her bedroom with her shoulder-length blond hair gathered up in a twisty-towel and a bath towel tied around her. She'd spent more time under the spray of hot water than she expected, but it was well worth it because she felt warmer. She guessed that, having been chilled to her core, her body would take a while to thaw out. Waiting for her was Howard. He was stretched out on the bed. He lifted his head and made eye contact with her.

When she'd first moved into the apartment, the cat made himself scarce. It'd taken weeks to coax him out with bribes, but eventually, he'd warmed up to her. Either he liked her or he realized she was his only chance at survival. After all, who else would feed him?

She moved over to the bed and scratched his head, eliciting a purr. His contentment did a lot more to warm her than the shower had. Howard rolled to his side and licked a paw. So much for their bonding time. He was done with her—for the time being.

She walked to her closet and opened the door. The closet was about the same size as the one she'd had when she lived in the city, and just like then, she had to use rolling garment racks for extra clothing storage. She hated the messy, unkempt, and nomadic look. After a few weeks of living in the one-bedroom apartment, she'd scoped out space where she could add a closet and not lose too much living square footage. Now she needed the money for her new project. With a bunch of other expenses ahead of a new closet, she accepted she'd be living with rolling garment racks galore.

Her cell phone rang, and she dashed to the nightstand. When she lifted the phone, she saw Mark's name. She hesitated a moment before accepting the call.

"Hey." She walked back to the closet.

"Hey, yourself. I heard what happened. Are you okay?" His voice was thick with concern, and she suspected he'd drop whatever he was doing and come over if she asked him to. She wanted to, but she was a big girl and could weather the unfortunate incident on her own. Well, maybe a pint of chocolate chip ice cream would help.

She couldn't help but wonder if he was referring to finding Diana's body or to talking with his sister. She figured it was the former. "Okay, I guess. I still can't believe someone murdered her."

"I'm relieved the killer wasn't still there when you arrived. Why did you go to her house? Was she a customer?"

Kelly waded through her dresses. After the morning she'd had, she wanted something comfy, yet she wanted to look like the owner of a fashionable resale boutique. Who happened to have found a dead body only hours ago. A long-sleeved dusty green A-line dress caught her eye. She pulled the hanger from the rod.

"Kelly, are you still there?"

"Yes. Sorry. Diana bought a dress here the other day. I went there . . . wait, you mean you didn't hear about what happened at my uncle's party last night?"

"No. I've been in the city since Friday and got back early this morning. What happened?"

She filled Mark in on the highlights of the party as she moved to the full-length mirror that had come with her granny's bedroom set. She held the dress up in front of her. She'd gotten the dress at a trendy retail chain store that catered to the under-thirty and on-a-budget set. Not the best quality, but pretty good for the price.

"Wow. Those women sound very . . . interesting."

"Talk about an understatement." She stepped back from the mirror and went to lay the dress on the bed.

"I'm glad you're okay. Maybe we can get together for coffee or something. No pressure."

"I'd like that. Thanks for calling." She disconnected the call and set her phone on the bed. Her eye caught a little shimmer from the dresser. Her granny's faux baubles.

Martha Blake had been a collector of many things over the years. Kelly was now wading through the collections and the memories of the one person in her life who always believed in her. Why on earth had her granny collected those gaudy necklaces and rings? Set out on a tarnished silver tray, they caught the sunlight when it streamed in through the room's two windows. The flash of shimmer took Kelly back to finding Diana's body. The beautiful shimmery gown had been stained with so much blood.

She shook her head hard to chase the image out of her mind.

When her head steadied, her gaze landed on a framed photograph of Juniper. The baby was a beautiful little angel. Rosy cheeks, a lyrical laugh, and the happiest smile. Shouldn't a happy, healthy baby, a good marriage, and a successful fitness studio be enough for Juniper's mom? Why did Summer want to be on *LIL*?

A coldness lodged in Kelly again, displacing the warmth that was there just moments ago. Maybe it wasn't Wendy who'd killed Diana. Maybe there was an obsessed fan or disgruntled *LIL* wannabe who killed Diana. If so, could Summer be in danger?

It was official. Kelly's imagination was working overtime. There wasn't some deranged murderer targeting *LIL* cast members. Unfortunately, it probably was Wendy or someone else close to Diana. Maybe her soon-to-be ex-husband. Wasn't a husband most likely to be responsible for his wife's murder?

She had to stop thinking about murder. She had a business to run and an employee who was leaving for the day, so she needed to hustle. At her jewelry box, she pulled out a handful of bangles and her gold-tone watch and then dashed into the bathroom to blow-dry her hair, letting its natural waves do their thing, and applied her makeup. She'd added a multi-color blanket scarf around her neck and let it drape down the front of her dress, and she'd slipped on a pair of Sam Edelman suede knee-high boots in a golden caramel color. She finished her cozy chic look with simple stud earrings and her bangles and watch.

Less than an hour later, she was ready to head back downstairs to the boutique. Walking out of the bedroom, she took one final look at Juniper's photograph. Even though her earlier thoughts were very unlikely, she had to make sure Summer was safe for her daughter's sake.

* * * *

By Monday morning, Lucky Cove was abuzz with speculation and theories since news had broken about Diana's murder the day before. The Internet wasn't far behind. Celebrity websites, pop culture bloggers, and fan sites shared every detail of Diana's riches-to-fame-to-dead story. Kelly tried her best to stay off those sites while working on her article for Budget Chic, but it was hard not to click and travel down the rabbit hole of gossip and conjecture.

She should have been writing the last two paragraphs of her article, not looking at photographs of Diana when she was a young bride. She was beautiful and clueless about how her life would turn out and eventually how it would end. The groom standing and smiling beside her was handsome and years older. Aaron Delacourte had had wealth, power, a mansion, and a brand-spanking-new bride to replace his first wife.

What happened to the first Mrs. Delacourte? None of the articles Kelly read talked about her in any detail.

Staring at the wedding photograph, Kelly wondered if there wasn't a little voice somewhere deep inside Diana that whispered to her she'd end up like his first wife, cast aside for a replacement?

Kelly gazed off into space. Did Summer ever have those thoughts since she was Uncle Ralph's wife number three?

"I thought you were going upstairs to work on the apartment." Pepper entered the staff room and walked to the sink, where she refilled her water bottle.

"I'm heading up now. I wanted to finish the first draft of this article."

"Have you finished it?" Pepper turned to face Kelly and leaned against the countertop. She took a swig from her bottle.

"Not really. I got sucked into all these articles about Diana." Kelly closed out of the website she was on and lowered the top of her laptop.

"Talk about a waste of time. It's all gossip."

"How's business?"

"Steady. Nothing I can't handle." Pepper pushed off from the counter.

"I'm sure. Guess I'm procrastinating. There's a lot to go through upstairs. I've been trying very, very hard to think of Granny as a collector, but the word 'hoarder' keeps creeping into my brain."

Pepper laughed. After taking another drink of her water, she walked to the swinging door. "Collector. Hoarder. Tomato. Tomahto. Don't work too hard." She pushed the door and stepped out into the small hall that led to the upstairs staircase and the main room downstairs.

"Let me know if you need help!" Kelly doubted Pepper would send up an SOS if things got busy. The woman was thirty years older than her and had more energy than she could ever imagine possessing.

She stood, picked up her laptop and six-key holder, and headed out of the staff room. A locked door enclosed the staircase. Granny hadn't had the budget to create a separate entrance to the apartment, and the door was the best option to keep shoppers from popping up into her living space. The staircase was also close to the changing rooms, which were modest spaces with simple curtains for privacy. Updating those areas was top on her to-do list.

"I can't believe someone murdered Diana yesterday," a woman said from behind a curtain in the first changing room.

"Seriously? Have you been living under a rock? She'd gotten so messed up, it was only a matter of time before something bad happened to her. You know, I think her husband did it. I think he didn't want to pay her anything," said another woman from behind a curtain in the second dressing room.

"Or maybe his new fiancée did Diana in. Not only would she get rid of the obstacle to her wedding, but that also would ensure that Diana didn't return to *Long Island Ladies*."

The second woman gasped. "That's a terrible thing to say. She's my favorite one."

"And did you hear? I think the woman who owns this shop found Diana's body yesterday."

The second woman gasped again. "No. I hadn't heard. Is it morbid to want to know what it was like for her finding the body?"

Yes, it is morbid.

Kelly quickly unlocked the door and dashed inside the small landing, the size of a closet. After relocking it, she hurried up the stairs and arrived inside her apartment, letting out a whoosh of relief.

She set her laptop on the dining table. Her plan was to continue to declutter the dining area. So far, she'd torn up the carpet in the living room area with the help of Gabe and Liv. She was grateful the hardwood floor was revealed to be in good shape; maybe she'd purchase an area rug to warm up the space. The three of them had also rearranged the furniture. While not her style, it was free, so it stayed. She was looking online for sales on slipcovers. Perhaps white slipcovers for a shabby-chic vibe. She'd ordered a new refrigerator and stove, and they'd be arriving within a couple of weeks.

She was keeping most of the furniture, but there were a few pieces she wanted to move out and store in her granny's storage unit until the spring. She planned on having a tag sale in the parking lot behind the boutique. One of the items on the sell list was the domineering hutch in the dining area. Tall, wide, and not retro-cool, it was an eyesore that was a catchall for countless knickknacks.

Decluttering the hutch was a project she'd started weeks ago, before Halloween, but thanks to nonstop workdays and coming face-to-face with a killer who intended for her to be the next victim, clearing out the hutch had fallen to the back burner.

She propped her hands on her hips and stared down the space-guzzling monster piece of furniture. How her granny had gotten it up the staircase was beyond her. A twinge of guilt hit her when she thought of Gabe and Liv's brother, the only person she knew with a box truck, lugging that monstrosity back down the stairs.

She'd definitely have to have a lot of food to feed them on moving day.

Time to stop thinking, and time to declutter.

She approached the hutch and opened the glass doors and sighed. So many memories of her granny flooded her, and her eyes misted.

Don't go there.

She couldn't think about her childhood, about the lazy days of summer on the beach with Granny or the cold, wintry nights cuddled up on Granny's big sofa with hot cocoa and a book. No, she needed to stay focused on the job at hand because time was short, thanks to her never-ending to-do list.

For the next twenty minutes, she removed all the small knickknacks from the shelves and set them on the dining table. She had to wipe down the items, along with all the shelves. Even with the doors closed, a thick layer of dust had settled on every surface. She wrapped the knickknacks in layers of tissue paper and stored them in plastic bins she'd purchased. Yeah, that was a purchase she hadn't budgeted for, but she didn't want to risk breaking anything by using a cardboard box.

Set center on the middle shelf was the gaudiest floral-pattern platter she'd ever seen. It seemed her granny had had the platter forever but never used it. The dish only served as a decoration. A gaudy decoration. But it still brought a smile to Kelly's lips.

Martha Blake had had eclectic tastes and a borderline hoarding problem, but every item she owned she loved. Torn, Kelly wasn't sure if she wanted to store the platter.

No. I'm starting fresh.

She reached for the platter. She'd wrap it securely, store it, and then revisit it. She was certain she'd be displaying it somewhere, but it was now important to stand firm on her plan.

When she pulled the platter from the glass shelf, she discovered a plain white envelope with her grandmother's name written on it, stuck to the back wall of the hutch.

She set the platter on the table and peeled the envelope from the hutch and studied the printed return address.

The Chapel of the Rose. Las Vegas, Nevada.

What was the Chapel of the Rose? Why on earth did her granny hide the envelope behind the platter?

Her fingers began to unseal the envelope, but they stopped.

Opening her granny's mail seemed intrusive. Not to mention nosy and wrong.

She set the envelope down and stepped back. She leaned against the table and glowered at the envelope. Why did she have to clean out the hutch? If she'd left all the knickknacks alone, she wouldn't be wrestling with an ethical dilemma.

Ethical dilemma?

She was being dramatic and overthinking the situation. Maybe she should audition for a spot on *LIL*. She reached forward and snatched up the envelope and unsealed it.

She pulled out the trifold document and unfolded it.

It took a moment for her brain to catch up with her eyes as she scanned the document. The official certificate listed her granny's name, the name of a man, and the name of a reverend.

Then the date.

Five years ago last March.

It was a marriage certificate.

Kelly swallowed hard, falling onto a chair and letting the certificate fall from her grasp.

Her granny had remarried? To Marvin Childers? Who the heck was he? Why hadn't Granny told anyone? She'd been a widow a long time, and certainly no one would blame her for remarrying.

Well, except for Ralph, because he would've been fearful of losing what he considered rightfully his.

Then the realization slammed her chest. If Granny was married to this Marvin Childers guy before her death, did that mean she'd lose her inheritance? Her home?

Chapter Five

A good old-fashioned cry and finishing off what was left in the pint of chocolate-chip ice cream didn't leave Kelly feeling much better. She kept the ice cream on hand for emergencies, and lately she'd been having a lot of emergencies. Maybe it would be more economical for her to buy a gallon the next time she was at the store.

After she scraped the bottom of the container, she tore into the bag of M&Ms she kept stashed away for earth-shattering emergencies.

Learning that your grandmother had been secretly married and thus threatening your new home and business was earth-shattering.

A text message from her friend Ariel Barnes stopped her from inhaling the whole bag of candy.

Just barely.

Kelly pushed the bag of candy away and reached for her phone. Ariel was asking to meet her for dinner. She glanced at the table. An empty pint of ice cream, a spoon, and the open bag of M&Ms. She considered passing on the invite, preferring to hit Doug's Variety Store to stock up for a long, sad night of preparing to leave her home.

But she decided not to pass on dinner. Instead, she replied she'd meet Ariel in an hour. She needed to snap out of her funk, and meeting up with a friend she'd lost contact with for close to a decade was a perfect way.

The decision to attend a summer party ten years ago had ended tragically. Kelly had snuck away with Davey, leaving Ariel to get into a car with a drunk friend to go home. What happened next was a horrific car accident. Ariel was paralyzed from the waist down and forced to live the rest of her life in a wheelchair. Kelly was guilt-ridden for abandoning her. Davey left Lucky Cove before the start of the new school year. The fallout wasn't pretty. The driver went to jail, Kelly's family made it clear they were fed up with her flighty behavior, and her sister had put up a wall because she agreed with Kelly—Ariel's paralysis was her fault. Moving back to Lucky Cove meant more than Kelly keeping her granny's consignment shop open; it also meant she had to face her past, including Ariel. Renewing a long-dormant friendship wasn't something that happened overnight. The two had to work through feelings, emotions, and baggage. So far, they were headed in the right direction. They had met a few times since the middle of October for lunch or dinner. Ariel occasionally stopped by the boutique on her way home from her part-time job at the library.

Kelly was tempted to throw on a jacket and head out the door as she was, but she needed a little pick-me-up. She closed the bag of candy and went to her closet. She pulled out a cream-colored pencil skirt and selected a chunky, blush-colored turtleneck sweater from a dresser drawer for dinner. She added dangling earrings and a pair of nude leather booties.

She checked herself in the mirror. Her mood lifted a bit. Good food, good friends, and a good outfit always did wonders for a gal.

She shrugged into her coat and grabbed her camel-colored suede shopper tote, a significant purchase even with her Bishop's thirty-percent-off employee discount. Aside from doing a job she loved, she truly missed the employee discount.

She dashed across Main Street to make the short trek to Gino's Pizzeria, where she found Ariel at a table. Ariel had pulled her chestnut brown hair back into a ponytail, and her bangs grazed her large brown eyes.

"Okay, I feel underdressed." Ariel glanced at her distressed jeans and fleece top.

Kelly waved away the silly notion. "You look fine. I needed something to lift my spirits."

A waiter approached their table and took their orders for personal-sized pizzas. Kelly asked for a vegetable pizza, while Ariel ordered sausage and extra cheese.

"Considering what happened the other day, I understand you need something to brighten your mood." Ariel reached for her water glass and took a sip.

She'd probably assumed Kelly's funk was about finding Diana's body, and since Kelly didn't want to talk about her granny's secret marriage and how it could turn her life upside down, she let Ariel continue with her thought.

"I know Diana wasn't the first person you've discovered murdered, but it still had to have been a shock."

"It was." Kelly was preparing herself to push away the bread basket that was approaching their table.

Their waiter arrived beside the table. Gino's made the best bread and always served it warm with soft butter. Ariel dove in, breaking off a substantial chunk, and gestured for Kelly to join her.

"I'm almost full. I had some ice cream earlier." *Some* ice cream? Talk about a fib. It was more like the whole container plus a half a bag of M&Ms, but she didn't want to publicly admit to that.

"Have you heard Wendy Johnson was officially interviewed about the murder?" Ariel popped a piece of bread in her mouth and chewed.

"I'm not surprised. They had a big argument at the party and have a long history of animosity. Though, the more I think about it, the more I find it hard to believe Wendy tracked Diana down and stabbed her to death."

"You know better than anybody that people are capable of heinous actions, given the right circumstances." Ariel finished her piece of bread and drank more water, then she caught the eye of their waiter and asked for two glasses of wine for them.

"True. But Wendy had already humiliated Diana at the party. Why kill her? I feel those women like the publicity their online and on-screen feuding gets them. So why resort to murder?" Kelly had a hard time imagining Wendy trading her designer clothes for a prison jumpsuit.

Ariel shrugged. "Maybe Wendy was in a rage. You know, where all you see is red and there's no reasoning."

Their waiter returned with their wine, and Kelly took a drink. Good call on Ariel's part. She needed wine but in a bigger glass.

Kelly leaned back. Gino's was all decked out for Christmas. A tall tree in the vestibule with a life-sized family of snowmen had greeted Kelly when she arrived. Wreaths hung throughout the dining room, and evergreen swags draped entryways, while instrumental holiday music drifted from wall speakers. She cringed. There were no Christmas decorations at the boutique. Well, except for the mini snowmen Pepper had set on the sales counter. She still hadn't taken down the autumn decorations yet. They needed to be stashed away, either in the minuscule storeroom in the boutique or in the storage unit she'd inherited along with the business. There she'd found two bins of her granny's holiday stuff, but she wasn't sure if she'd have enough. She hoped there were more hidden somewhere. It would save her money, but searching for them and decorating would cost her time.

"Kelly. Yoo-hoo."

Kelly snapped out of her thoughts. "Sorry. What did you say?"

"Where did you go? We got our pizzas." Ariel smiled and slid a slice onto her plate.

"That was fast." Kelly reached for a slice of her pizza.

"Thank goodness. I'm starving." Ariel swallowed her bite of pizza and then wiped her mouth with her napkin.

"I'm sorry I'm distracted. I have a lot on my mind." She bit into her slice and got a mouthful of spinach and onion and bubbling hot cheese.

"Understandable. At least now you can stop worrying about the murder investigation. You're not involved anymore. You gave your statement. And it's not like Diana was a friend. All of your energy needs to be on the boutique. Are you going ahead with the holiday event?"

Kelly wiped her mouth after she set her slice down. "The Edit? I think so. I've been making notes, and I've gotten in some good inventory for holiday parties and events. I need to set a date."

"What exactly is an Edit?" Ariel lifted her wineglass and sipped.

"The theme is holiday parties. I'll pull items from what's available for sale and merchandise them for inspiration. This way every attendee will have an idea of how she can wear a garment, and she saves time because she doesn't have to wade through racks and racks of clothes."

"Kind of like a fashion show?"

Kelly nodded. "Without the models. Of course, everyone is free to browse the other merchandise, but the actual event is specific."

"Consider this my RSVP. I'll be there. Oh, I also have clothes I'd like to consign. I didn't realize how many scarves I have. Way too many for one person." Ariel glanced at the chair next to her and the thick plaid scarf draped over her bag.

"Awesome. I can come over and get the clothes." Kelly reached for her wineglass and took a drink. Setting the glass back down, her thoughts drifted back to Wendy. She was the most obvious suspect, but what would be her motive? It seemed more likely Diana would kill Wendy, considering the leaked photographs and scathing blog posts. Maybe that was what happened. Maybe Wendy was defending herself and accidentally killed Diana.

"Kelly. Kelly."

Kelly snapped out of her thoughts again. "Sorry. I can't stop thinking about Wendy. I don't think she's guilty."

"It's not your job or your responsibility. However, if she has the slightest motive for murder, then she'd better make sure she has a good lawyer, because we all know Detective Wolman will follow the smallest breadcrumb to build a case."

Kelly leveled a look at her friend. Ariel was right. Wolman's job was to close a case, and to close a case she needed to charge someone with the murder. So if Wolman got a whiff of a reason for the murder, she'd follow the scent until she had a case and someone in handcuffs.

"Enough talk about Wolman and Diana's murder."

"How's Mark doing these days?"

Kelly groaned. Leave it to Ariel to bring up another topic she didn't want to talk about. "Have you started your Christmas shopping yet?" Her not-so-subtle change of subject earned her a disagreeable look from Ariel, but her friend took the hint. They finished their dinner talking about the various holiday events in Lucky Cove and their plans for the coming year. Kelly passed on dessert, while Ariel indulged in a slice of chocolate cream pie. They left the restaurant and went their separate ways.

All dressed up with no place to go. Not much had changed since Kelly was a teenager in Lucky Cove. Now twenty-six, she was all dressed up but had no plans. Again. After dinner with Ariel, she expected to go back to her apartment, change into her flannel PJs, and curl up in bed with the rest of the M&Ms, while Howard judged her.

Hyped up on sugar and wine, she called her cousin to find out what he was up to. Lucky for her, Frankie was at home, decorating, and he invited her over. All dressed up, and now somewhere to go. Even if it was her cousin's place, she'd take it.

Behind the wheel of her Jeep, she drove to her cousin's condo a few miles outside of Lucky Cove. During the drive, she tried to remember what had happened to Wendy after Diana left the party. She couldn't recall seeing Wendy after her run-in with Diana, but maybe Frankie had. It was possible, with all the guests—and there were plenty—that she and Wendy had never crossed paths again. If Wendy had stayed at the party and depending upon the time of death, Wendy could have an alibi.

She parked in one of Frankie's two assigned spaces. The two-bedroom condo was way beyond her cousin's financial reach. His restaurant, Frankie's Seafood Shack, was successful, but it was seasonal, which meant that, in the winter, he did private chef work to pay the bills. The condo was a gift or a bribe, depending upon how you looked at it, from his father.

While most parents would be proud of their son if he'd graduated at the top of his culinary class and then studied in Paris, Ralph wasn't.

He wanted Frankie to come into the family business. Unfortunately for Ralph, Frankie didn't love real estate development. He loved to cook. He also loved the condo.

His father had dangled the residence as an incentive to get Frankie to try working at the office for six months. Ralph was sure his son wouldn't be able to walk away from all the perks being the boss's son offered or the financial reward of wheeling and dealing in real estate. When Frankie's trial was up, the condo was his, free and clear—no matter what he decided. Frankie had decided to quit. With his housing taken care of, he had enough money to open his small restaurant.

He might not have liked real estate, but he had learned how to work a deal from his father.

"What took you so long? Wow, did you have a date or something?" Frankie walked away from the opened front door into the living room. With bare feet and dressed for a cozy night in shredded jeans and a baggy thermal top, he picked up a box of ornaments. "I think I should've bought a shorter tree. What do you think?"

Modern renditions of holiday music classics filled the condo, giving Kelly a little holiday jolt. She smiled as she shrugged off her coat and dropped it, along with her tote bag, on Frankie's sofa, which he had decorated with festive needlepoint pillows and a giant Santa Claus throw. She joined Frankie at the tree, which he'd placed in the corner between the fireplace and the built-in cabinet that housed the mega-sized television.

She crossed her arms over her chest and checked out the tree from base to top. She doubted the topper would fit in the small space between the top of the tree and the ceiling.

"What were you thinking?" She peered around the branches. She inhaled the fragrance of the freshly cut tree and immediately was transported back to a time when all she had to worry about was whether Santa got her letter in time for his elves to make her toys. What she wouldn't give to have her childhood innocence back for one day.

"That I was buying too short of a tree." Frankie grinned.

Kelly's nose wriggled. Another aroma caught her attention. "Cookies? You're baking?"

Frankie's grin got bigger. "Yes, I am. Help me finish decorating the tree, and I'll share some hot-out-of-the-oven sugar cookies."

Kelly's knees weakened. "My favorite." Great, more sugar.

Frankie laughed. "There isn't a cookie that's not your favorite." He shoved the ornament box into her hands and then went to grab another box. "Earn your food."

"You think you can boss me around?"

Frankie made a show of thinking for a moment, tapping his chin with his finger. "Yes." He turned to the tree and hung a medium-sized round ornament. "Get trimming. And tell me why you're here."

"Obvious?" She hung the ornaments. Frankie had a story for each one, like his mom used to. Tradition was important to Frankie. Maybe if Ralph and Summer respected the traditions Frankie valued, they'd have a better relationship. Then again, it didn't seem like good parent-child relationships were a strong suit in the Blake family. Her own relationship with her parents was still strained, and she had no idea how to repair it.

She gingerly pulled out a glass ornament in the shape of a stand mixer and hung it on a branch. Frankie had inherited their granny's collecting gene and now had dozens and dozens of food- and cooking-related ornaments.

"After Diana left your dad's house, did you see Wendy later in the evening?"

"What difference does it make?" Frankie stepped back from the tree and inspected it. "More filler." He grabbed a handful of poinsettia picks and inserted them into bare spots.

"Because she's been officially interviewed in Diana's murder."

"Not unusual. Look, Kell, you have a lot going on right now, so you don't need to go looking for trouble."

Kelly set the box down and padded over to the sofa and dropped onto the cushion. She stared at the gray brick fireplace. Frankie had draped garland above the firebox. The sliver of the mantel was bare of any knickknacks or decorations. She fell back into the deep cushion and crossed her legs.

Frankie looked over his shoulder. "I thought we had a deal."

"I want to renegotiate."

A timer dinged, prompting Frankie to set down the box and dash into the efficient kitchen. The noise coming out of the kitchen told Kelly he was pulling the cookie sheets out of the oven and plating the cookies.

"Don't forget the milk," she called out.

The refrigerator door opened and closed, and so did a cupboard door. A few moments later, Frankie appeared with a tray he set on the oversized coffee table. It held a plate of cookies and two glasses of milk.

"I should let them cool." He lifted the plate for Kelly.

"Can't wait that long." She picked up a cookie and took a bite. Her eyes rolled upward as the buttery, sugary cookie melted in her mouth. But it was hot, hot, hot. Yet so worth the moment of discomfort.

Frankie took a cookie and then returned the plate to the tray. After he finished his cookie, he washed it down with milk and then reclined back into the sofa. "What's going on, Kell? Why are you asking questions about Diana's murder? You have no stake in it."

"You're right. I don't. I guess there's a part of me that feels responsible. I mean, the last few moments of her life will be remembered as a nasty catfight between her and Wendy because she shopped in my boutique."

"You need another cookie." Frankie reached for the plate. "And you need to stop blaming yourself."

Kelly lifted a cookie off of the tray. She'd have to add another mile to her run in the morning after her poor food choices. She bit into the heavenly cookie. So worth every calorie.

Chapter Six

Kelly suppressed a yawn after she set her travel mug down and opened her laptop. She'd stayed at Frankie's house longer than she expected last night. Her plan to run off the calories from the pizza and sugar cookies hadn't happened. Instead, she'd hit the snooze button more than once and fell back to sleep each time. It was Howard's meowing in her face that woke her. The cat didn't understand personal space or boundaries.

Because she was thirty minutes late, her morning routine was a blur. She raced from bedroom to bathroom to kitchen. Finally dressed and with Howard fed, she filled her travel mug and raced down the stairs to open the boutique.

Thanks to her harried morning, she'd had little time to think about the dark cloud that had appeared yesterday while she was wrapping up her granny's tchotchkes for storage.

The dark cloud had a name—Marvin Childers.

In the middle of the night, she woke with a thought. She could destroy the marriage certificate and not say a word to anyone. If her granny was married to this man, wouldn't he have shown up when she died? More curious, why hadn't he shown up while she was alive?

The whole situation seemed bizarre. No one would be the wiser.

She tapped on the computer's keyboard and navigated to the boutique's online account on the Mine Now Yours website. She glanced at her watch. Pepper should arrive any minute. It would be her and Kelly in the boutique today. Breena had a full day at Doug's.

It took a moment for the website to come up, and she pulled the stool closer to the sales counter and sat. She logged into her account and checked the sales.

Holy cow!

All of Wendy's dresses had sold.

She'd been confident the dresses would sell, but she hadn't expected them to sell so fast. Her elation was replaced by the added work she needed to squeeze into her day. She had to package the dresses and make a trip to the post office. After she created the account, she'd purchased a box of pretty note cards, each with a different fashion illustration, to write a personal thank-you to her online customers. She'd be writing a lot of thank-you notes during the day.

Not a bad problem to have.

Her cell phone rang, and she reached for it. She swiped the phone.

"Hey, Pepper." Kelly grabbed her travel mug and took another drink but was disturbed by a hacking cough she heard on the other end of the line. Her mug landed on the counter with a thunk. "Pepper, are you okay?"

"No . . . I'm sick. I was feeling a little tired yesterday, and I woke up this morning . . ." Pepper stopped talking and coughed hard.

"I hope you're calling to tell me you won't be in today." She wasn't only Kelly's employee; she was also a dear friend she'd known since childhood and had been her rock since her granny had died. Hearing Pepper's weak voice and coughing made Kelly nervous, and instantly her mind drifted to a worst-case scenario. *Stop it. She'll be fine. It's only a cold.*

"I'm sorry. I know Breena isn't working today—"

"It's okay. Don't worry. I want you to rest and take care of yourself. Do you hear me?"

"I do. And I will rest."

"Good. Oh, I have a question. Do you know a man named Marvin Childers?" Kelly crossed her fingers Pepper knew him so she could get some information on the guy. Her step-grandfather?

Pepper coughed again and made a sound, then Kelly heard Pepper drinking.

"No, the name isn't familiar. Why are you asking about him?"

Kelly sighed. "No reason. I came across his name, and I'm curious."

"Where did you come across his name?"

The bell over the door jingled, and when Kelly looked up, her breath caught. Wendy Johnson? What on earth was she doing there?

"Kelly?"

"Gotta go. Take care, and call me if you need anything." Kelly ended the call and set her phone down. She inhaled a fortifying breath and stepped out from around the counter. "Hi, Wendy. I didn't expect you'd come back here after what happened at the party."

The door closed. Wendy stopped and pulled off her aviator sunglasses. She tilted her chin upward with practiced ease. She was used to making an entrance, and even dressed down in athleisure wear and bare of any makeup, she still commanded attention.

"Tell me about it." Wendy slipped her sunglasses into her nylon cross-body bag and stepped farther into the boutique.

"I've sold all your dresses. You'll be receiving your consignment check next week." Kelly walked toward Wendy and stopped at a circular rack of blouses. Wendy was a lot calmer than the last time Kelly had seen her, but she'd just arrived.

"Whatever. It's not like I need the money." Wendy tilted her chin even higher, giving the impression she was staring down her slender, patrician nose at Kelly, the local shopgirl.

"Then why are you here?"

"I'm here because you have to help me."

Have to help her? Kelly wasn't sure how Wendy had come to that conclusion. She was curious to hear what the privileged housewife had to say.

"What do you need help with?"

Wendy flipped her hair and cocked her head sideways. "Duh. This whole mess I got caught up in, thanks to you."

Duh?

How old was Wendy? She was old enough to have a better vocabulary, but Kelly wouldn't take on that topic because there was a bigger one to deal with straight on—Wendy blaming her because she was a murder suspect. Frankie was right last night when he told Kelly she had had no part in what went down between the two reality-show housewives. Their argument Saturday night wasn't the first one, and they had deeper issues than a dress.

"I don't understand why you're blaming me for what happened."

Wendy sighed. "I really need to spell it out for you?"

"Apparently."

"If you hadn't sold Diana my dress, we wouldn't have had the argument."

"I doubt that. It seems like drama follows you and your castmates around. I'm sure if the two of you hadn't fought about the dress, you would've fought about something else."

"Do you have any idea who you're talking to?" Wendy's intense, ice-blue eyes narrowed on Kelly.

"I don't have time for this. I have a business to run." Kelly turned to walk away.

"Just like your uncle's wife, Summer. She has a Pilates studio to run, and she'd love to expand it."

Kelly stopped and looked over her shoulder. "What are you saying?"

"Being on a national television show like *Long Island Ladies* would be a boon to her business. I see a franchise of Pilates studios in Summer's future. But . . ."

Kelly's stomach flipflopped as she turned around. "But what?"

"There are other contenders for the open spot on the show." Wendy stepped forward. "I'd love to be able to put in a good word for Summer. You know, like endorse her."

"Then go ahead."

"I won't be able to if I'm arrested for Diana's murder. I heard you did a little sleuthing last month when there was another murder. Seems you were instrumental in capturing the killer. I want you to do that again. Help me clear my name."

While Kelly might have been interested in the current murder investigation, she wasn't looking to come face-to-face with another killer.

"I still don't see how this is my fault and why I owe it to you to help clear your name." Nor was it Kelly's responsibility to help get her aunt onto the reality show.

Wendy closed the small gap between them. "If you don't help, I will make sure Summer knows you refused to help me and that's why she was taken out of the running for the show. How do you think she'll react? You know how difficult it can be dealing with family members who have their dreams crushed because of your actions or inactions." She crossed her arms over her chest, jutting out a hip and waited.

The thought of living with Summer if Wendy followed through on her threat was painful. Summer would never, ever let Kelly forget she caused her to lose out on a chance to be on television. Forget flipflopping, her stomach was churning violently now.

Wendy snapped her fingers. "I don't have all day. Are you in or is Summer out?"

Kelly gritted her teeth. "I guess I'm in. But I don't know what you're expecting. I'm not a detective."

"But you're nosy, and you like to dig into people's lives."

Kelly opened her mouth to protest, but Wendy shushed her.

"There's also a little something for you in clearing my name, Kelly. Once this matter is all cleaned up, I'll introduce you to women who can definitely improve the level of inventory in your little shop. You'll be consigning some of the most exquisite and expensive merchandise on the island."

Kelly could definitely use connections to help her get into the to-die-for walk-in closets of Long Island's wealthy socialites. She hated herself for thinking about business when one woman was dead and another was a prime suspect.

"Then let's start. Where did you go after Diana stormed out of my uncle's house?"

"I went to the restroom to freshen up and then rejoined the other guests. When I left, about an hour later, I went straight home."

"Why did you leave so early?"

"I wasn't feeling well. My assistant had a cold, so I thought I was coming down with something." Wendy unzipped her purse and pulled out a lipstick. After taking off the top, she moved over to one of the full-length mirrors Kelly had added to the sales floor; looking at her reflection, she swiped the color over her lips.

"What time did you get home?" Kelly followed and stood behind Wendy, looking at their reflection. "Can anyone confirm your story?"

"You sound like that awful detective, Wilson, Wood, Wolman! My husband was in Boston for business. And, no, I don't have live-in staff." Wendy swung around and waved her lipstick. "Any more questions?"

"Not at the moment."

Wendy snapped the lid on her lipstick tight and dropped it back into her purse. "I have to go. We'll check in. I'll text you." She spun around and walked out of the boutique, the bell jingling on her exit.

Kelly looked back to her reflection. Had she made a deal with the devil? Or a murderer? Just to not suffer Summer's wrath and help her boutique's bottom line? Yeah, she probably had sold her soul.

Kelly returned to the sales counter and grabbed her travel mug. She needed more coffee. Her day wasn't starting as she'd expected. To be honest, she wasn't sure what she expected after the past few days. The bell jingled again, and this time a customer entered. Kelly quickly plastered on a smile and greeted the petite brunette. She was looking for an outfit for a tree-trimming party, not an investigator to clear her of murder.

*   *   *   *

Kelly grabbed her key fob and cell phone from the console between the two front seats in her Jeep. Thirty minutes before closing the boutique for the day, she'd gotten a text message from Summer. Her aunt insisted she come over right after work. She considered declining. There was plenty of work to do upstairs in her apartment, but then she'd miss an opportunity to see Juniper.

The front door opened, and the housekeeper greeted her and then led her to the sunroom, where the lady of the manor was waiting.

Upon entering the room, Kelly noticed immediately that something looked off. Summer was lounging on the sofa with an arm stretched along the back of the sofa, talking on her cell phone. That wasn't what seemed odd. It was her exaggerated facial expressions, and the not one but three tosses of her head. Kelly followed Summer's gaze and found the reason for the weird behavior.

Standing in the opposite corner was a man with a video camera.

A cameraman?

"What's going on?" Kelly continued farther into the room. Okay, she was confused. According to what Wendy had said earlier, Summer wasn't on the show . . . yet. So, why was there a cameraman in the sunroom?

Summer lowered the phone. "Kelly, dear, I'm glad you could come by." She set the phone on the coffee table, never losing eye contact with the camera.

"Were you fake-talking on the phone?"

Summer laughed as she leaned back. "I'm practicing."

"You're practicing to talk on the phone?"

"I'm practicing being filmed. I hired Philip to follow me around. I'm getting used to being filmed. I think I'm adapting well. Don't you think so, Philip?"

Kelly caught Philip grinning, but he soon recovered his professional demeanor. "You're doing very well, Mrs. Blake." He gave a thumbs-up.

Summer ate up the praise. She crossed her legs. "Come, sit, and let's chat." She patted the cushion next to her.

"With Philip filming us?"

Summer nodded. "He's following my every move today." She patted the cushion again.

Yeah, but did he have to follow Kelly's every move? Against her better judgment, she joined Summer on the sofa, setting her phone and key fob down next to her. "How does it feel to have a camera follow you around?"

Summer tucked a lock of her blond hair behind her ear. "Honestly, it was a little odd at the beginning, but after a couple of hours, I forgot Philip was around. He's very quiet, and I got involved with things. This isn't only for practice. He will put together an audition reel for me if

Hugh asks for one. But I doubt he will. After the party Saturday night, I'm a shoo-in. There was so much drama, and we weren't even trying!"

"Speaking of the party, after Diana left, did you see Wendy later?" Since she was there, Kelly might as well find out what Summer remembered from the party. And to make sure Wendy hadn't lied to her.

"Let me think." Summer took a dramatic pause, tapping her chin with a finger. "Yes. She was mingling with the other guests. At some point, she was huddled with Hugh's wife, Tracy. But since I was the hostess, I was busy all evening with our other guests and didn't have much time to talk to Wendy. Why are you asking?" She lowered her hand to her lap.

"Wendy stopped by the boutique this morning. She asked for my help." Shoot. Summer was right. It was easy to forget you were being filmed. She twisted and looked at Philip. "Do you think you can delete what I just said?"

"This isn't about you. Nobody cares what you said." Summer gave a dismissive wave.

"Geez, thanks," Kelly said.

Philip gave another thumbs-up.

"I don't understand why Wendy is asking for your help. You're the reason she's in this mess. If you hadn't sold Diana the dress . . ."

"I didn't. I didn't know she'd come into the boutique until after she left. But I'm pretty sure there's a lot of footage between the two women to give the police reason to suspect Wendy. Were you and Diana friends?"

"No, not really. We were members of the same club. She also came into the studio for a few classes. She could've used regular classes. Just like you, dear. Your posture is that of a seventy-year-old. A few classes and you'll not only look taller, but you'll also feel taller."

Another sales pitch for pricey Pilates classes, even with the family discount, wrapped in the guise of concern.

"Aside from Wendy, could another *Long Island Ladies* star have had a motive to kill Diana?"

Summer tossed her hair again, flashed Philip and his camera an ominous look and held it for a beat, then returned her attention to Kelly. A touch overdramatic.

"You're being absurd. Nobody on the show killed Diana."

"How can you be certain?"

"Because she was off the show. My guess is her one-on-one with Hugh was to try to get back into his good graces and slink herself back on the show."

"What one-on-one?"

"She had lunch with him last week." Summer looked over to Philip and shook her head.

Kelly tamped down her irritation. She was trying to have a discussion with Summer, while her aunt only wanted face time with the camera. Kelly definitely wouldn't want a camera following her around or to be mic'd up all day. What about privacy? Like right now. She shouldn't be having a conversation in front of a camera.

"But, as you know, Hugh is looking for new blood for the show. Someone like me." Summer's face lit up. She really did want the job.

"In the few times you've talked with Diana, did she ever mention being threatened or in fear for her life," Kelly asked.

"No." Summer angled her head so she was looking directly at the camera. "She did mention her soon-to-be ex-husband, Aaron. He cheated on her several times, but the last time, the fool went and fell in love with Janine."

"She's on the show?"

Summer nodded. "She's the youngest. And apparently one sneaky little girl. She claims Diana's marriage has been over for a long time. Guess it's her way of justifying breaking up a marriage."

"Do you think she or Aaron Delacourte could have killed Diana?"

"You know, I really don't like talking about this morbid stuff. I have to check on Juniper. Want to come with?" Summer stood.

"Are you talking to me or Philip?"

"Both." Summer headed out of the room.

Kelly snatched up her car key and phone. She flashed the cameraman a smile. "Come on, Philip."

He gave his thumbs-up signal and followed.

In the kitchen, the housekeeper was unloading the dishwasher, while Juniper was seated in her high chair. Kelly took advantage of Summer filming her "confessional" with Philip and played with her cousin.

Summer later explained the "confessional" was the moment in the show when the cast members talk directly to the camera about their castmates or what was just shown to the audience. Even though Kelly had her reservations about Summer joining *LIL,* she had to admit that the few times she'd indulged in the guilty pleasure of watching reality shows, she loved the "confessionals." It was when the ladies backstabbed each other, wiggled their way out of compromising situations by making excuses, and traded some good old-fashioned trash talk.

Would any of the *Long Island Ladies* use the "confessional" to admit to murder?

Chapter Seven

On Wednesday morning, Kelly hurried downstairs to the boutique. She wanted to get in before Pepper and go through the tasks of opening the boutique for business. But Pepper had already arrived. She'd already opened the cash register, unlocked the front door, and tidied up the snowmen on the sales counter.

In the middle of wiping the counter, Pepper turned her head as Kelly approached and offered a faint smile. Despite wearing a festive holiday sweater and trying to brighten her face with makeup, she still looked tired.

"How are you feeling?" Kelly set her travel mug on the counter.

"Better. I slept most of yesterday." Pepper returned to cleaning the workspace. She reached for a spray bottle and gave the countertop a spritz and a wipe. A black headband pulled her shoulder-length blond hair off her face. Kelly figured Pepper had been too tired to fuss with styling her hair, but the simple style seemed to suit her.

"I'm glad you're feeling better." Kelly hugged Pepper.

The woman was like a mother, and having her ill, even with a little cold, was scary. Pepper was a strong woman, much like Kelly's grandmother. Martha had been the pillar of strength Kelly leaned on to get through the dark period of Ariel's accident. Maybe that was why when she got the news her granny had died, she was so blindsided. She never thought her granny would die. She was too strong. But Kelly was wrong, and that was why Pepper's illness had tangled up her insides so much.

"I'm not dying." Pepper pulled back from the hug. "There's no need to fuss. It's only a cold. Besides, I'm supposed to worry about you, not the other way around."

"You need not worry about me. Things are going well. Wendy's dresses have sold out. In fact, because I didn't get the chance yesterday, I have to run out to the post office to mail the packages. We also had a decent number of customers come in, and they bought stuff."

Pepper discarded the paper towel in the trash bin under the counter. "Hallelujah! Hopefully, this holiday season will turn things around for the boutique. Since we're on the topic of the holidays, when are you planning on putting up the decorations?" Pepper reached for a tissue and blew her nose, and then pumped a dollop of sanitizer on her hands.

"Today?" It was more of a question than commitment. Two boxes of decorations were in the staff room, waiting to be opened and used.

"Good. Clive will stop by later with some outdoor decorations. We can't be the only business on Main Street without them."

Pepper hadn't meant to, but the comment stabbed at Kelly's heart. In years past, her granny had changed out the decorations from autumn-themed to Christmas in every nook and cranny and then some—all in the blink of an eye. Now Kelly was dragging her feet.

"Does Clive know how much I love him?" Kelly was indebted to the Pepper and her husband for so much, and she wondered if she'd ever be able to repay them for the kindness. "Though, I don't want you decorating outside or inside. You're not to exert yourself."

"I'm not a baby."

"Got it. Still doesn't change what I said. Maybe I'll ask Liv to come over tonight, and we can have a boutique decorating party. Sounds like fun, right?"

"It does." Pepper stepped out from behind the sales counter. "Did you want to change any displays this morning?"

"No. I did the window yesterday and the mannequin in the accessory department."

After she'd cleared out the home accents and the square room was empty, it became a blank canvas for Kelly's wildest fashionista ideas. She'd spent hours online, browsing images to fuel the remodel, though her budget was tight, almost nonexistent. With her ideas in check, she'd stuck to a few cosmetic changes and roped in her friends for help.

A fresh coat of paint and revealing the windows behind a few large pieces of furniture made a huge difference in the boxy room. She added two freestanding mirrors she leaned against the walls and set out two tufted ottomans for trying on shoes or just taking a breather after a hard day of shopping. Her most recent addition was a crystal chandelier she picked up at a tag sale. She'd spent days cleaning it and had replaced the old, boring fixture right before Thanksgiving. All in all, the space had come together nicely.

"When I go out to the post office, I'd like to drive over to Diana's house." Kelly lifted her travel mug and took a long drink.

"What on earth for? Your part in the matter is all done. You gave your statement to the police."

Kelly shrugged and set the stainless-steel mug down. "I'd like to express my condolences to Diana's family and to Nanette, her housekeeper. The murder must have been a shock for her."

Pepper propped her hand on her hip. "I'm sensing you're not being entirely forthcoming. Why do you want to talk to the housekeeper?"

There was no getting around it. Kelly had to share what Wendy asked—no, correction, what she had blackmailed—Kelly into doing. Halfway through the story, the Pepper glare surfaced and contorted into a whole other look Kelly hadn't seen before. Yikes.

"You've got to be kidding me. You will really help this woman?"

"I doubt I can help her, but if I don't try, she'll make sure Summer doesn't get on the show. You know what she's like. Can you imagine what she'd be like if she knew I was the reason she didn't get on the show? Plus, Wendy has connections, and we need inventory. Good, quality inventory."

Pepper threw her arms up in the air. "I'm at a loss for what to say to you."

"That's a first."

Pepper wagged a finger at Kelly. "Don't get fresh."

How many times had Kelly heard Pepper say that? She pressed her lips together to keep from smiling.

"Look, I will ask a few questions. Enough for Wendy to believe I'm helping her." She used air quotes around the word *helping*. "It'll satisfy her, she'll talk Summer up to Hugh, and she'll introduce me to socialites who want to clear out their closets."

Pepper shook her head. "Do you hear yourself? You're sounding like one of those horrible reality people."

"Am not." Okay, how old was she? That wasn't the appropriate response for a twenty-six-year-old.

"Are too." Pepper threw up her hands and turned away. She walked toward the accessory department but stopped and looked over her shoulder. "You go do what you need to do. Don't be surprised when you realize you're all covered in dirt because that's what happens when you lower yourself to their level."

With that snippet of wisdom dancing around in her brain, Kelly collected the packages to mail and left the boutique. She arrived at the post office, and on the way to the counter, she caught snatches of conversation as she passed by a cluster of old-timers who hung out at the post office. Those guys made their rounds from the post office to Doug's Variety Store and the community center.

Kelly walked up to the counter. She was greeted by the postmaster, a woman in her late sixties with an obvious dye job. The deep auburn shade of her hair looked unnatural against her pasty skin tone and barely there eyebrows. While scanning the packages, the postmaster pumped Kelly for information about finding Diana's body, and no doubt, she'd pass on whatever she learned to the next customer. Small towns tended to be like that, and Lucky Cove wasn't any different.

With her packages mailed and her lips still sealed about finding Diana's body, Kelly stepped out into the cold air. December was a few days away, but its weather had already arrived. A strong gust swept by, sending Kelly's hair swirling in all directions, and left her shivering. She'd forgotten her hat when she rushed out of the boutique. But she'd remembered her gloves, and she slipped them on. Next on her to-do list was visiting Nanette. Hopefully the housekeeper would talk to her. She turned to head back to the boutique for her Jeep, and that was when she bumped into him.

"Oh, hey, Kelly." Mark caught her with both hands and flashed the sexy grin that had earned him the nickname Smokin' McHottie Lawyer.

"Hey, yourself." Kelly stared at his dark-as-midnight eyes, and the coldness she'd felt a moment ago vanished. "What . . . what are you doing here? I mean, I know you work close by . . ." She pressed her lips together. She was fumbling her words, so it was best to stop talking.

"Checking my PO box." Amusement flashed in his eyes. Clearly, he felt no awkwardness.

"Right. Lots of people have post office boxes here." *Way to go. State the obvious.* Since their date after Halloween, she'd made it a point to avoid him. Run-ins with exes—though he wasn't an ex because it had been only one date—were difficult. And it was so much easier in the city. Five boroughs and millions of people. Avoiding someone was a piece of cake. But in Lucky Cove? No such luck.

"Excuse me," a voice from behind Mark said.

Kelly and Mark murmured apologies to the woman and stepped to the side of the entrance. The little sidestep gave Kelly the opportunity to break free from Mark's hold, though it had felt nice.

"I have an idea."

"You do?" Against her better judgment, she was interested.

"How about we go get a coffee?"

"Now?"

He nodded.

"I'm sorry. I can't. I'd like to. Really. But I have an errand to run, and I have to get back to the boutique. I don't want to leave Pepper alone too long. She's not feeling well."

"I'm sorry to hear that. Of course, you have to get back to work. I should too."

"Call me, and we can set up a time for coffee." Her heart was racing, and butterflies fluttered in her stomach. Getting involved in a relationship wasn't a smart thing to do. She had too much on her plate as it was, and he was Detective Wolman's brother. The woman didn't like Kelly, and when a guy's family didn't like you, the relationship was doomed. She'd learned that lesson when she'd dated a medical student whose two sisters thought Kelly's interest in fashion was frivolous. They made Kelly's life a living nightmare for the five months she'd dated the guy. She could only imagine what Wolman could do to her.

"Sounds good. I'll call you. Have a nice day, Kelly." He leaned in for a kiss on her cheek and then continued into the post office.

Her gloved hand touched her cheek, and she smiled. Why did he have to be Smokin' McHottie Lawyer and Wolman's brother?

With a heavy sigh, she propelled herself forward to walk back to the boutique and get her Jeep for the drive over to Diana's house.

* * * *

On the drive to the crime scene, Kelly passed the small weathered cottage. Today the old man and his dog were nowhere to be seen. Maybe they were hunkered inside, a smart choice considering that the temperature hovered around twenty degrees. With the wind chill, it felt ten degrees colder. Technically it wasn't winter yet, but it seemed Mother Nature hadn't gotten the memo. If this was any sign of what real winter would be like, she needed to get thermal underwear.

She arrived at Diana's house and parked her Jeep in the circular driveway. She grabbed her tote bag and stepped out into the cloudy, bitter cold. Her steps were quick as she walked to the front door. As she pressed the doorbell, she prayed her visit wouldn't be a repeat of Sunday, when Nanette had shut the door in her face not once but twice. Moments passed before the door opened. Nanette appeared with a scowl etched on her face. Her cropped black hair was sleek, and her outfit was a pair of black trousers with a cream-colored, button-down shirt. In one hand, she held packing tape, and the other hand rested on the doorknob.

"Good morning, Nanette. I was hoping to speak with you. I promise it won't take long." Launching into her sales pitch came easily for Kelly. She wanted her visit to be brief. Pepper had said she was feeling better, but Kelly heard her coughing as she left for the post office. When she got back, she'd insist Pepper take the rest of the day off.

"I'm very busy." Nanette began to close the door. Déjà vu all over again.

Kelly held out her hand to stop the door from closing—a bold move she didn't expect to make, and now she had to follow through. What she'd told Pepper was true. She would do just enough to let Wendy believe she was helping to clear her name. What she didn't share was that she was curious why Nanette hadn't known her boss was dead and lying in the snow for most likely the whole night.

"Please. I promise I'll go away once we talk."

Nanette's heavy eyelids drooped over her pale blue eyes, and her face was drawn with exhaustion. Even her attempt to shut the door on Kelly seemed half-hearted, as though she didn't have the strength to close it hard and storm away.

"You're persistent." Nanette released her hold on the front door and turned. She walked into the living room, which was open to the foyer, thanks to an arched doorway.

Kelly entered the house and closed the door behind her. As she passed through the two-story foyer, she didn't inspect the space; she didn't want to waste any time since the clock was ticking on the housekeeper's reluctant hospitality.

In the living room, several packed moving boxes were stacked in front of the empty built-in bookcases and the fireplace mantel, which was barren of decorations. What was left in the shell of a room was the furniture, floral and stripe patterns mixed together, while the pale wood items were bare of accessories. Nanette shuffled over to an opened box and resumed wrapping a lamp in Bubble Wrap.

"It seems so soon to be packing up Diana's things." Kelly dropped her tote bag on the sofa.

"We've been packing for weeks. Diana was up to her eyeballs in debt. Most of this is going to an auction house." Nanette didn't look up. She continued to work on wrapping the lamp, then gingerly set it in the box. She then added a bunch of tissue paper for added security.

"That's why she bought a dress from my boutique? Because she didn't have the money for a new designer dress?" So much for living more eco-friendly and the book deal. "I thought she was doing research for an upcoming book about recycling and sustainability."

Nanette stopped packing tissue paper into the box and looked up. "What are you talking about?"

"Diana didn't have a book deal?"

"Ha! That would have been a godsend. Reality stars get huge advances for their books." Nanette returned to packing. "She shopped in your store to save money. She'd already sold most of her evening wear, and she probably didn't want to be seen in a dress she'd worn before. Then she buys one that Wendy owned."

"Appearances were important to Diana?"

"You have no idea. When Aaron walked out on her two years ago to be with Janine, the backstabbing witch, he cut off Diana's monthly allowance." Nanette closed the flaps on the box and ran the roll of tape over the seam.

"How did she keep up with the other ladies if she didn't have the money?" There was an old saying in suburbia about keeping up with the Joneses. When Kelly got into fashion, she learned that keeping up with or besting a neighbor was child's play compared to what it was like in the world of privileged, Upper East Side socialites. She could only imagine that the same held true for the Long Island Ladies.

The housekeeper's eyebrows arched. "Good question. I could use a break. Would you like a cup of coffee?"

"I'd love one." Kelly hadn't expected Nanette to mellow so quickly. Maybe she wanted someone to talk to.

While Nanette prepared the coffee, Kelly texted Pepper to check in and let her know she'd be a little late getting back to the boutique. Pepper assured her all was well and there wasn't any need to hurry back. Kelly was still worried and promised herself she wouldn't stay any longer than she had to.

Nanette returned to the living room with the coffee, and they both sat on the sofa. She'd chosen two *LIL* mugs. "Diana squandered all the money she did have to keep up with the other ladies. The designer clothes, the fancy car—which, by the way, has been repossessed—the vacations. Dinners out and parties to attend to be seen. Nobody wants to tune in to watch you sit in your house night after night. Social engagements meant new dresses, shoes. All such a waste, if you ask me."

Kelly blew on the steaming cup and then took a sip. "When she was fired from the show, she lost the only income she was receiving?"

"Exactly. Diana was broke, and she blamed Wendy."

"Because of the blog post and those photographs. Do you know why Wendy did such a thing?"

"Sure do. Wendy was desperate to stay on the show. Did you know she faked a story line about being romantically involved with some European count? Then she faked a pregnancy scare? At her age! Talk about absurd." Nanette shook her head before lifting her mug to her lips. "Then this past season, when she married, she planned this whole over-the-top wedding that cost close to a million dollars."

"Wow. All of that sounds extreme." Kelly took another drink of her coffee. A million-dollar wedding? How was that even possible? It was a ceremony and dinner. A million dollars? She'd always dreamed of marrying on the beach in a vintage dress. She'd love to find a gown made by the same dressmaker who'd made Jackie Kennedy's dress. Or maybe a vintage Priscilla of Boston gown. She'd love one of those.

"Wendy had no choice. On the show, Diana was her biggest competitor for attention and sympathy. Diana didn't have to embellish one thing about her marriage's breakup. Her pain was real. Her husband cheated on her with a friend. If you ask me, even though she lost pretty much everything, Diana was better off without him. He'd been very mean to her. The entire world saw him berate her. Horrible man."

"What about the other ladies? What was Diana's relationship like with them?"

Nanette sipped her coffee. "Diana got along with everyone, except for Wendy. And it was because of Wendy's insecurities. Janine is busy planning her wedding to Aaron. Looks like there's nothing standing in Janine's way now."

"What do you mean?"

Nanette lowered her mug. "Diana was fighting the divorce. She had no intention of making it easy for Aaron or his mistress. Now she's dead, and Aaron is free to remarry any time he wants to."

Interesting. It sounded as if both Aaron and Janine had a motive for murder. They had a lot more to gain than Wendy. In fact, other than the argument Saturday night, Wendy didn't have a motive. She'd already gotten Diana off the show. Detective Wolman should look at the estranged husband and his girlfriend, not Wendy.

Kelly set her mug on the glass coffee table. "I have one more question. When Diana didn't come home—well, I mean, come inside Saturday night—why didn't you try to find out where she was? Why didn't you call the police?"

Nanette also set her cup on the coffee table, pressed her palms against her thighs, and drew in a deep breath. "I'll never forgive myself. If I'd called the police, maybe she'd still be alive. But you have to understand Diana's lifestyle. It wasn't unusual for her to stay out all night at parties and with the occasional date."

"Was she dating anyone when she died?"

"No. She hadn't been on a date in months. Not after those awful photographs surfaced. Though she liked her men younger." Nanette stared off toward the fireplace. "It was cold on Sunday morning, so I didn't venture outside. Had I gone out, I would have found her." Tears streamed down Nanette's face, and she wiped them away with the back of her hand. She stood and walked to the end table and pulled a tissue out of the box. "To think she was lying in the snow and died all alone." She buried her face in her hands and sobbed.

Kelly stood and guided Nanette back to the sofa. She remained for another half hour, and when she left, Nanette was calmer and had gone back to work packing up the living room. Kelly's heart was heavy with sadness for the housekeeper. She genuinely seemed to have liked her boss.

Sliding behind her Jeep's steering wheel, she realized she'd told Pepper she wasn't really going to investigate on Wendy's behalf. Reason number one was that she wasn't a detective. Reason number two: the last time she stuck her nose into a murder case, she almost became a very dead fashionista. Reason number three: she owed Wendy nothing. All superb reasons. Solid reasons, if she said so herself. So why was she itching to talk to the lady who wanted to step into Diana's Jimmy Choos and marry Aaron Delacourte?

Chapter Eight

Kelly returned to the boutique. Pepper was assisting two customers at the changing rooms, while three more browsed with armfuls of clothing. Now that was how to put a smile on a gal's face. She greeted the browsing customers, and each one mentioned Diana's death. Not wanting to discuss the topic, she guided the conversations back to the clothing. By the time two of the women were ready to try on their selections, Pepper had rung up the two customers she was working with.

After the customers left the boutique and they had a quiet moment, Kelly filled Pepper in on her visit with Nanette, leaving out the part where she was considering paying a visit to Janine.

"Now, since you've gotten *it* out of your system, let's talk about the holiday event you want to have. I spoke with Betsy at the candle shop. She can donate a few jar candles for the goody bags." Pepper stepped out from behind the sales counter with three blouses and rehung them. She then walked to what was originally the dining room and now housed circular racks, all filled with pants and skirts. Kelly had wanted to rearrange the merchandise in the store for a better flow and to encourage impulse buying, but she'd been involved with the accessory department, so she hadn't gotten to the rest of the boutique yet. She made a plan for after New Year's to tackle a new layout.

It wasn't out of her system yet. But Kelly opted not to share that little tidbit. Like the tidbit about Marvin Childers. Even being consumed with a whodunit and holiday sales couldn't keep her mind from fretting over the dark cloud named Marvin Childers.

The boutique's telephone rang, and Kelly picked up the handset. "Thank you for calling the Lucky Cove Resale Boutique. This is Kelly."

"Just the person I wanted to speak with. This is Janine Cutter. I'd like to consign some clothes. I heard you sold all of Wendy's dresses." And just the person Kelly wanted to speak to. Talk about perfect timing. "Yes, we did. I'm happy to meet with you about consigning your clothes. We do in-home estimates. Would you be interested in scheduling one?" Kelly squeezed her eyes shut and hoped Janine said yes.

"Sounds perfect. I'm busy packing for an upcoming move, so the sooner we get this over with, the better."

Kelly glanced at Pepper. Could she leave her alone again? She seemed okay. She hadn't coughed since Kelly had gotten back, and the color in her face looked better. "Not a problem. I can be there in a half hour."

"Excellent. I've already sorted out the clothes I want to consign, and I know they'll sell out as fast as Wendy's. The only difference will be is people will want my clothes because they're fabulous, while they only bought Wendy's dresses because of the murder. See you in thirty."

"I'm looking forward to it." Kelly jotted down Janine's address, then said good-bye. She set the phone down. She couldn't help but wonder if it was truly perfect timing or too much of a coincidence? Could Janine have known Kelly had talked to Nanette earlier and the housekeeper had shared her suspicions about the husband-stealing reality star?

Pepper came back to the sales counter. "Your granny always hung stockings over the fireplace." She nodded in the direction of the fireplace. It sat squarely at the center of the house and separated the two front rooms.

Kelly crinkled her nose. Big red felt stockings weren't the look she was going for.

"Don't worry. I'm not talking about those quilted stockings Martha has had for years. I found the most fashionable stockings. White and gold with ruffles. You'll love them. Trust me." Pepper continued past the sales counter and disappeared into the small hall that led to the staff room.

"Guess it's decided then."

"Heard that!"

Kelly laughed. Her jovial mood passed quickly when she realized she had to tell Pepper where she was going. She expected Pepper to think she'd initiated the appointment. She was right. Their conversation was anything but brief, and by the time Kelly left the boutique, she still wasn't sure Pepper believed her.

Kelly arrived at Janine's ranch-style house with a couple of minutes to spare, which gave her time to do a quick Internet search on the youngest cast member of *LIL*. Right out of college, Janine had landed a spot on another reality show, *The Next Entrepreneur*. She was cut in week five, but the show had given her enough exposure for her to launch her jewelry line. She returned to *The Next Entrepreneur* as a judge, and then she landed the job on *LIL*. A true reality-television success story.

Kelly navigated to Janine's website and was impressed by the jewelry. Feminine, delicate, and way out of Kelly's price range. She noticed the time on her phone. She closed the Internet and stepped out of her Jeep. A gust of wind slapped her, and she buried her hands in the pockets of her parka to make the short trek to Janine's front door.

A fresh-faced, barefoot Janine greeted her. Her faded denim shirt was as well-worn as her distressed boyfriend jeans. She looked like someone Kelly could hang out with, not a TV diva.

"Right on time. I like you already." Janine's thin lips slid into a smile as she stepped aside to allow Kelly into her small entry hall. Wisps of her glossy brunette hair had slipped from her ponytail and framed her diamond-shaped face.

"Thank you for inviting me over." For more reasons than one. "I know you're on a tight schedule."

"It's crazy town. Between work and moving and Diana's death, I barely have time to get a manicure. Follow me." Janine pushed her violet cat-eye frames up the bridge of her nose before she turned and led Kelly through the living room. Janine's steps were light and quick.

They entered the master bedroom. A king-size bed dominated the room and was flanked by two nightstands; a triple dresser anchored the opposite wall. Janine's toes were buried in the plush carpet as she walked to a rolling rack of clothes.

Janine did a Vanna White motion with her hand. "Here are all the clothes I want to consign. They're all in season."

In-season clothing was definitely a plus. Kelly stepped closer and did a quick scan of the garments. She liked what she saw. A nice selection of blouses, shirts, pants, and skirts and a couple of day dresses, though they were kind of short. She looked back at Janine, who stood about three inches taller than her. On someone of average height, the dresses and skirts would fall lower, closer to the knee. Not having been the owner of the boutique for very long, she wasn't sure how mini lengths would sell. On closer inspection, she noticed the clothes were all size zero. Didn't any of the *LIL* eat? Good thing she had her website to sell merchandise.

"What do you think? Better selection than Wendy's, I'm sure." Janine moved away from the garment rack and over to a box beside the dresser.

"You have great pieces here." Kelly pulled out her phone and calculated how much she could sell each item for and then how much Janine could earn. The items weren't high-end designer, so their price point for the boutique would be perfect. Kelly suspected Janine's wardrobe would get an upgrade once she became the new Mrs. Aaron Delacourte.

"I'm sure I'll have more stuff once I'm all settled in my new place. Those are items I know I don't want to keep." Janine covered a framed photo in Bubble Wrap and placed it in the box.

"Where are you moving, if you don't mind me asking?" Kelly glanced up.

Janine stiffened and paused before continuing with her packing. She picked up another photo and length of Bubble Wrap.

"I guess it's no secret. I'm moving in with Aaron." Janine's voice had hardened and sounded defensive. "I'm sure everyone will have an opinion about it."

"People talk about a lot of things that aren't any of their business." Kelly had experience in that area.

It seemed everyone in Lucky Cove had an opinion after Ariel's car accident, and most of those opinions were about Kelly. She gave herself a mental shake. She wasn't there to travel down memory lane. She was there to get merchandise for the boutique and see what she could learn about the reality show and Diana.

Janine nodded vigorously. "Sounds like you know what it's like to have your life out there for public consumption."

Kelly lowered her phone. "Sort of. But our situations are different."

Janine held up her palm. "I know. I chose to put my life out there on TV. You know, sometimes I regret the decision, but then I wouldn't have met Aaron." She lowered her hand, and her voice softened. "He's the best thing that's happened to me in a long time."

"What about his wife, Diana?"

"What about her? Their marriage was over long before I came on the show and met Aaron. She was just hanging onto her marriage for the show. Without Aaron being the bad guy, she had no story line. Her life was boring. Had I had the foresight to know my relationship with Aaron would prolong Diana's presence on the show, maybe I would've done things differently."

Like not pursue a married man?

Kelly gave herself another mental shake. *No judging.* She was there for merchandise and information. Judging was wrong, and it shut down a conversation faster than asking a woman if she was pregnant. Never do that. Let the woman tell you if she is. Lesson learned at her first job in retail.

"They fired her, so I guess it worked out for you." Kelly slipped her phone into her tote bag.

"Kind of. Diana was campaigning to get back on the show. She even tried to sell an angle of being all earth-conscious. She got herself a hybrid car. Talk about a load of bull. The only reason she got a hybrid was because her Mercedes was repossessed and she couldn't afford another luxury vehicle." Janine stopped packing up her dresser and walked to Kelly. "I wasn't the only one who didn't want Diana back on the show."

"You're talking about Wendy?"

"Absolutely. It thrilled her when Diana was canned. I have a theory."

"You do?"

"My theory is that Wendy and her new BFF, Summer, planned to make sure Diana never returned to the show."

"You think they killed Diana?" A heaviness settled in Kelly's stomach at the accusation. She wasn't a fan of Summer—never had been—but she was certain her uncle's wife wasn't a murderer. To suggest that was careless and damaging to Summer's reputation.

Janine gave a "you bet your sweet Louis Vuitton Speedy bag I do" smile as she nodded her head. "You can't deny that it makes sense. Wendy gets rid of Diana for good, and Summer gets on the show."

"There's another theory."

"Oh, yeah, what?" Janine crossed her arms over her chest.

The smugness reverberating off of Janine reminded Kelly of the attitudes of high school cheerleaders. She was one for two years, so she knew what they were like. Well, not all of them. Most of them. She'd lay money on Janine once being a cheerleader.

"The other theory is you killed Diana. Maybe you two got into a fight because she was still dragging her feet with the divorce. Or maybe Aaron killed his wife for the same reason. Or maybe you two did it together."

"That's absurd!! You're way off base." Janine turned around so fast, her ponytail nearly whipped Kelly in the face.

"Am I?"

Janine tramped to the open bedroom door, and she spun around, placing both hands on her slender hips. "I've reconsidered consigning my clothing in your shop. You may leave now." With that dismissal, she lifted one hand from her hip and pointed to the hall.

So much for getting merchandise for her boutique. Why did Kelly have to defend Summer? She could've let it go and just pumped Janine for more information in a more subtle way than blurting out her possible motive for murder.

Kelly gave a final look at the rack of clothes before exiting the room. She thought maybe she could salvage the deal, but the stern look on Janine's face told her otherwise. There'd be no deal. She was leaving empty-handed. Once Kelly passed over the threshold and out into the short hallway that led to the living room, Janine disappeared from sight. It looked like she trusted Kelly to make her way out of the house on her own. No worries. Kelly was eager to leave.

As she walked past the coffee table, covered with magazines, file folders, and rolls of packing tape, a piece of a document peeking out from a folder caught her eye. It looked like a legal document.

Kelly looked over her shoulder. No Janine. Curious about what the document was, she bent and flipped open the folder. It was a legal document. Not wanting to linger too long, she pulled out her cell phone, snapped a few photos, and then closed the folder. She raced to the door.

Outside, she hurried to her car and slid in behind the steering wheel. After starting the ignition to warm up the Jeep, she opened the photo on her phone and enlarged it. From her limited knowledge of legalese, she could make out that the paperwork was a restraining order placed on Janine on behalf of Diana.

Whoa!

Maybe Kelly's theory wasn't too far off. Maybe Janine broke the restraining order and confronted Diana and then killed her.

Her cell phone rang, jolting her out of her thoughts. The caller ID told her it was Ariel calling.

"Hey, you won't believe what I found out," Kelly said.

"Tell me later. I'm at the bistro on Seabreeze, and Yvonne Patterson just came in. Want to meet me? Maybe you can talk to her."

Kelly considered the time. She'd been away from the boutique for over an hour. But she had to eat something. She thanked Ariel and told her she was on her way. Before pulling out of the driveway, she texted Pepper to see if she wanted anything from the bistro. Pepper replied no thanks; she had soup.

By the time Kelly arrived at the bistro, a quaint little restaurant set on an adorable street off Main Street, Ariel had to bail. She got called into the library for a last-minute staff meeting. Bummed she couldn't be there in person to see Kelly in action, she texted that she'd settle for a recap later in the day.

Kelly pulled off her sunglasses after entering the bistro and scanned the dining room for Yvonne. Thanks to her Internet search on Janine earlier, she knew what Yvonne looked like. All the Long Island Ladies had popped up during Kelly's scroll through data about Janine. She spotted her. Yvonne sat at a table for two by herself, sipping coffee and reading something on her cell phone through a fashionable pair of readers. Not a size zero like the rest of the cast, Yvonne was mature and not ashamed of it. Her short and side-swept hairstyle was both easy and elegant. Her hair color was a light gray with white highlights, and while it was appropriate for her age, Kelly was confident the color was boosted by a standing appointment with a hairstylist.

Kelly approached Yvonne's table, and when she arrived in front of Yvonne, she was at a loss for what to say. She should have prepared something, but she hadn't. It looked like she would wing it.

Yvonne peered at Kelly over the rim of her readers. "Can I help you?"

"Yes, no, I mean . . . I'm Kelly Quinn. I own the Lucky Cove Resale Boutique and was just at Janine's house to do an estimate. She expressed an interest in consigning with my boutique." Expressed and then changed her mind. But Kelly didn't want to bore Yvonne with the details of the meeting.

"How nice for her." Yvonne's voice was as cool as her lavender-striped, button-down shirt. The color played well against her coloring and gray hair. Her jewelry was tasteful; she'd limited herself to stud earrings, a chunky necklace, and a wedding band. There wasn't anything blingy, flashy, or showy about Yvonne.

"I'm hoping she'll consign. I've revamped the boutique and am attracting a broader customer base."

"Ambitious. It's always nice to see a young woman engaged in entrepreneurship. Would you like to join me?" Yvonne set her phone down and removed her readers. "I'm between appointments."

"Thank you. I'd love to." Kelly pulled out a chair and shrugged out of her coat after setting her tote down. A waiter appeared and took Kelly's order for a coffee. She was hungry but didn't get the vibe from Yvonne that she wanted a lunch companion.

"You're Ralph Blake's niece, aren't you?"

Kelly paused a moment before answering. She wasn't sure how people felt about her uncle. He was a shark in business, which made him a lot of enemies but also made many people rich. Kelly wasn't sure which camp Yvonne fell into.

"I am." Before she could ask how Yvonne felt about her dear uncle, the waiter appeared with her coffee. She added a dash of cream and stirred. "How did you like his holiday party?"

"I couldn't attend. I had a prior engagement. This time of the year, the invitations are endless. Ralph must be proud of you being a young businesswoman."

Proud? Not exactly the word Kelly would use to describe her uncle's feelings about her. Disappointment. Annoying. Problem. Those three words were more like it. He was disappointed that she wouldn't sell the building and annoyed that he was the estate's executor, which meant Kelly was one big problem. Definitely not proud.

"My uncle admires business owners." While she had her differences with her uncle and his wife, she didn't want to air them publicly.

"I heard you used to work at Bishop's in the city. Do you know Serena Dawson?"

The name Serena Dawson still sent a wicked chill through Kelly.

Serena was the person she least wanted to talk about. (Uncle Ralph came in second place.) From her first day on the job, she'd never clicked with the high priestess of fashion, and their relationship hadn't improved while she was there. Maybe Serena didn't like her pedigree as the granddaughter of a consignment shop owner. Whatever the reason, Kelly never got the chance to find out. Because after a series of events on what was a rather normal day—she'd returned with the wrong coffee order, picked up the wrong sample skirt from a designer's showroom, and missed confirming an appointment that left Serena arriving at another showroom with no one there to greet her—she was terminated.

Another chill snaked through Kelly at the memory. It had been late in the afternoon when Serena returned to the office. She had marched over to Kelly's desk and, without warning— mostly thanks to her regular Botox injections, which meant she showed no emotion, so there wasn't a heads-up for Kelly—she was fired in front of everyone in the women's buying office. Everyone.

"I know Serena. She's a legend on Seventh Avenue." Kelly took a long drink of her coffee. The woman was indeed a legend on Fashion Avenue. She was better known as the dragonista of retail. The last thing Kelly wanted to do was bad-mouth Serena.

"She's quite a force of nature. When I go into the city, she arranges a personal shopper for me. Then we have lunch." Yvonne leaned into her chair. "What is it you want, Miss Quinn? Do you want me to consign with your little shop?" She arched a colored brow.

Yvonne was as direct and condescending as Serena was. No wonder they were friends.

"Only if you're interested."

Yvonne leveled a flat stare on Kelly. "I'm not."

She was as blunt as Serena too. "Consignment isn't right for everyone."

"As I said, I'm between appointments. I don't have the time nor the desire to play games. I will guess you're here to talk about Diana's murder. It seems everyone with idle time on their hands is interested."

Kelly tamped down her irritation toward Yvonne. The older woman had a lot in common with Serena, in addition to the already identified attributes. They both seemed to have no problem insulting people. In fact, they both acted like it was their duty.

"When was the last time you saw Diana before her murder?" Kelly pushed her half-empty cup forward and rested her hands on the table.

Her own boldness shocked Kelly, and Yvonne almost looked amused. "Even though it's none of your business, I'll tell you because you have the guts to approach me and to insinuate I'm a suspect. I saw Diana a few days before the party. We met for lunch. Satisfied?"

"Where?"

"Right here. If you're keen on finding out who murdered Diana, then I suggest looking at Janine and Aaron. The poor sucker thinks he's in love, but Janine is just as conniving as Diana was."

"What about Wendy?"

Yvonne shook her head. "She's not a killer." Yvonne lifted her classic Chanel quilted leather bag off the table and stood. She slung the chain strap over her shoulder. "I have a daughter about your age, so take my advice to heart, dear. Focus on your shop, and stay out of this ugly business of murder."

Kelly remained seated as Yvonne wove her way through the round tables in the dining room to the hostess station, where she was handed her coat. She said a few words to the hostess before disappearing out the doorway. Kelly decided to finish her coffee, giving herself time to think.

Yvonne had given her some solid advice, but Kelly was focused on her business. By helping Wendy, she was helping her boutique. That was the deal they'd made, and so far, she'd held up her end of the bargain. She'd asked questions and was confident she was drawing the same conclusion as Detective Wolman—that Janine and Aaron were the most likely suspects. Wolman was far too competent a detective not to see the writing on the wall.

As Kelly swallowed her last drink of coffee, her cell phone buzzed with a text message from Breena. Her eyes nearly bugged out of their sockets when she read the text.

Need you here now. Trouble.

Chapter Nine

Kelly dug through her tote, pulled out her wallet, and slapped down a few dollars for the coffee. She shrugged back into her coat and darted out of the bistro. When she arrived in the boutique, Gabe was seated at the table in the staff room, drumming his fingers on the table. A grim expression was etched on his face.

He was the *trouble* referred to in the text.

"Hi, Gabe. What's going on?" She unbundled herself from her coat, scarf, gloves, and tote bag, dropping them all on her desk. She'd tidy up later, after finding out why Gabe looked so serious.

Gabe stopped drumming his fingers. His beachy-blond hair had been cut. Gone were the soft waves he'd had since childhood. The almost buzz cut gave him a more mature look. "What's going on? You're doing it again."

Kelly pulled out the chair at her desk and sat. "Doing what? I've been at a consignment estimate."

"Asking questions about Diana Delacourte's murder. It's a police matter, and you can't be poking around."

"What makes you think I'm doing that?" Kelly crossed her arms over her chest and eyed the swinging door to the sales floor. Now would have been a good time for an interruption.

Gabe leaned forward. "Then why did Janine Cutter call Wolman and tell her you harassed her?"

"What? That's outrageous!"

"I believe she feels the same way. Kell, I know how you get— "

"Whoa, whoa . . . hold on there." Kelly uncrossed her arms and pointed a finger at Gabe. "She invited me to her house for an estimate on clothes she wanted to consign. She's the one who brought up the show and the other ladies and her affair with Aaron. We were talking. I wasn't harassing her."

Gabe rubbed his hand over his head. His kind eyes flickered with annoyance. "Kell, do I need to remind you of what happened last month? How you almost got yourself killed?"

"No, you don't. It's still burned into my brain." Until recently, she'd had nightmares of the incident and how close she came to being the late Kelly Quinn.

"Good. There's a lot of work to be done in the boutique. You stayed here in Lucky Cove to build a business and a life. Getting involved in the investigation could put you in danger again, and you could lose everything if you're arrested. You know how much lawyers cost."

When had the goofy boy Kelly had grown up with become so smart? It must have been while she was pursuing her now-faltered fashion career.

"Thank you for caring." .

"It's more than caring, Kell. You're like a sister. I'd hate to arrest you. Again."

Ouch.

She didn't want to think about that fateful night when the stars had aligned and she'd landed in handcuffs. Liv's mother still hadn't forgiven Kelly for getting her baby girl arrested. Ever since then, Mrs. Moretti muttered in Italian when she saw Kelly, and Liv refused to translate.

"I promise I'm doing nothing that will get me arrested." She stood and walked to the table. She sat across from Gabe and reached out for his hands. "I'm not going to risk this boutique or my life . . . again. You have my word."

Gabe stared at Kelly, and she sensed he wanted to believe her. She also sensed he believed she was withholding something too. Damn, he was a good cop. She hadn't wanted to tell him about Wendy's offer or the fact she'd made a deal with the reality diva. If she told him, he'd stay and lecture her and probably arrest Wendy for something, maybe tampering with a witness? She had no clue.

"Okay, okay." Gabe patted Kelly's hand and then stood. "I've said my piece. Consider yourself warned when it comes to Wolman." He grabbed his leather jacket off the back of the chair and put it on. He pulled out a pair of gloves from his pocket and slipped them on.

"On a different note, how's your mom feeling? She's been sick, but she keeps telling me she's fine."

"Yeah. She tells me too. Dad and I are keeping an eye on her."

"I'm doing the same. I don't want her to overdo it. I love having her here, and she's beyond helpful, but I want her to be healthy."

"Maybe you need to be here more and not out chasing killers. Maybe then she can feel like she can take time off. She feels responsible for this shop." Gabe zipped his jacket.

Kelly lowered her eyelids. Gabe's words were harsh but true. Pepper had a deep sense of responsibility, not only to the shop, because she'd worked there for twenty years beside Martha, but also to Kelly.

"I didn't mean for it to come out like that, Kell. Sorry." Standing beside her, he rested his hand on her shoulder and squeezed.

"You're right. I'll do better. I promise." She officially felt like last year's must-have now hanging haphazardly on a discount store's markdown rack, like one of the items people mocked after a season and whose only purpose would be as part of a Halloween costume. She patted his hand to affirm she wasn't angry with him. "Thanks for warning me about Wolman and what Janine told her."

He let go of her shoulder and left through the back door, allowing cold air into the staff room. Kelly shivered and wrapped her arms around herself. She rubbed her arms vigorously to warm up. She had a lot to think about, but she was also hungry. She stood, walked back to her desk to get her phone out of her tote, and texted Liv to see if she wanted to have Chinese for lunch. She walked out of the staff room. It was time to get to work and send Pepper home for the day. Liv texted back and said she'd pick it up and be there soon.

Lunch plans with a friend put a smile on Kelly's face, and it broadened when she saw more than a handful of customers browsing with garments in hand. Maybe things were turning around for the boutique without her extra efforts. Well, a little thanks needed to be given to the refurbishing and to the targeted advertising she'd done. She gave a little shrug. What mattered was the fact that she had customers.

A snafu at the bakery had Liv running behind and texting she'd arrive with lunch as soon as she could. To tide herself over, Kelly snagged a protein bar from her stash of snacks in the staff room. It should be enough to hold her over until lunch arrived. By the time Liv showed up with Chinese takeout, Breena had reported to work and insisted she'd be fine on her own while Kelly ate. If she needed help, she'd text Kelly. Kelly appreciated the offer, especially because she wanted to discuss the Marvin Childers situation with her friend and didn't want to risk anyone overhearing them.

Liv looked confused when Kelly told her they'd be eating upstairs rather than in the staff room, where they usually ate lunch.

"Get out! Your granny remarried and told no one?" Liv's look of astonishment must have been how Kelly had looked when she'd discovered the marriage certificate. How and why did someone keep a marriage a secret? What could have been the reason?

"I know for certain she never told me. I'd think she would have told Pepper because they were as thick as thieves for as long as I can remember." Kelly drizzled duck sauce over her egg roll and then took a bite.

"They were besties, like us. Can you imagine us at their age? What secrets will we be telling each other then?" Liv took a mouthful of her chicken lo mein. She didn't want to share Kelly's Szechuan chicken because it was too spicy for her taste buds.

After Kelly swallowed her bite of egg roll, she set it down and wiped her fingers with a napkin. "Maybe something like one of us got hitched in Vegas."

Liv laughed. She set her chopsticks down. She worked them with precision while Kelly fumbled with hers, always had, and that was why she used a fork. She scooped up rice, along with a piece of chicken.

When Liv had arrived with the large shopping bag of food, Kelly realized they might have over-ordered, because there was enough food to feed not four but six people. Lucky for Howard. He appeared at the smell of the chicken and gave Kelly sad kitty eyes, and she caved like the new pet-mommy she was and broke off a few bits for him, careful to remove all the sauce.

"Do you know Marvin Childers?" Kelly prepped another piece of chicken for Howard. Yes, she was setting a bad precedent of feeding the cat while she was eating her meal, but he was being adorable and she wanted to bond with him as her granny had.

"He's your granny's husband?" Liv stopped dishing out more lo mein and stared at Kelly.

"Don't call him that. Wait, do you know him?" Kelly set down the pieces of chicken for Howard, and he ate them in a dignified manner, though she was certain he wanted to pig out.

"Not really. He used to live out by the water and was an illustrator. He's retired now. The library had showings of his work over the years. I don't know where he is now." Liv filled her plate with more noodles and chicken.

"What were they doing in Vegas?" Kelly stroked Howard's head, and he purred, melting her heart.

He was becoming more loving with each passing day, and it was what she'd hoped for. Little did she know a month ago that she'd be trying to have a cat love her. Go figure.

Liv lifted her wineglass and took a drink. "My guess is they went as part of the Senior Center's annual trip. The Center stopped doing it a few years ago after one of the seniors got hurt on the trip."

"Then I should be able to verify it, right? Who runs the Senior Center?" Kelly took a sip of her wine. She normally didn't drink wine with lunch, but it'd been a rough day, and one glass wouldn't be too bad. At least she hoped not.

"Harriet O'Neal. She can be a little ornery. Be sure to pick up a couple of her favorite cupcakes from the bakery before you see her. They'll soften her."

"Ornery? Great." Kelly took a gulp of her wine. Sipping just wasn't working.

"Don't worry. This will all work out. I'll also see what I can find out about Marvin, like where he's living these days."

"Thank you. I can't lose my inheritance." A soft meow had Kelly looking at Howard. He'd positioned himself by her chair at the table. "Or Howard."

"You'll never lose Howard. And you won't lose the boutique or your home."

Kelly gave her best friend a knowing look.

"You're worried that if Marvin is the rightful heir, he'll sell to your uncle?"

Kelly nodded.

Liv reached forward, lifted the wine bottle, and topped off Kelly's glass. "We won't let it happen. But we shouldn't get ahead of ourselves."

Too late. That train had already left the station. Kelly's mind was a hamster wheel of worry and a nonstop film reel of finding Diana's body.

"Hey, let's talk about something more festive." Liv set the bottle down.

Kelly cringed. No, she'd rather talk about the strong possibility that she would lose her fragile livelihood and home either to an old man she didn't know or to Wendy's bad-mouthing her to everyone who followed her on social media.

"When are you going to decorate your apartment?" Liv took an exaggerated look around the living room. "Hang a stocking for Howard?"

Kelly pressed her lips together to form a pseudo-smile—part-happy, part-displeased, and part-annoyed. Her entire world was again on shaky ground, and her best friend wanted to talk decorating? How could she hang ornaments in the boutique or in her apartment when, at any moment, she could lose everything?

Kelly reached for her wineglass and took a long drink. She was being overdramatic, and she needed to ratchet it down a notch.

"Having a little crazy time in your head?" Liv lifted her glass, leaned back, and took a sip. She knew Kelly all too well. "Everything's going to work out fine. You have to believe that. And what may help is a little holiday spirit. Let's plan to decorate soon. Okay?"

Kelly studied Liv over the rim of her glass. Her friend's optimism was palpable. Adding some holiday cheer to her apartment might help Kelly not think twenty-four/seven about the murder or her business. She might enjoy being in the moment—something she hadn't been able to do since her firing from Bishop's and her granny passing away.

"Sounds good. While we're at it, we can decorate the boutique too. Pepper found some stockings to hang on the fireplace. How about tonight?" She'd had fun decorating Frankie's tree the other night, and the sugar cookies were an extra bonus. She wondered if she could get Frankie to bake her a batch for her own decorating.

Liv frowned. "No can do. I'll be at the community center all night. I'm organizing a gingerbread house decorating event. We have a ton of stuff to go over."

"Bummer. Well, then soon. Or I'll never hear the end of it from Pepper."

"You've got it." Liv leaned forward and held out her glass. "Here's to holiday cheer." She clinked her glass against Kelly's.

"Holiday cheer," Kelly repeated.

They finished lunch and cleaned up their plates right before the impending storm hit the island. What had started out the night before as a prediction of a few flurries had turned into a full-fledged snowstorm with varying reports of accumulation. The weather people couldn't agree on how much snowfall the island would have by tomorrow morning.

When Kelly said good-bye to Liv at the back door downstairs, the snow was already coating the road. She hurried from the door to the sales floor and instructed Breena to leave for the day, before the roads got too messy and dangerous. She would close the boutique at six.

Breena left without an argument. Kelly considered closing early, but there was still traffic on Main Street, so there was a chance she could get a few customers before closing, though she was doubtful she'd have many first thing in the morning if the snow continued to fall at this steady clip, because most people would be digging out.

Chapter Ten

Kelly woke with a start, shifting Howard from his cozy spot, curled up along her legs, which earned her a glare. Her gaze darted around the bedroom and up to the ceiling. Okay. It was only a dream, a terrible Christmas-decorating-induced dream. The pieces of the dream that woke her came together.

She was tangled up in silver garland. The garland was so tight she couldn't move her hands or feet. It trapped her. Beside her was a tree so tall it broke through the ceiling—a big gaping hole through to the attic space and roof.

Wendy had also been present in the dream. Handcuffed, she was shouting she'd destroy the boutique since Kelly didn't help her clear her name. Summer was also there, lying on the floor, doing leg circles with expert precision. Between inhales and exhales, she shouted repeatedly that Kelly had ruined her chances of getting on *LIL*.

In her dream, Kelly had struggled to free herself from the garland, and a piece of fabric slipped from the top of her head. It wasn't any piece of fabric. It was the scarf from Diana's body. Kelly struggled harder and called out to Pepper to help her. Pepper was too busy hanging ornaments and humming Christmas carols to pay her any attention.

Her only hope was Frankie, but he was dashing around the room with a plate of sugar cookies, insisting everyone take one. And off in the distance, Janine stood draped over a man Kelly didn't recognize but guessed was Aaron. Janine grinned like a woman who'd gotten away with murder.

Kelly shook her head. It wasn't a dream; it was a nightmare.

A nightmare that could come true. She threw off the covers and righted herself. After slipping into her cozy slippers, she reached for her cardigan. In the winter months, she preferred a chunky cardigan to a robe. Snuggled in the cardigan, she padded over to the window and pushed back the drapes.

The early morning sun revealed several inches of fresh snow all across Lucky Cove and, no doubt, its neighboring towns. Mother Nature wasn't playing around. She was making sure the East Coast had a white Christmas.

She let the drapes fall back and turned to walk into the bathroom. After a quick freshening up, she headed for the kitchen. The bright side of the snowfall was that she didn't have to go for her morning run. She'd given herself permission to take snow days off from exercising. With the coffeepot prepared, she pressed the ON button and then pulled out a box of cereal from the upper cabinet. She didn't have to run, but she had to clear the paths to the boutique, both out front and in the back. It looked like she had to exercise after all.

Howard made his appearance, weaving his way through her legs and pressing his body against her. Apparently, all was forgiven on his end about his abrupt wake-up. The cat didn't hold grudges.

"Hey, little dude. Sorry about earlier. It was a bad dream. Everyone was shouting at me or ignoring me, and someone wrapped me up in garland. It was awful."

Howard responded with a comforting meow, and she scooped him up.

"Thanks for understanding. I'm guessing you'd like some breakfast."

She set the cat down and filled his bowl with kibble. She then cleaned and refilled his water dish. While he ate and she drank her first cup of coffee—liquid gold, it was—the conversation she had with Gabe yesterday about Diana's murder replayed in her mind.

While Howard finished his breakfast, she settled at the dining table with her mug and her laptop. She turned on the computer and checked her e-mails while Gabe's words echoed in her head. Their conversation was hanging around.

Was she risking too much by asking questions about Diana's murder and helping Wendy? The answer was probably yes, but she hated to admit it. Her curiosity was overwhelming. She'd already inserted herself into the investigation by going to Janine's house and asking her questions. Looking back to the day before, she hadn't been a hundred percent honest with Gabe. She had had an ulterior motive when she went to Janine's house, but she was telling the whole truth about Janine bringing the topic up. Then the woman had the nerve to call Wolman. The reality star was a tattletale.

Whoa. Kelly was reverting back to a tween.

By the time she finished the last of her coffee, she'd decided to continue to help Wendy however she could. Her Christmas nightmare had included a gloating Janine with Aaron, and it reinforced her gut feeling Janine was guilty of more than stealing Diana's husband. She had to be careful and stay under Wolman's radar.

With her coffee finished, she padded into the bathroom and took a shower. She then dressed for work, keeping in mind that she had to do some shoveling. She chose a pair of skinny jeans and a three-quarter zip fleece top. She eased her feet into her snow boots, pulled on a hat, and grabbed her gloves, along with her parka. Coming off the last step of the staircase, she opened the door and entered the boutique. First thing, she turned on the lights. On her way to unlock the front door, she dropped her gloves and parka on the sales counter. Continuing to the door, she saw the outline of a person waiting on the other side.

Early bird shoppers on a snowy morning. That put a spring in her step. Her spirits were definitely lifted.

And all in one sweeping moment, her spring was gone and her spirits plummeted when she got a good look at the woman waiting outside.

Detective Wolman.

Kelly unlocked the door and then opened it after flipping over the OPEN sign.

"Good morning, Detective. What brings you here this morning?" She knew the reason for the visit. But she didn't want to let on that Gabe had forewarned her. Kelly stepped aside to allow the detective to enter the boutique and then walked toward a round rack to straighten up. Browsing through clothing could leave a rack messy. Shoveling snow would have to wait until the impromptu visit from Wolman ended. Meanwhile, she'd tidy up.

"I've had a complaint lodged against you, Miss Quinn. It seems you were harassing Janine Cutter." Wolman unzipped her wool coat, revealing a stark white shirt tucked into a pair of boring plain black pants. The detective lacked any fashion flair. But then again, before being promoted to a detective, she was a patrol officer who wore a uniform every day, so she probably didn't know how to express her own fashion sense and found comfort in a new uniform of boring basic pieces.

Kelly rested her hand on the rack. "I did no such thing. She called and invited me to her house to do an estimate for consignment."

"Why were you asking questions about Diana Delacorte's death?" Wolman rested a hand on her hip, sweeping back the side of her coat.

While her clothes were basic and uninspired, her makeup was spot-on. Her subtle smoky eyes were daytime appropriate, and a shimmer of blue on her lashes caught Kelly's attention. Wolman used a colored mascara. Good for her!

"She brought up Aaron while I was doing an estimate on her clothes. Diana's death came up in conversation. I can't believe she's making it sound like I grilled her. I didn't." Not completely a lie. She didn't have time to probe for more answers.

Wolman dropped her hand and closed the space between her and Kelly. "I doubt you were just making conversation, given your history with murder investigations. I will give you one more warning to stay out of this matter. Stay out of my way. Have I made myself clear this time?"

Kelly didn't appreciate Wolman's advance into her personal space but made the smart decision—it happened every now and again—not share her irritation with the detective.

"Crystal."

"Good. I expect this will be the last time we'll have this conversation." Wolman backed up and headed to the exit, but stopped on her way and turned back to Kelly. "Are you going to do any holiday decorating? Make the place a little more festive?"

Festive. Kelly was starting to hate that word.

"It's on my to-do list."

Wolman gave a sharp nod and left the boutique.

"On my to-do list. Geez, like everything else," Kelly muttered on her return to the back of the boutique after she relocked the door. She stepped out into the small drafty mudroom off the staff room and grabbed the shovel as she huffed. She'd been prepared as a shop owner to stock inventory, clean the boutique, and spend hours on bookkeeping—but shoveling? Nope. But there she was, plodding through at least four inches of new snow.

The strenuous work of clearing paths helped work out her frustration with Detective Wolman. The various scenarios fluttering around in her head fueled her swift movements with the shovel. Scenarios of a family dinner with her, Mark, and his sister.

The image of being seated across from Marcy Wolman and asking her to pass the peas, only to receive a glare, had Kelly tossing a shovelful of snow to the side a little more aggressively than she intended, resulting in a sharp pain along her side.

She needed to reign in her doom-and-gloom scenarios. Even if she and Mark met for coffee or lunch or dinner or whatever, there was no guarantee they'd make it to the stage in the relationship where he'd take her home to meet his family.

Ignoring the pain in her side, she stabbed the next patch of snow with the shovel. The truth was, she wanted to be in that stage of a relationship with him. He was the first guy she'd met in a long time that she wanted to be with all the time.

Of all the guys on Long Island, why did she have to fall for Wolman's brother?

By the time Breena showed up for work, Kelly had cleared the paths in both the front and the back of the boutique. She expected the plow service to show up within the hour to clear the parking lot.

Breena shook off the cold as she unwrapped herself from her coat and chunky scarf. "Can you believe all the snow? And it's not even the first day of winter yet. I'm afraid to think of what will happen then."

"There's a fresh pot of coffee." Kelly settled down at her desk and checked her cell phone. There was a text from Ariel. Before Kelly went out to shovel, she'd texted Ariel and asked her to dig up all the information she could on all the *LIL* cast members. Working part-time at the library and being a freelance writer, Ariel had information-gathering skills Kelly didn't possess. According to the text, Ariel had gathered the information and suggested they meet for lunch later. Shoveling definitely worked up an appetite. She replied, and they set a time to meet.

Breena poured a cup of coffee and stirred a packet of sugar into it. "Is there anything special going on today?"

Kelly stood with her cell phone in hand, and before she could answer Breena, Ralph's voice bellowed through the building. Dread settled on her like a cement block.

"Is that your uncle?"

"I'm afraid it is. What's he doing here?" First, snow. Then, Wolman. And now, Ralph. Her day kept getting better and better.

He bellowed again, and Kelly was tempted to do rock-paper-scissors with Breena but resisted. Sending her part-time employee to deal with her uncle would be cowardly. She slipped her phone into her back pocket and pushed off to find out why her uncle was paying a visit.

"Well, it's about time. I was wondering if anyone was here. Seriously, Kelly, do you think this is any way to run a business?" Ralph didn't bother with pleasantries or salutations. No. Rather, he went to the place he always went—reminding Kelly that she was too inexperienced to run the business.

"I just came in from shoveling. What brings you by?" Kelly walked to the sales counter but kept a watchful eye on her uncle.

Ralph approached the sales counter, unbuttoning his full-length wool coat. The charcoal gray garment was expertly tailored and must have set him back a fair chunk of change. His chubby cheeks were red from the cold, and his bushy eyebrows needed a good waxing and combing.

"I have good news."

Kelly eyed her uncle warily. Ralph never came by with good news, at least not for her. "What are you talking about?"

"I got us an offer on this old house. Emilio wants to buy this place. And he's offered a decent price." Ralph beamed with satisfaction.

"Emilio who?"

"You met him at the party the other night. Remember?"

"No, I don't."

"I introduced you to him and his wife. Kelly, he's a business contact and you need to pay attention and remember people like him. See. Another reason why you're not cut out to be a business owner."

Kelly took a deep breath and mentally counted to ten. "I met many people at your party. You know, it doesn't matter, anyway. I'm not selling." Kelly pulled out a disposable cleaning cloth and wiped down the counter.

"Use your head, Kelly. It's a good offer. You'd have a lot of money to do what you want." Frustration had slipped into Ralph's voice. Since the day Martha's will was read and Ralph learned his mother had left her biggest asset to someone else and saddled him with being the executor, he'd been trying to get Kelly to sell the house and business. He'd made it clear the responsibility was a nuisance, and she didn't doubt for a minute he'd find a way to profit off the sale.

"I'm already doing what I want to do. Tell Emilio thanks but no thanks." Kelly tossed the cleaning cloth into the trash bin and then powered on the cash register and tidied up the shopping bags.

"Why are you so stubborn?"

"Why are you so thick? I've told you how many times I don't want to sell. Granny left me this business, and I intend to make it successful, despite your attempts to sabotage me."

"Sabotage you? I don't have to sabotage you because you're doing a fine job of that on your own. Like getting yourself arrested last month. What about the roof? Has it been repaired yet? Owning a retail business is more than wasting time with fancy displays and frilly merchandise."

Kelly opened her mouth to respond but closed it and mentally counted to ten, again. Her uncle left out the fact that she hadn't been charged with a crime and was let go. Also, the roof was patched well enough to withstand another winter.

"I'm not selling, so stop trying to find a buyer."

"When you finally come to your senses as this thrift store continues to spiral into the red, you'll thank me because I have buyers." He huffed, his cheeks puffing out and his beady eyes narrowing. "Can't understand how you and your sister are so different." Shaking his head, he turned and headed for the door.

"Wait." Kelly came out from behind the counter, and her uncle turned around so quickly he lost his balance and teetered for a moment. She realized she must have gotten up his hopes that she'd changed her mind. Oops. "Do you know a Marvin Childers?"

"Why? Has he made an offer on this place?"

"No. Do you know him or not?"

"Never heard of him. Why?"

"Nothing, really. Be careful driving." Kelly walked to a table where two torso mannequins were displayed, each wearing an ivory sweater. Each sweater had its own stitching; one was a classic fisherman's pattern, and the other was mixed-stitched with a side slit. Displayed along with the mannequins were more sweaters, all folded. To make herself busy, she refolded the sweaters and waited, hoping she'd hear the jingle of the bell over the front door.

The lyrical sound of the bell finally sounded, indicating Ralph had left and she could stop with the busy work. She had real work to do. Merchandise she'd sold on the website needed to be packaged and mailed. She then would find out what Ariel had dug up on the *LIL* cast.

Breena poked her head out of the hallway. "Is he gone? What did he want?"

"He's gone. It's safe. He got an offer on the building." Kelly gave a final touch to the sweaters before walking away and going back to the sales counter to check the cash register. All looked good. She began the process of preparing the cash drawer for the day.

"You're not going to sell, are you?" Breena dashed to the counter. Her dangling snowflake earrings bounced with her quick steps, and her eyes were glossed over with worry.

"I'm not selling. He's trying to wiggle out of his responsibilities of being executor. My guess is if I sold, he'd have a lot less work to do—maybe nothing at all, because then the biggest asset would be sold." Kelly tucked the bank bag under the counter and closed the cash drawer.

"Phew. I really like working here. What's the game plan for the day? Were there any online orders?"

"Nice earrings. They're very seasonal."

Breena gave her earring a little pat. "Couldn't resist. I should get you a pair; then maybe you'll finally get in the holiday spirit. Look at this place." She swept her hand around. "Humbug."

Humbug?

"Scroogista. You'll be known throughout Lucky Cove as Scroogista. Do you want to be known as Scroogista?" Breena asked, waving a finger at Kelly, her eyes alight with merriment.

Kelly cocked her head sideways and tried to hold back her smile. "You like saying the word, don't you?"

Breena's head bobbed up and down. "Clever, huh?"

"Very. And yes, we have merchandise to package and ship today. I printed the orders. If you can take care of the packaging, I'll run out to the post office around lunchtime."

"Absolutely." With a salute, Breena twirled and headed back to the staff room, leaving Kelly to greet the first customer of the day. The rest of the morning flew by, thanks to a steady stream of customers and three new consignors.

While assessing the clothing brought in for consignment, Kelly mentioned her idea for a Holiday Edit event, and each lady thought it was a fabulous idea.

Feeling surer with her idea, she sat down at the sales counter when the store was quiet and worked on the event.

She reached for the calendar and considered which date would be best for closing the shop early. She pulled her phone out of the back pocket of her jeans and checked Lucky Cove's town website for events over the next few weeks and took those dates out of the running.

Based on the jam-packed schedule, Lucky Cove was big on Christmas. She glanced around the boutique and frowned. Her granny would have had all the decorations out and holiday music playing in the background while the fragrance of freshly baked gingerbread cookies drifted from the staff room.

While decorating wasn't on the schedule for today and baking would risk burning down the building, she definitely hadn't inherited her granny's baking gene, Kelly could play music. She hopped off the stool, got her phone out, tapped on her music app, and found her holly, jolly playlist. Yes, there was a time when she had enjoyed the season. She turned up the volume, set the phone down, and returned to planning the Holiday Edit event.

She was all smiles during the brainstorm session until she remembered she'd have to give away goody bags. What was the old saying? You had to spend money to make money. With no data to show whether an event like the one she was planning on doing would be successful, she hesitated to spend money. But she knew her guests would expect a little something.

She had Betsy's offer to donate jar candles from her shop. It was a start. Now she needed a few more items. She jotted down the hair salon, Liv's family's bakery, and the card shop. She was confident they'd donate because they all had adored her granny and, unlike her uncle, wanted Kelly to succeed. Once she had their donations, she'd budget to buy a few more small items to fill out the bags.

Satisfied she had everything under control for the event, she let herself relax a smidge and hummed along to the Christmas carol playing. The holiday spirit was slowly seeping back into her as she swayed to the music, and she belted out a few of the lyrics. Heck, she was alone, why not?

Her sing-along came to a screeching halt when the door opened.

Surprised by the unexpected visitor, Kelly fumbled to turn off the music and stood.

What on earth was he doing there?

Chapter Eleven

Hugh McNeil's gaze appraised the sales floor before meeting Kelly's. "Miss Quinn, what a lovely shop you have. Very charming."

"Thank you. What brings you by?" She stepped out from behind the counter and crossed her arms over her chest. She hadn't had the chance to speak to Hugh at length at her uncle's party, but she knew the type of guy he was.

While living in the city, she'd had her run-ins with guys like him and guys who wanted to be like him—a successful television producer who was chauffeured around town during the week and the Hamptons on the weekends. A flash of a Rolex watch and a black credit card got guys like him far in New York's social circles and up the ladder of success.

"No small talk. You're direct. I like it." He flashed his toothy, salesman-sleek smile as he unbuttoned his gray cashmere coat. At Bishop's, Kelly wasn't in the menswear buying office, but she'd had a lot of male colleagues and learned firsthand what fine-tailored men's clothing looked like. She was looking at a perfect example, from Hugh's outerwear right down to his polished leather loafers. Her uncle's outerwear and footwear were expensive, but Hugh's were off-the-charts big bucks. "I want you!"

"Excuse me?"

"For *Long Island Ladies*. You'd be a perfect addition to the show." He stepped forward and raised his hands in a sweeping gesture. "A struggling young businesswoman selling used clothes from the wealthy to the middle class. Some type of fashionista Robin Hood. We can tweak the angle. It'll be a breath of fresh air for the show." When he finished his sales pitch, he froze in place and looked expectantly at Kelly.

Kelly wasn't sure whether or not to be flattered. She didn't see herself selling clothing from one class of people to another. She sold good-quality, pre-loved merchandise. Wait. What was she thinking? The offer wasn't of any interest to her. She had no desire to be on television. Or to be part of the current *LIL* cast.

He lowered his arms, looking slightly dejected. He must have expected Kelly to fall all over him with gratitude for offering to make her a reality-television star.

"Come on. You're not loving the idea? What's not to love? I'll make you a star. We'd have to spruce up this place for filming. I've got a name, and she'll take care of the renovation for you."

"Hold on there. I didn't agree, and honestly, I don't think the show is for me. But thanks for the offer." It was nice to be asked, but his story-line idea didn't appeal to her. He could peddle his pitch to some other shop owner.

"Honey, nobody can pass up television." He cocked an eyebrow as his gray eyes shadowed over with a hint of anger. She guessed he wasn't a man used to being told no. If so, he had a lot in common with her uncle.

"My name is Kelly, not *honey.*"

"I apologize. I didn't mean to offend you. I call everyone honey."

"I'm sure you do." Oh, yeah, she definitely had his number. He was as slick as the thin coating of ice she'd almost slipped on when she was outside shoveling. "I appreciate the offer, but it's not a good fit for me. I also don't think I'd fit in with the other ladies."

He waved away her concern. "That's what makes the magic in reality television. Viewers love watching when there's friction, differences between the cast members."

"Friction? Is that why Janine had a restraining order placed on Diana?" Kelly watched Hugh's response.

His head twitched, and his lips pressed tightly together. She sensed he was trying to check his temper.

He reached into his coat pocket and pulled out his leather gloves. "How did you find out about the restraining order?" His tone had hardened, and gone was the sales pitch.

"I thought everyone knew about it. Did Diana threaten Janine?"

He cleared his throat as he slipped on his gloves. "Consider my offer. It could make your little shop here famous." He turned and walked out of the boutique.

Kelly dashed to the door and looked out. She spotted him approaching a Mercedes sedan. After opening the driver's side door, he slid in behind the wheel. She was curious to why he didn't comment on the restraining order, considering what he'd said about friction being good for the show. There had to be a heck of a lot of friction to warrant a restraining order. What had gone down between those two women? And was it bad enough to lead to murder?

* * * *

"Oh, my gosh. How did you know I love beef stew?" Kelly licked her lips as she watched steam rise from the deep bowl of stew Ariel had placed in front of her. Along with the stew, there was a loaf of warm sourdough bread and softened butter. She made a mental note to have more lunches at Ariel's house. To give the stew time to cool, she reached for the loaf and broke off two pieces, one for her and one for Ariel, and slathered butter on hers. She wished she could eat lunch like this every day. Before she popped a piece of bread into her mouth, she realized that lunching like a queen would mean going up a few sizes in her jeans. "You shouldn't have gone to so much trouble. I usually get a wrap and a soda."

"It wasn't any trouble. I used my pressure cooker." Ariel dunked her spoon into her stew.

Kelly looked up from her bread. "You used a pressure cooker? Granny tried cooking in one of those years ago. It wasn't pretty."

The centerpiece on the kitchen table was a wreath with a Santa carrying a red sack over his shoulder plopped in the middle. The decoration was jolly and simple and yet another reminder for Kelly to get moving on decorating the boutique.

Ariel laughed. "Those were scary. These days, pressure cookers are digital and safe. You can't blow it up. But you can have stew in less than an hour. And what better meal for a day like today? Cold and snowy." She scooped up a spoonful of the stew.

Kelly glanced out the window over the sink. Fluffy snowflakes were falling. According to the latest weather report, snow showers would happen on and off until late evening.

"Wow. I can't believe it's so fast. Maybe I should get one. I probably should cook more."

"You are remodeling your kitchen." Ariel reached for her water glass and sipped.

"Not really a remodel. The cabinets and countertops are staying. I've ordered a new stove and refrigerator. The new fridge is energy rated. It'll save me a little money. And the stove—well, two of the burners didn't work. I figured I might as well since I'm staying."

Ariel reached out and patted Kelly's arm. "I'm glad you are. I've missed you."

"Same here. I've wanted to reach out so many times, but I was scared. I'm sorry."

"No, don't be sorry. I could have reached out too, but I was scared." Ariel laughed again. "Look at us, two scaredy-cats."

Kelly laughed. "I'm happy we've rebuilt our friendship." They had a ways to go. Even though Ariel had insisted the accident wasn't Kelly's fault, Kelly still had carried a lot of guilt over the years, and shedding it wouldn't be an easy task.

"This is a working lunch. Let's talk about all of my research, shall we?" Ariel navigated her wheelchair away from the table to the island; she reached up for the notepad and returned to the table.

Kelly caught a glimpse of all the notes scribbled on the pad. "You got a lot done. You're like a research ninja."

"I am, aren't I? I love this stuff." Ariel set the pad on the table and ate another spoonful of her stew.

"Guess there was a lot of information online about the show and cast." Kelly took a bite of her bread.

"You're right. The show and those ladies are very popular. I admit I've indulged in watching a few episodes. I guess you can call it my guilty pleasure." Ariel laughed at her confession. "Back to business. There was a ton of stuff about them on Lulu Loves Long Island."

The mention of the website almost wiped out Kelly's appetite, but the stew smelled too delicious for that to happen. Lulu Loves Long Island tried to pass itself off as a one-stop resource center for all of the best cultural events on the island, but it was really a big gossip fest, with snarky innuendos and "gotcha" photographs leaving little to the imagination. Unfortunately, Kelly knew firsthand the damage the website could cause.

"Not surprising."

"I know. There was an article about a month ago that Diana's stepdaughter danced way into the wee hours of the morning in some nightclub." Ariel slathered her slice of bread with a thick pat of butter.

"Diana has a stepdaughter?"

Ariel nodded, swallowing her bite of bread. "Beryl Delacourte. From Aaron's first marriage. She's been divorced three times and now runs an art gallery out in California. Anyway, does the name Patrice Garofalo mean anything to you?"

Kelly swallowed her spoonful of stew. She seriously needed a bigger spoon. And the recipe. "No. Should it? Who is she?"

"She was a production assistant on the show, and when the cast was down in Florida filming, she was arrested at the airport for cocaine possession."

"Not exactly a smart move, huh?" Kelly dipped her spoon back into the stew and lifted out a chunk of meat and a carrot.

"Most criminals aren't smart. We learned that last month, didn't we?" Ariel was referring to the pseudo-brains behind the murders they both got tangled up in. "What caught my eye was the fact that Diana convinced the production company to pay for Patrice's defense."

Kelly set her spoon down and reached for her water glass. She sipped her water. "From my limited exposure to the cast and the producers, no one on *LIL* does anything out of the kindness of their hearts."

"What could Diana have gotten out of helping Patrice, a production assistant?"

"Is Patrice still on the show?"

"No. According to the articles and blog posts I found, she went on leave during the trial and then quit. She still lives in Queens, though." Ariel helped herself to another slice of bread and took a bite. "I found out through her social media that she's a waitress and is back in school."

"You were very thorough. Did you come across anything regarding Janine's restraining order against Diana?"

"No. It looks like they kept it quiet. Which is hard to believe because it's so juicy. Why not get some buzz out of it? It's not like them to pass up a scandal."

"Whatever happened, it seems no one wants to talk about it. Hugh clammed up."

"The producer? When did you see him?"

Kelly shared the details about the unexpected visit from the producer as they finished lunch. While Kelly helped clean up, Ariel filled her in on the rest of the information she'd found about the show and its stars, but it wasn't anything Kelly hadn't already caught a whiff of—late-night partying, adultery, drinking, and over-the-top spending. The ladies weren't shrinking violets; they were more like the cast from the *Little Shop of Horrors*. Which prompted Kelly to ask if Ariel wanted to do a girl's night with movie and popcorn and invite Liv. Ariel loved the idea. She suggested they do it soon and watch *White Christmas*.

Kelly had been thinking more along the lines of a romantic comedy, not a Christmas movie. But not everyone was like her. Most people had Christmas on the brain. Glancing around Ariel's kitchen, it was clear that she had Christmas on the brain in overdrive. Snowmen crammed every nook and cranny, and a wreath hung on the window; even the dishtowels were reindeer themed.

Before Kelly left, she took the bag of clothing Ariel wanted to consign. She'd get an estimate back to Ariel, and since the items were all in-season, they'd be displayed ASAP so Ariel could get some quick cash for holiday gift shopping.

Kelly gathered her coat and wristlet, along with the bag, and promised to set a date for movie night. She stepped out into the cold afternoon and tugged her parka's collar closer to her face. She walked to her Jeep and, once inside, blasted the heat for her drive back to the boutique.

At the boutique, Kelly hung up her parka and dropped her wristlet on the desk before making her way out of the staff room to the sales counter, where she set down the bag of Ariel's items. She'd sort through them later. Breena finished up with a customer, a woman Kelly had seen in the boutique before. A little zing of happiness had her smiling. Repeat customers. She loved it.

"Oh, hey, glad you're back." Breena stepped away from the counter after the customer exited the boutique. "Pepper went home. She looked bad. Really bad. Like maybe she needed to go to the hospital bad."

Kelly had learned that Breena had a flair for the dramatic. Once an actress, always an actress. Because of that, Kelly was cautious to jump to the worst-case scenario. She'd call Pepper and find out how ill she was. She blew out an aggravated breath. If she hadn't been at Ariel's house getting the lowdown on the cast of *LIL,* she'd have been there to see firsthand how sick Pepper was. But no. She was meddling into a police investigation yet again.

"Hey, Kelly, did you hear me? Pepper left sick."

"I heard you. I'll call her." Kelly turned and went back to the staff room. She'd just unzipped her wristlet to pull out her phone when it buzzed.

"Hello, Summer." Kelly sat on the chair and tapped on the speakerphone command. With her phone set on the desk, she sorted through the day's mail. Bills, invoices, junk mail.

"I can't believe you'd do something so underhanded. What have I done to you to make you want to hurt me?"

Kelly stopped sorting the mail. Summer's accusatory tone hit her like a slap. "What are you talking about?"

"Don't play dumb with me."

Kelly leaned back and shook her head. She'd lay money on Hugh being the source of Summer's meltdown. What was he thinking?

"Why does Hugh want me to convince you to be on the show?" Kelly groaned. "I have no idea."

"You know exactly what you did. The show is mine. Not yours!"

"The show isn't like a toy you can claim and run off with."

"Don't lecture me."

"I'm not. And you know what else? I'm not having this conversation with you. It's absurd."

"You joining the cast would be a nightmare."

"I couldn't agree more. Give my love to Juniper." Kelly tapped the END CALL button and tossed her phone down. What was Hugh up to? Going to Summer and asking her to work Kelly into submission? Dragging Summer into the fray wasn't winning him any points with Kelly. She'd already told him no, and now she was even more emphatic about her decision.

She took a deep inhale and then exhaled, releasing the tension between her shoulder blades. Another inhale and exhale, and more tension released. She shut her eyes and remained silent for a moment to regroup. She hadn't been a fan of meditation—actually, she wasn't even sure if what she was doing counted as meditation, but she needed something to clear her mind. She took a few more deep breaths, and clarity surfaced.

She opened her eyes and reached for her phone. She wanted to check in on Pepper, and then she'd tackle the one thing, besides Diana's murder, that had been dogging her.

Her conversation with Pepper lessened her fears. Pepper wasn't in need of a hospital. She needed rest and a dose of the cold medicine she'd hesitated to take because she was driving. She assured Kelly she wasn't on death's doorstep and would take tomorrow off. Relieved, Kelly ended the call and set out to add some holiday cheer to the boutique.

The bins of decorations had been pulled out of the storeroom and waited to be opened. She lifted the cover of the plastic bin and pulled out a nutcracker. Her finger traced the outline of the wood figure. In the ballet, the nutcracker was transformed into a handsome prince. No one knew for sure if it was a dream or if the magic of Christmas had come to life for Clara. Either way, it was one night for Clara and her prince. Much like Kelly's one night with Mark.

Oh, how silly her thoughts were getting. She was acting like a lovelorn teenage girl. Now wasn't the time to swoon over some guy. *Swoon?* Who said that word anymore? With a shake of her head, she set the nutcracker back into the bin with the other nutcrackers her granny had collected. She replaced the lid and carried the bin out to the front of the boutique. It was time to get to work.

Breena clapped her hands with excitement when she saw Kelly appear with the decorations. She played holiday tunes on her phone and joined in with the decorating.

While the nutcrackers weren't Kelly's thing, she wanted to honor her granny and lined them up on the fireplace mantels in the two front rooms. Once the nutcrackers were in place, she tucked in greenery. There were swags and ribbon in the bins. Her granny had draped the swags along the mantels and then added ribbon and finished with a layer of ornaments. She'd have to find that bin next.

While decorating, a few customers came in and complimented Kelly on the progress so far. Encouraged by the kind words, she and Breena finished the mantels with the three-foot nutcrackers on either side of the hearths and hung an artificial wreath over each fireplace. When all the decorating was done, she had four empty bins, and she decided to visit Patrice Garofalo.

Kelly stacked the bins together and carried them back to the storeroom. She then firmed up her plan to take a drive to Queens to talk to the former *LIL* crew member tomorrow. Breena said she would come in and cover Pepper's shift. The extra pay would help buy a doll her daughter wanted for Christmas. With the boutique dealt with, Kelly hoped her drive into the city would result in some information that could help clear Wendy.

Clearing Wendy took a back seat to a spur-of-the-moment decision to meet Mark for dinner. Yes, they'd discussed meeting for coffee, but after a text exchange at closing time for the boutique, they agreed that, since they both had to eat, the only logical decision was that they eat dinner together.

No pressure. It was only dinner.

"No pressure. It's only a meal, not a date," Kelly repeated to herself while tossing aside dress after dress, blouse after blouse, and skirt after skirt. She wanted a casual, stylish, it's just dinner look but not too casual or too stylish or this really isn't an important meal look. By the time she finally decided on what to wear, she was running late, and her bedroom looked like a tornado had roared through it.

She fed Howard in record time, grabbed her wool coat from the hall closet, and dashed across the street to Gino's. After shrugging out of her coat and hanging it up, she found Mark seated at a cozy table with a bottle of wine, waiting for her. She made her apologies, and they awkwardly kissed on the cheeks. On their one and only date last month, they had said good night with a kiss that left her body tingling, right down to her toes.

A kiss on the cheek seemed so unsatisfying, but it probably was a smart thing, considering they weren't on a date. They were just having dinner. "You look beautiful." Mark pulled out a chair for Kelly.

"Thank you." She'd finally decided on a Peter Pan–collared jersey top and a tweed skirt with her wedge-heeled tall boots. Short on time, she'd swept her hair up into a messy bun and freshened her makeup. "I'm sorry I'm late."

Mark returned to his seat. He wore a V-neck sweater and chinos. Unless he was meeting with a client, he had a very casual dress code in the office. "No problem. I only got here a few minutes ago. I had a last-minute call with a client. Wine?" He lifted the bottle.

"Yes, please." With her glass filled, she lifted it and gazed over the rim at Mark. The flicker of the candle on the table, the low lighting in the dining room, and instrumental background music all came together and created a magical moment. She was sitting across from the man . . .

"Mark?"

An all-too-familiar voice interrupted Kelly's thought.

"What are you doing here?" Detective Wolman had approached the table from behind Kelly and continued to her brother, coming into full view of Kelly. "Miss Quinn, isn't this a surprise?"

Kelly couldn't have agreed more.

"Hey, sis." Mark smiled as his gaze traveled between his sister and Kelly. But his smile quickly vanished. Kelly guessed he was seeing that neither woman was pleased at the moment.

The magical moment was definitely gone.

"I didn't realize you two had started seeing each other again," Wolman said.

"We're not . . . it's just . . ." The legal eagle was at a loss for words.

Kelly took a gulp of her wine. "We're having dinner, Detective Wolman." Kelly set her glass down while silently praying Mark wouldn't invite his sister to join them.

"Please, join us," Mark said.

Kelly cringed inwardly. Why, why, why?

"Thanks, but I'm picking up takeout. Late night at the office. I have a murder to investigate." The detective's lips pressed into a thin line, and her eyes narrowed on Kelly.

"Terrible thing. Any leads, yet?" Mark seemed oblivious to the tension bubbling off of his sister. Or maybe he was accustomed to it and no longer acknowledged it.

Wolman turned her face toward her brother. "You know I can't discuss an ongoing case. Especially in front of a witness."

Kelly leaned forward. "That would be me." She took another gulp of wine. Mark's brows knitted in confusion. "Well, don't let us keep you, sis." Wolman stared at Kelly and Mark for a beat. "Have a nice dinner." She turned and continued to the takeout section of the restaurant.

Kelly's shoulders slumped, and she leaned back. *Fat chance of having a nice dinner now.*

"Are you okay?" Mark pushed aside his glass and reached for Kelly's hand.

She liked the touch of his warm hand on hers. She also liked his kisses. And his Smokin' McHottie Lawyer sexy grin. What she didn't like was his sister.

"She hates me."

"No, she doesn't. She's protective."

"And suspicious."

He nodded. "It's part of her job. A part she takes home with her. Give her time. She'll warm up."

"You promise?"

He grinned. "I do. Now, how about we order? I'm starving."

"Sounds good." She let go of his hand and opened the menu their waiter dashed over with. She peeked over the top of the menu and smiled. Maybe they were on a date after all.

Chapter Twelve

Breena arrived to open the boutique and said she could stay until Kelly returned. She didn't have to work at Doug's Variety Store until Sunday. Knowing she didn't have to rush eased Kelly's nerves about driving into Queens and meeting Patrice Garofalo.

She'd messaged Patrice on social media and asked to meet. Kelly had a hard time explaining why she wanted to talk because she wasn't sure herself. She had a feeling in her gut that Patrice could help shed light on Diana's murder, at least where Wendy was concerned. Then again, if that were the case, the police would've talked to the former *LIL* employee. However, in one of Patrice's messages back to Kelly, she said they hadn't contacted her. So this might be a complete waste of time on Kelly's part.

They agreed to meet in a small coffee shop around the corner from Patrice's apartment building in Jackson Heights. When she entered the shop and approached the table, Kelly recognized the twentysomething from her online profile picture.

"Hello, Patrice. I'm Kelly. Thank you for meeting with me." Kelly pulled out a chair, and it scraped along the battered floor. As she sat, a larger man brushed by her and grunted.

"I'm not sure how I can help you." Patrice's dark hair fell loosely on her shoulders, and her brown eyes were hooded and bloodshot. In front of her was a large coffee and a tablet she tapped to close the document she had been working on.

"Neither am I right now." After a quick inspection of the table, Kelly chose to set her tote bag on her lap. She wondered when was the last time anyone had wiped down the tables in the coffee shop.

Patrice nodded as she lifted her disposable cup. Her fingers wrapped around the cup, giving Kelly a full view of her high-maintenance manicure. Her stiletto-shaped nails must have required frequent appointments. One finger on each hand had an intricate design of miniature crystals. Patrice had also loaded her fingers with silver-tone rings. Feeling a little self-conscious, Kelly slid a glance at her own hands. They hadn't had a proper manicure in months.

"I'm sorry Diana died. She was a nice lady. Well, at least to me." Patrice took a long drink of her coffee.

"She wasn't nice to the crew or her castmates?"

Patrice laughed—but not in a jovial way. No, her laugh was dark. "No one on that show is nice. But it is what it is." She shrugged. "People love to watch the lives of those uppity ladies who spend more money on one lipstick than I spend on a day's worth of food. They don't want to see someone like me struggling to pay the bills. No, they prefer to watch the lifestyles of women like Diana and Wendy."

"Do you know Wendy is a prime suspect in Diana's murder?"

Patrice's mouth fell open. "You're not serious? She couldn't have murdered Diana."

"They had a public feud. It sounds like it was nasty."

"All of those women had feuds. It was good for ratings. Not one of them has ever regretted starting a fight. Look, the best thing to have happened to Diana's career was her cheating husband leaving her. The whole incident made her relevant again, which infuriated Wendy. She wanted to be the queen bee."

"But not enough to want to kill Diana?"

Patrice shook her head. "I got the feeling Wendy was all bark and no bite. But I guess I could be wrong."

A screaming toddler drew Kelly's attention to the counter. His mother fussed to quiet him, but he kept wailing, forcing her to retreat from the shop. Kelly turned her gaze back to Patrice. Dressed in a well-worn denim shirt, unbuttoned to reveal her ample cleavage, the young woman seemed to be okay with talking about the show, and Kelly hoped she'd be okay with talking about the incident at the airport. If she wasn't, Kelly couldn't blame her. She knew what it felt like being handcuffed and hauled off to jail, though Kelly wasn't placed in a cell or officially arrested, only detained for an interview.

"I hope you don't mind me asking about the incident in Florida. Why did Diana help you?"

"The *incident*? Nice way to phrase it. My arrest. Talk about bogus. Those weren't my drugs. I swear. I have no idea why Diana stood beside me and forced Hugh to pay my legal expenses."

"Did you ever ask her?"

"Several times, and she would only say I didn't deserve what happened. And she didn't deserve to die. Look, I'm sorry for what's going down with Wendy, but I don't know how I can help you. Why are you even asking about this? Are you a relative of Wendy's or something?"

Kelly would be option number two—or something. "No, I'm not a relative. She asked me to help her."

"Wow. Wendy asks no one for help. She must be mellowing or she's terrified. Probably scared. She's not going to mellow. Ever." Patrice drained her coffee cup.

"Do you think it's possible someone on the show planted the cocaine on you?" Kelly wasn't sure where the question came from. It just popped into her head.

Patrice nodded. "Yes. Absolutely. I can't think of any other way it got into my bag. I didn't put it there. Look, whatever motivated Diana to help me out, I certainly appreciated it. I wasn't in a position to afford a decent attorney. It has turned my whole life upside down, though it's not completely ruined."

"I admire your positive outlook."

"Hey, sometimes life throws you a curve. But I learned one thing. One very important thing."

"What?"

"Never. Trust. Anyone."

Those weren't the words of wisdom Kelly expected to hear. But considering what Patrice had gone through, she had reason to be wary of people—that was, if she was set up. Kelly couldn't imagine living her life never trusting anyone. She'd be one lonely gal.

Patrice leaned forward. "For what it's worth, my money's on Janine as the murderer. She wanted Diana out of the way."

"Do you know anything about a restraining order Janine had on Diana?"

Patrice let out a low whistle. "Restraining order? No idea about it. Sounds like their animosity had sunk to a whole new level. Or Janine was just being overly dramatic."

"For ratings? Then why has it been kept a secret? There's nothing online about it."

"How did you find out about it?"

Kelly worked her lower lip. Should she confess to snooping through Janine's papers? Probably not. "I heard someone mention it."

Patrice nodded her head. "Sure you did."

Patrice's tone and skeptical look told Kelly she wasn't being believed for a minute. "Thank you for meeting me."

"Not sure if I was much help." Patrice stood, swept up her cup and tablet, and walked away.

Kelly dug into her tote bag to check her phone. There was a message from Julie, her closest work friend from Bishop's. She returned the call.

"What's going on in Lucky Cove? Serena is bat crazy," Julie said.

"Why?"

"A television producer called wanting information on you. He told Serena you're going to be on a reality show. You've been holding out on me."

Kelly could hear the pouting in her friend's voice. "No, I'm not. His name is Hugh McNeil, and I've told him I'm not interested in his show."

"Are you bat crazy? Why not? It could be a great marketing opportunity for the boutique. Girl, you need to reconsider."

"I appreciate the advice, but my answer is still no." Kelly stood and slung her tote bag over her shoulder. She made her way through the crammed tables to the exit and emerged out onto Astoria Boulevard.

"Party pooper. Here I thought I'd know someone famous." Julie laughed.

"Sorry to disappoint. Look, I've gotta go. Call you later." Kelly disconnected the call and returned the phone to her bag. Now she could zip up her coat. The air was cold and biting. She walked along the sidewalk to where she'd parked her car but stopped when she came to a nail salon. She looked at her hands. She'd been working nonstop since taking over the boutique, and it was high time for a little pampering. She headed for the salon's entrance.

* * * *

The holiday spirit was kicking in. Kelly splayed her fingers and admired her manicure. She'd opted for the Candy Cane, alternating stripes of red and white nail polish. For the drive back to Lucky Cove, she found a Christmas music station on the satellite radio and hummed along to many of her favorite songs.

By the time she arrived home, the Christmas spirit had infused her. Where were those stockings Pepper wanted to hang on the mantels? She had to find them because she was putting them up tonight. With the Jeep parked in its spot behind the boutique, she reached for her tote bag. Digging for her house keys, she found the tin of mints she'd been looking for. She dropped it into the interior side pocket. As she pulled out her keys, her phone buzzed with a text message. It was from Gabe. *You should know. Summer was in a car accident. Not hurt.* Kelly gasped.

When the shock settled, her fingers itched to text back to Gabe to let him know some news shouldn't be shared through text messages. Instead, she typed a generic thanks and opened her contacts app to call her uncle.

The news had knocked her holiday spirit to the wayside. Impatiently, she waited for her uncle to answer her call. While waiting, she said a silent prayer Juniper wasn't in the car with Summer when the accident occurred.

"Unbelievable day, Kelly," her uncle said in a shaken voice.

"What happened? Is Summer okay? Is she in the hospital? What about Juniper?" Kelly's questions were rapid, to match her heartbeat.

"Juniper was here at home when the accident happened."

Kelly expelled the breath she hadn't realized she'd been holding. "Thank goodness."

"Yeah, tell me about it. Summer lost control of her car. She said it happened so fast she's not sure what happened. She said it felt as if the brakes weren't working. They serviced the freakin' car a month ago! I swear, if I find out Chuck missed something . . . What? I'll be right there. I have to go, Kelly."

"Sure. I understand. I'll come by tomorrow before the boutique opens to see Summer." Kelly ended the call and stared out the windshield. Ralph took meticulous care of his vehicles. He was proud of them because they conveyed his status to the world. He had them serviced on schedule, had them washed regularly, and replaced them for newer models every two years. Summer's brakes wouldn't have just failed. An unsettling feeling settled in the pit of Kelly's stomach.

Summer was being considered for the vacant spot on *LIL* Diana had left, and Diana had been murdered. Was Summer's accident simply a case of mechanical failure or a murder attempt?

* * * *

After learning about Summer's accident, Kelly wasn't into holiday decorating. She let Breena go home early and worked until closing time. With the boutique locked up for the night, she climbed the stairs to her apartment. After a quick change into a pair of cozy fleece pants and a long-sleeved T-shirt, she swept her hair into a ponytail and decided to spend the evening working on her article for Budget Chic.

She had the best of intentions to work. Instead, she stood at the dresser, staring at her granny's collection of fashion jewelry, set out on a porcelain tray. She'd sorted through the jewelry, detangled the delicate necklace chains and organized the rings. She wasn't sure what she'd do with the jewelry. Perhaps buy a jewelry box to store the pieces in. None of them was her style, but getting rid of them didn't feel right to her.

A small smile touched her lips as she fingered one necklace. The faux stone was a deep purple set in a simple setting. She remembered her granny wearing it one Easter. Kelly's fingers moved over to the rings. She'd lined them up in a straight row. Over the years, her granny's ring size had fluctuated. Most of the rings coordinated with the necklaces. Martha had liked sets.

Though, there was one ring that didn't match any necklace. It was a simple gold band.

Kelly picked it up and studied it. It looked like a wedding band. Simple, thin, and gold. Kelly knew that Martha had been buried with the band Kelly's grandfather had given her on their wedding day.

Kelly's mouth gaped open. Was the ring she was holding from Marvin Childers? She stepped back to the bed and dropped to the mattress. She didn't take her gaze off of the ring.

"Why didn't Granny tell anyone? Why was it a secret?"

Why did she have to find the certificate?

* * * *

The next morning, before the boutique opened, Kelly drove over to her uncle's house to check on Summer in person. The front door opened, and the housekeeper greeted Kelly. Miriam maintained a stoic, unshakable demeanor at all times. Her intense observation unsettled Kelly; it was as though she was being appraised or judged.

"Mrs. Blake is in the kitchen." Miriam closed the door and led Kelly through to the large kitchen. "She has a visitor. The police."

Kelly paused and pressed her lips together. *Shoot.* The dark sedan outside had to have been Detective Wolman's vehicle. She sighed when she caught a glimpse of the visitor. She was right. The vehicle belonged to Wolman.

Seeing the detective first thing in the morning was becoming a habit. "I don't mean to interrupt." Kelly stepped into the kitchen as Miriam continued to the laundry room. "Good morning, Detective."

Wolman nodded and then returned her focus to Summer, who sat across from her at the table. "When I have more information, I'll be in touch. Thank you for the coffee." She gathered her notepad and pen and stood.

"Do you know what caused the accident?" Kelly asked the detective.

Wolman walked toward the doorway and stopped in front of Kelly. "Yes, we do. And it's now a police matter, which means that what I said regarding the Delacourte murder now applies to Mrs. Blake's accident." She flashed a warning smile, then walked past Kelly and disappeared out into the hallway.

"Police matter? What on earth is going on?" Kelly moved farther into the room and toward Summer, who had Juniper on her lap.

Summer was dressed in a pale pink hoodie and matching French terry pants. Her hair was braided, and she wore minimal makeup. She looked years younger without the heavy makeup she normally applied.

"Someone cut my brake lines. Someone sabotaged my car. Thank goodness, Juniper wasn't with me. I can't imagine what I'd do if anything happened to my baby girl." Summer sniffled as she fought back tears, and her chin quivered.

Kelly set her tote bag on a chair. She extended her hands to Juniper, and Summer relinquished the baby to Kelly. With Juniper in her arms, Kelly walked over to the French doors that led out to the spacious patio to give Summer a moment to compose herself. Several inches of snow covered the stone patio. Kelly pointed, and Juniper looked outside. "Soon you'll be building snowmen and making snow angels."

Juniper giggled, and Kelly's heart lit up. The baby was magical.

"I can't believe my brakes were tampered with," Summer said with a hitch in her voice.

Kelly turned back to Summer, who looked uncharacteristically vulnerable. Seeing her like that was a first—and uncharted territory for Kelly. Juniper giggled, and Kelly ran her hand over the baby's soft blond curls.

"Where were you before the accident?" Kelly paced with a bounce in her step because Juniper liked the motion and it made her giggle more.

"At the day spa. I had a massage." Summer reached for her cup of tea and took a sip. "The detective suspects that's when my car was tampered with. She's looking into whether the spa has surveillance cameras on the property."

"You didn't see anyone suspicious?"

"There? Of course not. What kind of place do you think I go to?" Summer shook her head as she reached forward and plucked a strawberry out of the fruit bowl on the table.

"Have you received any threats?" Kelly made a silly face, and Juniper's eyes widened with amusement.

"No. This doesn't make sense. Why would someone want to hurt me?" Summer bit into the strawberry.

Juniper flailed her chubby little arms out and closed them again on Kelly's face and giggled harder. Slapping her cousin seemed to delight the baby. Kelly gingerly removed the little hands from her face and kissed the baby on the forehead before settling her into her high chair.

Juniper fussed, prompting Kelly to give her a pacifier. With the baby settled for a few minutes, Kelly pulled out a chair at the table and sat across from Summer.

"I don't want to alarm you any more than necessary, but I can't help but think that what happened yesterday could be connected to the show. Maybe you should reconsider pursuing the vacancy."

"What you're suggesting isn't possible. You're being ridiculous."

"No? Diana was murdered and now you're being considered to fill her spot and your brake line was cut."

"Pish. There has to be another explanation."

"Until there is, please consider removing your name from consideration."

"Absolutely not. Being on the show means my Pilates studio will have national exposure. I could expand."

"Yes, it's a great opportunity, but is it worth risking your life?"

"At this point, we have no proof the show and my accident are connected. And I don't want you to go around town saying they are." Summer cast her eyes downward for a moment, and when she set her gaze back on Kelly, she looked determined. "This is an opportunity I can't pass up. Do you understand?"

Kelly nodded. "The decision is yours, but I think it's a bad idea." She glanced at her watch. "I need to get back to the boutique." She gathered her tote bag and stood. She kissed Juniper on the head and walked past Summer, whose determined look had slipped away. Back was the worried look Kelly had seen a few moments earlier.

Chapter Thirteen

Kelly arrived back on Main Street with enough time to dash over to Doug's Variety Store. It was official; she was addicted to the Holly Jolly blend. She was able to get in and out of the variety store in record time and started on her way back to the boutique. With her gloved hands wrapped around the cup, she passed the Gull Café, where morning diners leisurely ate their breakfasts.

Kelly's mom took her two girls to breakfast at the café during school vacations as a treat. Kelly spotted Paulette pouring coffee and stopped. She remembered how the café's longtime waitress had made a fuss over her and Caroline. The memory reminded Kelly to call Caroline, touch base with her, and ask if she wanted to join in on girl's night with Liv and Ariel.

A face appeared after a menu was lowered, and Kelly recognized Nanette and the other woman at the table. What were Janine and Nanette doing together? Kelly's spidey senses pricked up again. Why would the housekeeper of a murder victim be having breakfast with a woman who could be a suspect in the murder?

"What are you doing?"

Kelly jumped at the unexpected voice; she spun around and found Liv had come up behind her. "Geez, you startled me."

"What were you looking at?" Liv peered into the café's window. "Janine Cutter? Kelly! She's reported you to the police."

"I'm not following her. I was on my way back to the boutique from Doug's." She lifted her coffee cup. "And I saw Paulette and then those two." She pointed to Janine's table.

"Who's the lady she's with?"

"Nanette Berger."

"Diana's housekeeper?" Liv moved closer to the window and stared into the dining room. Kelly grabbed her shoulder and pulled her back. "Hey!"

"Don't stare like a weirdo."

"I wasn't . . . really."

"Walk with me. I'm freezing." Kelly walked away from the café with Liv in tow, and they crossed the street. "I was at my uncle's house, and when I arrived, Wolman was there."

Liv frowned.

"Exactly how I felt. Anyway, she said someone cut Summer's brake lines."

"No! Sabotage? Why? Who?"

"Summer has no idea. But my gut tells me it's connected to *LIL* and Diana's death."

"Come on, Kelly. That's a pretty big leap." Liv tightened the collar of the army green parka around her neck.

"Possibly. But if I'm right, then Summer is in danger. If I'm wrong, then it was a freak accident."

"I'm sure Wolman will sort it all out." Liv stopped walking. "I wanted to tell you I found Marvin Childers."

"You did? Where?"

"He still lives here in Lucky Cove, on Glendale Road."

"Wait, did you say Glendale Road?" When Liv nodded, Kelly was certain the old man outside the equally old cottage before Diana's meticulously maintained home was Marvin. "I can't believe he's Marvin."

"Who? Do you know Marvin?"

"No, I don't. It's a long story, and I have to open the boutique. Thanks for the information. Talk soon!" Kelly dashed to the boutique and opened up with seconds to spare. There wasn't a mob of customers clamoring to get in, but she liked to be consistent with store hours. Too many small businesses played fast and loose with their hours and ended up annoying their customers.

Annoyed customers shopped elsewhere.

With the boutique opened and Breena on the sales floor, Kelly busied herself with photographing items for the website. Pepper had the day off, and Kelly hoped she would rest and get over her nasty cold—that was, if Pepper would stay still for an entire day. Kelly worried that, at Pepper's age, a simple cold could turn into something more serious.

Kelly raised her camera to her eye and focused on the blue cable-knit sweater, not Pepper's illness. She pressed the button and took a flurry of shots of the sweater.

The space she'd carved out for the photo studio was tight but functional, and now it was starting to look professional, thanks to the backdrop she'd ordered. The heavy-duty vinyl backdrop was designed to look like old, weathered white wooden boards; through the camera lens, the look was very realistic. A background stand for the backdrop had been part of her order. Both items were within her budget, and she was confident they'd up her online sales game.

She'd steamed the garments she wanted to sell online, hung them, and snapped dozens of photos. She removed the sweater from the setup and took it off the hanger, refolding it and setting it on the table. There was one item left to photograph, a floral print flounce skirt, and her inner merchandiser told her the skirt needed to be shown on a body, not on a hanger. She could traipse out to the storeroom and drag in a mannequin, or she could slip the skirt on and take a few photos.

Short on time, she chose the latter. Within a few minutes, the camera was set to a timer to take photos, and Kelly was posed in front of the backdrop. She'd set the angle so only the lower half of her body would be photographed. With the remote discreetly placed in her hand, she continued to take more than a dozen photos before she checked the camera.

"What are you doing?" Breena had poked her head into the photo studio. "Cute skirt."

"Thanks. I'm finishing up photos for the website. I have an errand to run. Can you hold down the fort while I'm out?"

"Duh. Sure can. Where are you going?" Breena entered the room and browsed through the items Kelly had photographed. "We're getting so many nice pieces lately. How's the edit event going? Have you set a date? I can make flyers, and I can write up a press release and post it on social media. I like managing the social media for the boutique."

Having a marketing student for a part-time employee was a big win for Kelly. Breena was eager to build her skills. The downside was Breena's inexperience. Mistakes were bound to happen. Kelly accepted the risks because she herself was inexperienced when it came to owning a business.

"You're doing a great job, and yes, I've set a date. When I get back from my errand, we can go over what I have so far. And we can review what ideas you have to promote the event. Sound good?" Kelly shimmied out of the skirt and pulled on her jeans and boots.

"Don't be too long then. I want to get a plan into place. This is the busiest time of year for women, and we want to get onto their calendars ASAP. I want the event to be successful." Breena swung around and left the room.

It looked like Kelly and Breena wanted the same thing: success. Kelly shut off her camera and rehung the skirt. Before heading out to the Senior Center, she wanted to do a little of her own digging into Marvin Childers. She set the camera down on the table and then swiped up her phone and, against her better judgement, typed in a website address she vowed never to visit ever again: Lulu Loves Long Island. While it seemed gossip was its bread and butter, the website did report on the achievements of prominent members of the community. It took some searching, but Kelly eventually found a few articles on Marvin Childers. Liv had been right about him being an illustrator. Kelly found an article about his last showing and learned he'd been a widower for over a decade and had one son and two grandchildren. The few photographs of his work impressed Kelly. She huffed. She didn't want to like his work. She sighed. Now she was being childish.

Kelly closed the website and switched off the light as she exited the photo studio. She had answers to find.

* * * *

Kelly opened the door of the Lucky Cove Senior Center. While photographing garments for the boutique's website, her mind had churned over what to do about the marriage certificate she'd found. While a part of her wanted to shred the document, it wasn't the right thing to do. With Marvin Childers located, she needed to get information on the Las Vegas trip. Had her granny been a part of the annual trip and married Marvin then? Or had granny and her beau secretly run off on their own—had they eloped? The pit in her stomach deepened. She feared the worst-case scenario of losing everything she loved.

She stepped into the vestibule and shook off the cold. There was a large bulletin board covered with flyers advertising activities for local senior citizens. Beneath the bulletin board was a narrow table covered with brochures for services from home care to low-cost home fuel for seniors. After she wiped her boots on the mat, Kelly pulled opened the second door and entered the center.

The large open space was divided into areas for various activities. One area had round tables for dining, and another had comfortable seating and a television for relaxing; a small cluster of computer desks were arranged in the back corner for web surfing.

In each area, there were a few clients, and they all looked up when Kelly entered. Their gazes turned from her to each other, and they whispered before returning to their activities.

Feeling like the new kid in school, Kelly approached the lone desk in the corner of the space. The desk's location gave the director, Harriet O'Neal, a clear vantage point to see all and hear all. The name plaque on the desk confirmed that the gray-haired woman—buttoned-up in a blouse with a crisp tie at its high collar and with a pair of reading glasses perched on the bridge of her nose—was the woman Kelly was looking for.

The woman looked up from the document she was reviewing, over the rim of her glasses, and cast a dubious stare on Kelly. "May I help you?"

"I hope so." Kelly had followed Liv's advice and brought a box of two chocolate frosted cupcakes for Mrs. O'Neal. Her long strides put her in front of Mrs. O'Neal's desk before the woman could change her mind and not help her. While in the bakery, Liv's aunts had told her Harriet was more than just a little ornery, as she'd been cautioned earlier. She was a town employee who followed the rules, no exceptions.

"I'm Kelly Quinn. Martha Blake's granddaughter."

Harriet O'Neal's stern look softened. "Terrible loss. She was a pillar of this town. Beloved by many." However, her tone didn't convey sincerity.

"Thank you. I'm hoping you can shed some light on a trip to Las Vegas that the center organized five years ago last March."

Mrs. O'Neal's stern look returned, and she looked like she was about to tell Kelly to take a hike.

"I brought these for you. German chocolate cupcakes." She placed the box on the neatly organized desk.

"My favorite." Mrs. O'Neal lifted the lid of the box, and a smile emerged from her frown. "What a tasty little treat. What do you want to know about the trip?" She lifted a cupcake out of the box and set it on a tissue she plucked from its box.

Feeling victorious at passing the first hurdle, Kelly relaxed and settled on the chair in front of the desk. "My granny went on the trip. Was it organized? I mean, was there an itinerary set for the group, and was the trip chaperoned?"

Mrs. O'Neal crossed her arms on the desk. "There was an itinerary for the trip. There was some time in the casinos, shows to go to, and some sightseeing. We had guides with us, but no chaperones. This was a group of seniors, not wild teenagers."

Mrs. O'Neal might want to rethink the policy because two seniors on her watch had run off and eloped on a whim.

"What was on the sightseeing agenda?" A drive-thru wedding chapel? As tempting as it was to ask the question, Kelly left it unsaid.

"Due to their age, we had to limit sightseeing because it can be challenging for our members to get around. We went to the Hoover Dam. In fact, one member wanted to go to Carson City."

Kelly's eyebrow arched. Carson City was home to a very popular ranch for adult activity.

"That trip, in particular, was very challenging for me. I had to keep my eye on Marvin."

"Marvin Childers?"

Mrs. O'Neal nodded. "Do you know him? Well, if you do, you know he's quite a character. Though he doesn't come here as often as he used to. Why are you interested in the trip?"

"I found a note my granny left about it, and I was curious."

"He and your grandmother were good friends." Mrs. O'Neal leaned forward. "I think they were sweet on each other."

Enough to marry? Kelly opted to keep that question to herself too.

"Thank you for your time." Kelly walked away from the desk. She reached the exit at the same time Dorothy Mueller arrived. Mrs. Mueller had been one of her very first customers when she took over the boutique. Unfortunately, Mrs. Mueller's purchase hadn't been what she expected, and she'd returned it. Since then, she hadn't come back into the boutique.

"Good morning, Mrs. Mueller. How are you today?" Kelly held the door open so the elderly woman could enter.

Mrs. Mueller was a spry senior with a keen eye and vivid imagination. "Kelly, dear, so good to see you. I'm doing well. Though, with this snow and cold weather, I don't get out much. But today is book club, and we're having pot roast for lunch." She patted the hardcover book in her hand.

"Sounds like you'll have a lovely day."

"Why are you here? You're far too young to be hanging around here." Mrs. Mueller stepped farther inside and unbuttoned her coat.

"I was asking about a trip my granny took to Vegas a few years ago."

"I heard it was a wild one." She gestured for Kelly to lean in. "I heard from Louise two people got hitched. They took off on their own and went to one of those ridiculous wedding chapels. You know, the type with fake Elvis Presleys. They acted like impetuous teenagers. Eloping at their age. Utter nonsense. Or hopelessly romantic."

Kelly gulped. Was Mrs. Mueller talking about her granny and Marvin?

"Do you know who those two people were?"

Mrs. Mueller shook her head. "Louise kept it a secret. Took it to her grave. May she rest in peace. Well, I see Cora waiting for me. I better get over there. You take care, dear." She patted Kelly's arm before she walked away.

Kelly's gaze followed Mrs. Mueller cross the large space and then stopped at Mrs. O'Neal's desk. She was devouring one of the cupcakes. At least she had an appetite. Kelly's stomach was all knotted up now that her fear had been confirmed. Granny and Marvin were sweet on each other. There had been a trip to Vegas, and a couple had married. Now the next thing she had to do was introduce herself to Marvin Childers, her step-grandfather.

Chapter Fourteen

Kelly stopped at a stop sign. She waited for the town plow truck to go through the intersection. They'd arrived at the same time, but she yielded for two reasons. One, she was grateful the plows had been out clearing the roads; her driving skills were rusty, thanks to taking subways and Uber in the city for too many years. Two, the plow truck was a lot bigger than her vehicle.

The few moments she waited allowed her time to reflect on her visit to the Senior Center. Apparently, her granny had married an old man who'd wanted to visit an adult-only establishment. She squeezed her eyes shut at the thought of her granny marrying a dirty old man. Honking from behind snapped her out of the icky visual, and she proceeded through the intersection, on to meet her step-grandpa.

She turned off of Glendale Road onto the gravel driveway of Marvin Childers's shingled cottage. There wasn't much space. Someone had cleared enough width for only one vehicle. Observing the messiness, Kelly got the impression someone had shoveled rather than plowed. Had Marvin cleared the snow himself? At his age, shoveling could be dangerous—heart attacks, injuries, hypothermia, the list was extensive.

She parked behind the beat-up old station wagon and climbed out of her Jeep. She heard barking and looked around but didn't see the dog until her gaze landed on the covered porch, and there he was. Scruffy, white, and loud. The short path to the porch was barely shoveled but manageable, thanks to the sturdy tread on her boots.

Marvin might have lived on the same road Diana had, but their worlds were miles apart. She had lived in a big, beautiful new home, while he lived in a small, timeworn cottage. Kelly's best guess was he'd been a holdout interested in blocking development. The closer she got to the house, the louder the dog got. The front door swung open, and a man appeared, and all Kelly's thoughts about real estate vanished.

"Don't mind Sparky. He's all bark."

"Sparky? Cute name."

Marvin nodded. "While I appreciate a visit from a pretty young woman, I'm afraid I'm not buying anything today." He smiled and then took a drink from the mug he held. His shoulders were hunched, and he'd probably lost a few inches in the past few years. His white hair was thin and his matching eyebrows bushy. Over a plaid shirt and tan pants, he wore a gray, shawl-collared cardigan. His sneakers were scuffed and smudged with dirt.

"I'm not here to sell anything. My name is Kelly Quinn. I'm Martha Blake's granddaughter."

Marvin stared at Kelly a long moment, and then recognition flicked in his pale blue eyes, and he gave a knowing nod. "You're the one who went to the city. Your sister stayed here on the island. A doctor, right?"

"Lawyer. Caroline is a lawyer."

He shrugged. "I was close. Either way, she was left with a lot of school loans, right? Your grandmother and I were good friends. Come on in. I'm freezing my snowballs off out here."

Kelly held back a laugh. She wasn't there for a social visit. She was there to find out if her inheritance was about to be ripped away from her. *Snowballs.* Her granny would have had a good laugh at that line, though.

Marvin whistled and got the attention of his dog, who turned around and bounded back inside. Kelly followed into the two-story, cedar-shake cottage. The first floor was open concept; the kitchen, eating, and living areas were all connected. The dog trotted over to the sofa and leaped up. He rested his head on a pillow and closed his eyes while Kelly scanned the walls. She didn't know where to look first. Every inch of wall was covered with framed artwork. It was chaotic, overwhelming, yet beautiful. Off the kitchen, an art studio was set up.

A large wooden table, with an easel set in the center, was pressed up against a bank of windows. The view was of the open land that surrounded the cottage. The tabletop was cluttered with jars of paintbrushes, pens, and pencils, stacks of sketchbooks, tubes of paints, discarded rags, and paint palettes. A flat file cabinet stood where she expected a hutch would be situated, and two carts filled with more painting supplies were left standing in the middle of the room.

"I usually don't get much company these days." Marvin shuffled to the kitchen counter and took a mug off the drain board. "You're in luck. I just brewed a fresh pot."

Kelly wasn't sure how lucky she was, but she accepted the mug and dropped in a splash of milk from the carton Marvin had set out from the refrigerator. She took a drink and revisited her game plan. What was her ideal outcome from this meeting? Learning that the marriage certificate she found was a fake.

Marvin sipped his coffee. "Your grandmother always talked about you and your sister. She was proud of both of you."

Kelly swallowed down her sadness. A ball of sorrow landed hard in her stomach at another reminder of how much granny had loved her. Her granny was the one person in her life who had been supportive, even when Kelly didn't deserve support. She always believed in Kelly and pushed her to find what made her happy, even if it didn't meet the expectations of her parents or older sister.

"You knew my grandmother a long time?" With her mug in hand, she drifted over to the art studio.

"Decades. Your grandfather and I used to golf together."

"You and Grandpa were friends?"

"Until tee time. I always beat him. Back in the day, I had a heck of a swing." Marvin rushed to the table and tidied up. "Excuse the mess." He set the neatly ordered sketchbooks to the side of the table and returned the pens to their glass jar, then set his focus on Kelly. "I'm an old man, so I tend to be direct these days. You came here today for a reason. What's the reason, Kelly?

"I found a marriage certificate from Las Vegas."

"Las Vegas? Sin City." He let out a low whistle. "I went there for my bachelor party. What a weekend."

"You also went five years ago with the Senior Center. Do you remember?"

Marvin blinked, and he rubbed the back of his neck. "Senior Center? I haven't been there in years." He looked out the window and drank his coffee. "Wait . . . yes . . . we went on a trip to Las Vegas. Forgive my memory. Sometimes it's a little slow to recall events." He offered a weak smile. "Martha and I found a cheesy wedding chapel when we were casino hopping. It sounded like a fun idea."

"Eloping? You both thought it was a fun idea?" Now Kelly understood where she got her streak of spontaneity from. No wonder her granny always understood her.

"Yes, we did, young lady." Marvin chuckled as he wagged a finger at Kelly. "Martha looked so beautiful that day. I don't know any man who would've said no to her."

"You mean she proposed?" Kelly was peeling back a whole new layer of her granny. What else didn't she know about the woman who baked the best gingersnaps and made the best lemonade?

Marvin placed his bony hands on his hips. "Surprised me, for sure. But I was on board. It's not every day a man gets a second chance with an amazing woman. I miss my Trudy every day, but saying 'I do' to Martha helped me get past all the pain and hurt. I think it did her a world of good too."

"Getting over Grandpa's death?"

"Yeah, that too. I mean, having a man find her attractive."

Oh, boy. Oh, no. Kelly had no choice but to listen to details of the wedding ceremony so she'd know what she was up against when it came to her granny's estate, but listening to details about the wedding night? No. Nope. Not going to happen.

"My nickname for her was 'Hot Stuff.'" Marvin grinned at the memory. It seemed like he had no problem recalling that particular memory.

The pit of sadness in her belly from earlier had morphed into a glob of nausea. Maybe Mrs. O'Neal should have let him go to that adults-only ranch in Carson City and then he wouldn't have married her grandmother.

"Are you feeling all right, Kelly? You look deathly pale." Marvin set his mug on the table and reached out for Kelly.

She shoved her mug into his open hands and recoiled back. "I'm fine. Thank you for speaking with me. I should go." She spun around so fast it dizzied her, but she stayed upright and darted for the front door.

Stepping over the threshold, Marvin caught up with her. "Don't leave like this. You're upset." He followed after her down the porch steps.

"I'm fine. I'm sorry I intruded." Kelly continued down the steps until she landed on the walkway.

"No worries. You're always welcome here. Just make sure you don't speed."

Kelly looked over her shoulder. What was he talking about? "Speed? On this road?"

"This isn't a road you want to be driving fast on. Over the years, there've been a few accidents. Bad ones. Can't believe that Rolls-Royce didn't crash the other night."

Kelly turned around to face Marvin. "What Rolls-Royce? When?"

"The night the lady up the road was found dead." He pointed in the direction of Diana's house. "You heard about her?"

"Yes, I did. The night she was murdered a Rolls-Royce sped by your house? What time? Did you see the driver?"

"Nah. I was out with Sparky when the car sped by. It was real late. I'd dozed off watching the ten o'clock news. Gosh, I'm sorry I can't say exactly when Sparky woke me. I should have gotten the license plate number. Next time I will."

Kelly looked over her shoulder at the dirt road. Marvin might have seen the killer drive by. She turned around to face him. "You should let the police know if you see the car again. It could be important. Thank you for the coffee." She made her way along the snowy path back to her Jeep. She had a lot to think about. Correction. She had a lot to worry about. Just when she thought she could enjoy her first Christmas back in Lucky Cove, she was dealt a devastating blow. Everything she'd been working for was about to be yanked away from her.

Kelly traveled down the road with a heavy weight of doom and gloom pressing on her shoulders. The tension radiated up her neck. In a matter of minutes, the mother of all headaches would spread across her forehead. Exactly what she didn't need.

She reached an intersection and hesitated before flicking on her left blinker. Turning right would lead her back to the boutique. She grumbled at her spur-of-the-moment decision to go left. As much as she wanted to, she couldn't fight the draw to the last place she wanted to visit. Thirty minutes later, she'd arrived at the destination.

There weren't any words to describe the compulsion pumping through her as she pushed open the door of her Jeep and stepped out. The need to spend a few minutes alone with her granny overwhelmed her and scared her. She feared losing control and allowing a dam of pent-up insecurity and worry to burst. There was too much at stake for her not to be thinking clearly.

A cold wind struck her, and a chill snaked through her body, though the chill wasn't from the icy air. It was from all the death surrounding her.

She cast a wide glance over the top of her Jeep to what seemed to be endless rows of headstones and heaved a sigh as she buried her gloved hands deeper into her coat pockets. Undisturbed snow covered the graves and headstones. The haunting image laid out before her was part eerie and part beautiful.

The flat stretch of open land offered no barrier to the whipping wind that had borne down on the island. The road that cut through the cemetery had been cleared, but the staff hadn't shoveled out any walking paths. She trudged through the snow and arrived at the spot where her granny had been put to eternal rest.

Kelly pulled a hand out of her pocket, bent forward, and brushed off the snow on her granny's headstone. A strand of her hair escaped from the loose ponytail she'd gathered up after she left the boutique. MARTHA BLAKE. BELOVED WIFE, MOTHER, AND GRANDMOTHER The words etched in stone were forever imprinted on Kelly's heart. She'd never known such a selfless person. One day she would make her granny proud.

One day. I promise.

Tears welled in Kelly's eyes as she worked her lower lip. She had so many questions for her granny.

She slipped her hand back into her pocket and fingered the ring she believed Marvin had given Martha on their wedding day. She'd slipped the ring into her coat pocket at the last minute before leaving the boutique. She wasn't sure why she wanted to have it with her.

She stepped back from the stone. "Why didn't you tell anyone you remarried? What were you thinking? A Vegas wedding, really? Granny, what am I supposed to do now?"

Kelly waited for answers. None came. Only tears.

"Pepper wanted me to decorate the store like you used to. I did a little decorating. It's not the same without you. Without your gingersnap cookies. They're the best cookies." Kelly sniffled, wiped away the tears, and stared at the headstone.

The cold and stillness of the cemetery transported Kelly back to the winter after Ariel's accident all those years ago. Absorbed in guilt and self-loathing for abandoning Ariel for a silly boy who turned out to be a bad kisser, Kelly often found solace in the quietest place she knew, the cemetery. Back then she'd huddle beneath the big oak tree not too far from where Granny was now, and she'd let her mind wander and negotiated deals with God in hopes of Ariel regaining her ability to walk. She'd learned deals wouldn't undo the damage that was done in the accident. Today she didn't feel the peace she'd sought all those years ago. The stillness that hovered wasn't comforting. Instead, the hairs on the back of her neck stood up. Her body tingled; her nerve endings sent out an alert.

Her gaze darted across the openness, seeking the person who was watching her.

She shook her head and silently admonished herself for being dramatic. There wasn't anyone around. It was only her and the dearly departed.

She tucked the strand of hair that fell along her check back behind her ear. "How well did you know Marvin? Do you think he'll take the boutique away from me? I think my changes will help the business thrive. I'm trying to make you proud." She wiped her face with the sleeve of her coat. She didn't want to cry. She wanted to be strong. Strong enough to handle whatever would go down with Marvin. The past few months of being fired and taking over the boutique had made her tougher, more formidable. Was that the reason Granny had left the business to her? To fortify her resolve, her self-confidence?

Another chill skittered down her spine. She scanned the landscape again. Someone was watching her. She was sure of it.

"I guess I'll have to figure this out on my own. I love you, Granny." Kelly said a silent prayer before turning and walking back toward her vehicle. She tried to follow the footprints she'd made in the snow as she approached the grave. She pulled out her cell phone from her pocket and dialed Frankie.

"What's up?" He sounded out of breath.

She figured she'd caught him during his workout. "Do you have Granny's recipe for her gingersnaps?"

"I do. I'll be baking them for Christmas Eve. Why?" A loud crash in the background was followed by a chorus of curse words.

"Where are you?"

"I'm helping a friend. He's short a cook. I figured I'd pick up some extra cash." During the off season, Frankie worked as a personal chef and usually booked a couple clients each week. From time to time, he worked for friends whose restaurants were open year-round.

"I won't keep you. Could you e-mail me the recipe? I want to bake them."

"You?" he asked with a heavy dose of skepticism.

"Yes, me. How hard can it be?" When she reached her vehicle and made her way around to the driver's seat, she noticed a piece of paper slipped beneath the windshield wiper. "Some flour, sugar, eggs, and other stuff. Whip up in a bowl and bake. Easy."

"Not exactly."

She rolled her eyes. Leave it to a chef to think everyone needed a culinary degree to bake something. It couldn't be hard to bake a few cookies. She reached for the paper and pulled it out, then unfolded the note.

Kelly Quinn. Beloved daughter and sister. Rest in Peace.

She gasped. Her heart slammed against her chest, and her hands shook as she looked around, turning in a full circle. Nobody. She was all alone.

"Kell, you okay?"

Frankie must've heard her gasp. Shoot. She didn't want to tell him about the note and worry him. "Yeah, I'm good. I've gotta go." She disconnected the call as she stared out over the ominous landscape of headstones and mausoleums. Someone had been watching her. She shoved the note into her pocket and climbed into her Jeep. The person who'd been there and left the note was long gone. And it was time for her to be gone too.

Chapter Fifteen

Kelly's attempt to quell the uneasiness in her stomach by taking in deep inhales and exhales failed. After five breaths, she gave up. There was no quelling of anything. She hated to admit it, but she was a little freaked out. She'd received a direct threat, and the message came through loud and clear.

The drive back to Lucky Cove and the boutique was the longest thirty minutes of her life. She kept glancing in the rearview mirror to see if someone was following her. Why hadn't she paid more attention after leaving Marvin's house?

Between work, updating the apartment, decorating for Christmas, and finding the marriage certificate, she'd been distracted. No, she wouldn't have noticed if she was being followed.

But now she would pay more attention.

When she arrived back at the boutique, she sent Breena out to get lunch for them, even though she didn't have much of an appetite. She didn't want Breena to see her freak out. She'd prefer to have her meltdowns in private.

She looked at the note.

Kelly Quinn. Beloved daughter and sister. Rest in Peace.

Rest in Peace.

Definitely a threat. She gulped. The uneasiness in her stomach ratcheted up. She had to report it to the police . . . just in case. She grabbed her cell phone, but before she could hit Gabe's number, the front door opened and Hugh entered.

Good grief. What did he want now?

"We need to talk, Kelly. You and I need to talk." He flashed his toothy smile as he strode to the sales counter, unbuttoning his coat.

"I couldn't agree more." Kelly set her phone down.

He stopped mid stride, his eyes widened. "You've reconsidered my offer. Wonderful!"

Kelly raised a palm. "Slow your roll, Hugh. I have reconsidered nothing. I told you I'm not interested, yet you told Summer I brought up the idea of being on the show. You lied! Now she's upset with me."

"No, sweetheart. I didn't lie. I simply revised the conversation a fraction to elicit the desired response from her."

"What the . . . Do you hear yourself? Revised the conversation?" She sighed. "This is pointless."

"Lighten up. Summer will get over it. Trust me." He slid his hands into his coat pockets. "Besides, tension is good for the show."

"Why are you here?" Kelly had had enough tension with Summer and her uncle. She didn't need to add any more, thank you very much. She would spend either Christmas Eve or Christmas Day with them, and she didn't want the show looming over them.

"To make you an offer. Now, we rarely pay a lot to newbies, but I think your story, your struggle to make it in your new business and pick up the pieces of your tragic past—"

"My what?"

"The tragedy ten years ago when you left your friend and she wound up in a car with a drunk driver and was paralyzed. And then there's your humiliating firing at Bishop's. Wow! Serena Dawson fired you personally. We can probably get her to do a sit-down interview with us. Great stuff to work it."

"No, no, no. Not great stuff to work with."

"Look, there are many stories to tell on a show. Three of them are redemption, which is self-explanatory; walk away, you know where you walk away from a situation; and you're not alone, kind of a heartwarming tale that lets people know whatever they're going through, someone is right there with them. Those three stories are powerful, and let me tell you, sweetheart, you've got all three going for you. Millions of viewers will tune in week after week to see how you survive." He stepped closer to the counter.

"Survive?" Kelly turned over the threatening note to keep Hugh from seeing it. She came out from behind the counter. The quick touch of the torn piece of paper reminded her of the fear that had pulsed through her earlier. Someone had stalked and threatened her. Why? She'd only asked a few questions. The same questions many people in Lucky Cove were asking. So why target Kelly? First things first. She had to make it abundantly clear, in no uncertain terms, that she would not appear on *LIL*. "I don't care how much you offer me. I'm not going on your show." She hoped she was clear enough.

Hugh plastered on a cocky grin as he pulled out his phone from his pocket. He tapped on it and then showed her the screen. Her eyes nearly popped out of their sockets. That much money to let a cameraman follow her around? Holy cow.

No! Focus, Kelly. Focus.

"In your situation, this much money could come in handy." Hugh lowered the phone, taking a sweeping glance around the boutique.

Kelly fought back the tongue-lashing she wanted to give mister high-and-mighty reality-show producer, but she had questions, and insulting him would probably make him uncooperative.

"On second thought, maybe I've been too hasty."

Hugh's grin broke out into a full smile, and he nodded slowly. "You're being a very smart girl. You might as well cash in on your disasters now while you're still young."

Ouch. Reality television was brutally honest.

"Well, when you put it that way, how could I possibly turn down the offer?" Actually, it was easy—though stringing him along could help her get answers to her questions. "Since I'm seeing how lucrative the job can be, I need a little more time to think about it."

"If you're trying to hold out for more money, don't. I'm not open to negotiating any more money at this point." Hugh lowered his phone.

"I wouldn't offend your generosity by negotiating a higher rate. I need a little time since I've been so adamantly against it."

Hugh nodded. "Understandable. Don't wait too long." He turned to leave.

"Wait, I have a question."

Hugh stopped. "Promotion? You'll be featured on our website and across all of our social media platforms."

"No. I'm sure your company would do a thorough job raising my profile." Or, rather, exploiting her tragic past and life disasters, because if Hugh was willing to pay that much money, he had to expect to rake in a huge amount himself. "No, I'm curious why Diana helped Patrice Garofalo after she got arrested."

Hugh's eyes darkened, and his jaw set. "Poor girl got hooked on drugs. Really messed up her life. She left the show a couple of seasons ago. Why are you asking about Patrice?"

"It seemed out of character for Diana to help one of the production crew. She lobbied for you to provide legal services for Patrice. There had to be a reason. What was it?"

"Diana had a big heart when she wanted to admit it. I guess she felt a sense of responsibility to the younger woman. I wanted to keep Diana happy. Back then, she was an asset to the show, so I hired a lawyer for Patrice. I hope she's doing well, but sadly, many people who get caught up in drugs never get better. Now, you consider my offer."

"One more question." She stepped forward.

Hugh's gaze narrowed. His smile had slid away. She suspected he was growing impatient.

"Does anyone on the cast or crew drive a Rolls-Royce?"

"There's only one. Yvonne. Our viewers will find your curiosity charming. I, however, don't. Let me know what you decide." He turned and rushed out of the boutique.

The car Marvin saw belonged to Yvonne? Kelly's mind raced back to her conversation with Yvonne. What did she say about seeing Diana before the murder? Yvonne said the last time she'd seen Diana was a few days before the holiday party. She lied. Why?

Back at the sales counter, Kelly turned over the threatening note. Hugh wasn't the only person who hadn't found her curiosity charming.

Breena returned with lunch after Hugh's departure, and the rest of the afternoon was steady with customers and new consignees. The boutique's inventory was looking good, and one woman brought in a pile of Ralph Lauren sweaters, all with the tags still on them. They had never been worn. Merchandising ideas swirled around in Kelly's head. She entered the sweaters into the inventory system and would make a final decision tomorrow on how to best showcase them for a quick sale.

Kelly asked Breena to close up the boutique. She explained she had errands to run but didn't go into detail. Breena didn't pry and reminded Kelly she'd work on the marketing plan for the Holiday Edit event. She'd already made up a flyer, which Kelly approved on her way out the door.

On her drive over to the Lucky Cove Police Department, she called Liv. It was her day off from the bakery, and she spent it at the community center preparing for yet another holiday event. The Morettis always took part in community events.

"Can you believe he said that to me? He made me sound like some pathetic loser America needs to root for in order to turn my tragic life around. Maybe he's right. Maybe I should cash in on my disasters while I have the chance."

"Yeah, well, if you do, you're guaranteed to have another disaster on your hands, and the disaster's name would be Summer." Liv's voice was barely audible over the background noise of the other volunteers.

"Right." While Kelly had a hard time hearing her friend, being able to vent felt good. She flicked on her blinker to make the turn into the police department's parking lot. "Hey, I've gotta go. Thanks for listening."

"No problem. I have to go too. We're almost finished here, and I want to wrap things up. Call me later."

Kelly ended the call and pulled into a space. She grabbed her tote bag and dashed inside the one-story brick building. She'd hoped to catch Gabe during shift change but was too late. He'd already left work. Turning to leave, she was close to the exit when she was stopped by Detective Wolman.

"Is there anything I can help you with, Miss Quinn?" Wolman had emerged from the back of the building. She let go of the door behind her. As the door shut, she walked toward Kelly. She wore her usual uniform of dark pants, a crisp, white button-down shirt, and a tailored blazer.

"I was hoping to see . . . I found this on my windshield earlier today." Kelly pulled the note out of her tote bag and handed it to the detective. She figured Gabe would have to turn over the note to the detective, anyway.

Wolman read the succinct note and then lifted her unreadable gaze to meet Kelly's. "Where were you when you received this note?"

"At the cemetery. I was visiting my granny's grave."

"Did you see anybody?"

"No. As far as I was concerned, I was alone. I didn't even hear another vehicle. I guess I was too deep in my thoughts."

"Did anyone know you were going to the cemetery?"

"I didn't even know I was going there until I got there. Someone must be following me. Though I didn't notice anyone following me on my way over here."

Wolman lowered the note. "Do you have any idea of who or why?"

"I don't have a clue."

"Clue. Interesting word choice. Have you been meddling in my murder investigation?" Wolman squinted, and her brows furrowed.

"No, no, nothing like that." Well, okay, something like that, but Kelly didn't want to get into the weeds. "I've run into people who knew Diana, and we've had conversations about her and her death. I have spoken with Patrice Garofalo."

"Patrice Garofalo?"

"She used to work on the show until she got arrested for cocaine possession and Diana arranged for the show to pay her legal fees."

Wolman's nostrils flared as she stepped forward. "I warned you. You're a civilian with no training in law enforcement. Your nosing around can put not only yourself in danger but also those of us trained in law enforcement." Wolman took a breath. "Where were you before you arrived at the cemetery?

"I was at Marvin Childers's house on Glendale Road."

Wolman shook her head. "Where Diana lived? Why were you there?"

"I went to see him on a matter that relates to the boutique."

"He wants to consign clothing?"

"No. But you should know he told me that, the night of Diana's murder, he saw a speeding Rolls-Royce on the road, and Yvonne owns one. She said the last time she saw Diana was a few days before Diana died. It appears she lied."

"It appears you have been meddling." Wolman turned and headed to the interior office door. "Come on back to my desk, and you can file a report. And then I'll give you a tour of our holding cells so you can see where you'll end up if you continue meddling."

"Thank you." Kelly caught up with the detective and followed her through the doorway to file the report, though she'd politely decline the tour of the jail cells.

Chapter Sixteen

An hour later, Kelly exited the police department minus the up-close-and-personal visit to the holding cells. She told the detective she needed to get back to the boutique. Behind her back she crossed her fingers because it wasn't a small lie. It was a big fat lie, because her next stop was Yvonne's house—to find out why the woman lied about the last time she saw Diana.

However, there was a snag in her plan, thanks to Dorothy Mueller chasing after her in the parking lot. Bundled in a full-length puffy coat with a knitted hat pulled down over her ears, Mrs. Mueller waved a gloved finger at Kelly as she approached.

"Is everything okay, Mrs. Mueller?" Kelly's thoughts about Wolman and her next stop disappeared. The tone and urgency of the elderly woman worried her.

"No. Everything is not okay, Miss Quinn." Gone was the familiar greeting of Kelly's first name, along with the kind smile she'd offered Kelly earlier in the day. "What did you think you were doing?"

"When? What are you talking about?" Kelly burrowed into her coat. The late-day wind was whipping up and slicing through the air like a frozen blade. She chided herself for forgetting her hat.

"Don't play coy with me, missy. Why on earth did you badger poor Marvin about your grandmother?" Mrs. Mueller lowered her hand and rested it on her handbag, which dangled from her other arm.

"Badger? I did no such thing. I only asked him if he knew my grandmother." Kelly wasn't about to reveal to Mrs. Mueller her discovery of the marriage certificate. There was a chance this was all a bad dream and she'd wake up and learn her granny never knew a man named Marvin.

Okay, a very slim chance, but she wanted to hold on to it. "Wait, how do you know I went to see Mr. Childers?"

Could Mrs. Mueller have been the one who followed her? Left the threatening note? She shook her head, snapping her out of the ridiculous train of thought. Dorothy Mueller wasn't a stalker.

"He called me after you left. And what's this nonsense about him letting the police know if he sees a Rolls-Royce again?"

"It might be important to their investigation of Diana Delacourte's murder."

Mrs. Mueller frowned. "Where do you come up with this stuff? You know, he's not a well man. He's been sick."

"I'm sorry. I didn't know." Kelly shivered. She desperately wanted to get into her Jeep and crank up the heat.

"Now you do, and I suggest you leave him alone. Now, if you'll excuse me, I need to update the police on my security system." Mrs. Mueller brushed by Kelly and strode toward the building's entrance.

The tension headache that was building earlier had returned, and now it throbbed dead center in her forehead. She waited a moment before slipping into her Jeep. She wanted to make sure Mrs. Mueller got into the building safely. The woman was so petite Kelly could imagine her being swept away, and there were also some slippery patches on the pavement. When the woman entered the building, Kelly got into her vehicle and drove out of the parking lot.

By the time Kelly reached the highway, the sun had set, and the commuter rush hour was also in full swing. Traffic crawled, and forty minutes later, she reached her exit. Once off the highway, she followed the directions on her GPS.

Her visit to the cemetery and the sinister note had zapped whatever holiday cheer she'd begun soaking up after getting her Candy Cane manicure. Now, driving along the snowy roads, with homes looking like Christmas thanks to holiday lights and mega-sized inflatable Santa Clauses, a bit of seasonal cheer seeped back into her.

She wiggled her fingers on the steering wheel and smiled. Her nails were definitely festive.

The GPS announced her final turn before arriving at her destination. The left turn was onto a long, plowed driveway that led to Yvonne's home. Situated on what was known as the Gold Coast of Long Island, where the ridiculously wealthy at the turn of the twentieth century built lavish estates, Yvonne's house didn't disappoint.

"Holy cow!" Kelly shifted her vehicle into park and leaned forward on her steering wheel to take in the expansive house. "No surprise a Rolls-Royce lives here." She grabbed her tote bag and stepped out of her car.

The white colonial house—well over five thousand square feet, she guessed—was lavish, yet it had a down-to-earth vibe. White with traditional black window shutters, copper-roofed bay windows, a portico supported by massive columns, and meticulously trimmed evergreen hedges running the length of the house, it felt more like a home than a mansion. A heck of a big home.

She glanced upward and noticed a roof deck. Yvonne hadn't struck Kelly as a roof deck kind of gal.

Kelly forged forward, bracing for another encounter, all the while remembering how Yvonne had gotten her back up when Kelly had asked about the last time she saw Diana. Now Kelly would ask her why she lied.

Kelly pressed the doorbell and waited and shivered.

The door opened, and a uniformed housekeeper appeared.

Yeah, this was a lifestyle Kelly had no clue about.

"Hello, I'm Kelly Quinn, and I'd like to speak with Yvonne."

The housekeeper eyed Kelly from head to toe as if she were selling vacuums door-to-door or worse. "Is she expecting *you*?"

"No, she isn't. But it's very important that I speak with her." The last time she'd been rudely treated by household staff was the morning she'd found Diana's body. Nanette had shut the door on her twice and refused her access to the warmth of the house while she waited for the police to interview her. The staff of the reality show divas was as difficult as they were. Maybe they should get their own show.

"I'll see if she's available." The door closed on Kelly.

Here we go again.

Only, this time, Kelly wouldn't go looking around the property. Finding one dead diva was enough for her. However, since she wasn't in Lucky Cove, she would be out of Wolman's jurisdiction.

The door opened again, and the housekeeper gestured her inside. She led Kelly through the hall into an enormous room with floor-to-ceiling windows overlooking an expanse of snow-covered land. She wondered how many acres came with the house.

"I wasn't expecting you, Miss Quinn." Yvonne breezed into the room carrying a Louis Vuitton agenda. She wore a simple, knee-length black dress with a bright pink cardigan tied over her shoulders, giving a rosy glow to her face and complementing her gray hair. "This is what I use to track all of my appointments. When someone wishes to meet with me, they telephone or e-mail, and then I either accept or decline. When I accept, the date goes in here." She patted the closed agenda. "You are not in here."

This won't go well.

"I apologize for dropping by unannounced. You have a beautiful home." Kelly looked around the room. The tallest Christmas tree she'd ever seen indoors stood decorated beside the impressive fireplace, its polished dark wood mantel about the same height as Kelly.

"Thank you. I'm very proud of it. My husband and I purchased it right after we married."

Yvonne walked past Kelly, set the agenda on an end table, and then sat on the sofa.

"Not exactly the starter home most newlyweds begin with." Kelly clasped her hand over her mouth. She couldn't believe she'd said that out loud. "I'm sorry."

Yvonne looked amused and gestured for Kelly to have a seat on the opposing sofa. Kelly opened her coat, set her tote on the hardwood floor, and perched on the edge of the cushion. Her hand glided over the floral fabric.

Nubby silk. Very nice. Very expensive.

"I can see why Hugh wants to add you to the show. You'd be a breath of fresh air." Yvonne leaned back and crossed her legs, giving Kelly a glimpse of her red-soled nude pumps. Christian Louboutin. Kelly's heart did a little pitter-patter that kept her from responding to the comment about Hugh. "You're right. This isn't your typical first home. I had no idea my husband had bought this house for us. He surprised me by taking a drive; we ended up here, and he gave me the keys."

"How romantic. He made a wonderful choice with this house. It even has a roof deck."

Yvonne laughed. "It's not a roof deck; it's a widow's walk." She must have noticed the confused look on Kelly's face. "Also known as a widow's watch. They were common in the nineteenth century. Wives of sea captains watched out from the deck for their husband's ships to arrive back in port."

"Okay. Now I know what you're talking about." Kelly's thoughts drifted to a time when there were no telephones, no telegraph, or any other modern communication technology. Wives waited for their husbands to return for weeks, even months, after leaving for a journey. She imagined how much their hearts swelled when they first caught a glimpse of their husbands' ships.

"A wealthy merchant built this home when he moved his family from Massachusetts to New York. His eldest daughter had moved back home after her husband, a sea captain, died at sea. She had spent every day on the widow's walk of her home in Massachusetts and wouldn't move unless the new home had a widow's walk. She stood vigilant every day, looking for her husband, even during bad weather. It was right after a nor'easter that she came down with influenza and died."

Kelly hadn't considered the impact on a wife of never seeing her husband's ship return to port. The woman must have been unstable to wait every day on the widow's walk, especially when she was in another state.

"Alas, I don't think you came here for a history lesson on my home." Yvonne was perceptive.

"No, I didn't. I came to ask you a question. I've thought of how to ask this question without it sounding rude and accusatory, but I don't think it's possible. I'm just going to ask. What were you doing at Diana's house the night of my uncle's party? The night she died."

Yvonne opened her brightly colored lips, a deep pink with a warm hue, to say something.

Kelly guessed she was about to deny the accusation. "Someone saw your Rolls-Royce speeding down the road."

Yvonne's lips formed an O, and then she pressed her lips together. "Fine. I was there. I didn't see how it was any of your business."

"Understandable. But Wendy asked me to help her. And, earlier today, someone left a threatening note for me, so now it is my business."

Yvonne gasped. "I had no idea. Have you notified the police?"

"Yes. I also told them what the witness told me. You should expect another unannounced visit."

Yvonne pressed her hands on the skirt of her dress. "I didn't kill Diana. I went to see her because of the blowout she had with Wendy at the party. I tried to talk sense into her."

"What do you mean?"

"Diana wanted to get back onto the show in the worst way. I reminded her that acting out as she had at the party wasn't the way to do that. Like it or not, she needed to have Wendy on her side. Or, at least, not have her as an enemy."

"I take it your advice didn't go over well?"

"Hardly. Diana didn't want to hear anything I said. She was too worked up. She needed to calm down. I . . . I reached out to her, but she shoved me. I nearly sprained my ankle on the front step. I'd had enough. If she wanted to continue on her downward spiral, then so be it. I left. She was very much alive and angry when I did."

"The front step? When you left, she was at the front door?"

Yvonne nodded. "She wouldn't let me inside. I was freezing."

Then how did Diana end up outside? Did the killer lure her out under false pretenses? Or did Diana leave her house on her own, only to be surprised by the killer? But she wasn't wearing a coat when Kelly found her.

"If she was alive when you left, did you see anyone else around? Maybe someone passed you as you were driving away?"

Yvonne stared daggers at Kelly. "I don't appreciate being called a liar, young lady. I've been more than courteous to you, answering your prying questions and encouraging your Nancy Drew escapades, but I'm about done. It's time for you to go."

Kelly scrambled to her feet and grabbed her tote bag. This wasn't how she wanted to end her visit with Yvonne, but given the circumstances of the visit, it had turned out better than she'd expected. She was about to say something, but Yvonne gave her a warning look. Heeding the warning, she slung her tote over her shoulder and walked out of the great room. The housekeeper approached her and swiftly showed her to the door.

Yvonne's housekeeper was too classy to slam the door shut, but the sentiment was there as the door closed behind her. Darkness had settled completely over the island, and the temperature had dipped lower. She hurried to her Jeep and drove out of the driveway, heading home. Before she left the boutique to go to the police department, she'd checked her e-mail inbox and found the gingersnap cookie recipe from Frankie. Maybe she'd stop at the grocery store to buy the ingredients and then pick up something for dinner. It actually sounded like a good way to spend the evening. After all, she couldn't get into any trouble baking.

Chapter Seventeen

As she took the exit for Lucky Cove, she considered attempting to learn how to cook. If she was going to tackle baking cookies, she should be able to whip up dinner instead of buying it in a to-go container. Traffic wasn't as bad as she expected, and she got home with enough time to heat up her dinner of lasagna from the deli counter and lay out all the ingredients for the cookies. Rummaging through the kitchen drawers and cabinets, she found measuring spoons and cups. So far, so good.

She needed a cookie sheet.

Shoot.

She wasn't sure if there was one in the apartment. She couldn't remember seeing any when she moved in. Then again, she hadn't been looking for baking equipment. Her priority was to get the musty odor out of the one-bedroom apartment because it had been closed up for a few years. When her granny began having difficulty climbing the stairs, she rented a cottage a few blocks from the boutique.

Next was developing a relationship with Howard. The orange furball wasn't open to a new relationship, and he'd made that clear with a few swipes at her when she attempted to pet him. But, like most guys, he learned she was the one who controlled the food in the house, and it was in his best interest to be nice to her. She was also was trying to salvage what was left of her granny's business. 'Nuff said on that point.

A search of an upper cabinet yielded her granny's trusty cookie sheet.

With the ingredients ready to go and the mixing bowls set out, she opened the recipe on her phone.

"I'm already to get my bake on." She reached for the five-pound bag of flour and opened it. A puff of flour mist escaped the bag, and she pulled back. A meow drew her attention away from the flour mess on the counter. Howard sat with his head tilted sideways. His normally cool, indifferent gaze was replaced with a look of doubt.

"I can do this. It's not rocket science."

Howard continued to stare at his human.

"What could go wrong?" she asked with a shrug. She cracked an egg into a stainless-steel bowl. From that point, she continued following the directions with a newfound air of confidence. Frankie had made too much of a big deal about baking. It was easy-peasy. Before she knew it, she had six mounds of cookie dough sprinkled with sugar and ready to go into the oven. With the timer set, she went to check her e-mails.

She opened her inbox, found over twenty new e-mails, and began sorting through them. She was in deep concentration when she smelled something, and it wasn't the fragrant scent of gingersnap cookies.

Her nose crinkled at a hint of smoke, her heart slammed against her chest, and her mind raced with the worst-case scenario as she ran to the kitchen. Gagging on the smoke, she grabbed a pot holder and removed the cookie sheet from the oven. She dropped the flat pan with a clank onto the cooling rack and turned off the oven.

She stared at the burned cookies. What a mess. But she didn't have time to worry about the ultra-crispy cookies because the smoke detector had gone off, and the incessant, loud beeping had her covering her ears with her hands. She tried to get the thing to stop beeping after opening the windows.

It was no use.

The apartment turned into a freezer while the darn detector continued to beep.

She did the only thing she could think of and sent an SOS text to Gabe. Within minutes he arrived at her apartment.

"Make it stop," she screeched when she opened the door and pointed to the smoke detector on the ceiling.

He didn't hesitate. He climbed the chair she'd put under the detector and silenced the alarm.

"How did you do that?" Not waiting for an answer, she turned and walked to the thermostat. She cranked up the heat to get the deep chill out of the apartment while Gabe climbed off the chair.

"What made you want to bake suddenly?" Gabe replaced the chair at the table.

"It's not suddenly." She brushed by him, strode into the kitchen, and sighed at the sight of the burned cookies and the bowl of the remaining cookie dough.

"Did you leave them in too long?" Gabe had come up behind her.

"No, I didn't." She stepped farther into the kitchen and tossed the burned cookies into the trash. "I had the timer set. The oven was preheated, like the recipe said to do."

Gabe moved over to the old stove and studied the knobs. "You know. This could be broken. Your grandmother hadn't lived here for a few years. It's kind of old." He turned back to Kelly.

"I wasn't sure, but now I am. The new stove and fridge will be coming soon." She filled the dishpan with soapy water and then turned out the cookie dough onto a paper towel. "I won't be doing any baking tonight."

"Why the urge to bake? What's going on, Kell?" He'd come up and stood behind her. He was a force she couldn't ignore, nor did she want to.

She set the mixing bowl in the soapy water and wiped her hands. She turned to face Gabe. "I was thinking about Granny. How much she loved Christmas, and I thought baking her cookies would be a way to be close to her. Silly, huh?"

"Not silly at all." Gabe pulled Kelly into a hug. She buried her head in his shoulder and cried. She'd yet again made a mess of things. "Maybe you should leave the baking to Frankie and my mom . . . for now."

Kelly laughed. Gabe always had a way of making her laugh. He'd been a goofball throughout school, which got him called into the principal's office one too many times, but he'd also been her protector when things got ugly after Ariel's accident. He'd not only stood up for her; he'd also gotten into a fistfight with another kid while defending her. Gabe always had her back, and he was still coming to the rescue.

She pulled away and grabbed a napkin to dry her face. "Thanks for coming over and stopping that horrible beeping noise. How's your mom doing?"

"She's feeling better. I think she's realizing she has to slow down a little. Between work and volunteering, she's wearing herself down."

"I should cut back on her hours. I've been relying on her too much." She tossed the napkin into the trash can.

"Well, I think it would be a good idea, though I doubt she'd agree." Gabe leaned against the counter. "I'm sensing something else other than reminiscing is going on in there." He pointed to Kelly's head.

"It's scary how well you know me. Want tea?"

At Gabe's nod, she filled the kettle and set it on the stove. She filled him in on what had happened at the cemetery, her chat with Wolman, and her visit to Yvonne's house. To his credit, Gabe didn't interrupt her or lecture her. He also didn't have any insights, or if he did, he wasn't sharing, on why Diana was found outside without her coat.

"What's going on with you and Mark Lambert?" Gabe drained the last of his tea and leaned back, crossing his arms over his chest. "You two had dinner the other night?"

"Wow. Small-town gossip at its best." Kelly took a long drink of her tea to delay answering his question.

He cleared his throat, prompting her to set her mug down.

"It was dinnertime, and we were both hungry. Nothing more to it. Well, then Detective Wolman showed up. I can't believe they're related."

"Why?"

"He's nice, and she's not."

"Wolman isn't that bad. She's a police detective, so she's not looking to be everyone's friend."

"She doesn't like me. And she doesn't want me dating her brother."

"How do you know?"

"I feel like I'm being interrogated." She shifted on her chair. "Wolman told me. She was very clear. I'm to stay away from her investigation and her brother."

"Which you're not doing."

Kelly shrugged.

Gabe chuckled. "Nothing's ever boring with you, Kell." He stood. "Be careful, and lock up."

Kelly promised and closed the door behind him. She turned the lock and leaned against the door. Why hadn't Gabe lectured her? He'd had the perfect opportunity. Did he think she was good at sleuthing? After the last murder investigation she'd helped with, maybe he saw her potential as a detective.

A loud meow jolted her out of her thoughts.

"What? I did pretty well last time."

Another meow challenged her statement.

"Or maybe he knows lecturing me won't do any good."

Howard slinked by her legs, with his tail whipping in the air, and disappeared into the bedroom. She knew where he stood on the question about Gabe. She pushed herself off the door. Her cat was also right about going to bed. It'd been a long day, and tomorrow she was on her own in the boutique. Both Breena and Pepper had the day off. She needed to be well-rested and clearheaded.

After a double check of the door lock and windows—though she doubted a second-story man would come through any of the drafty old windows during the night—she followed her cat into the bedroom.

As she flicked off the light switches on her way, she prayed she'd be able to sleep with no bad dreams. Though the likelihood of her sleep being peaceful with someone leaving threatening notes and a killer on the loose was slim.

Chapter Eighteen

After Kelly opened the boutique, Breena showed up for her shift. The day before had been steady with customers. Juggling assisting her customers and answering questions about the Holiday Edit event kept Kelly busy. By the time she closed the boutique, she was wiped out. When Breena joined Kelly at the sales counter, she filled her employee in on how many reservations they'd gotten for the Edit. Breena wasn't shy about taking credit for the marketing plan. She began brainstorming ideas for the New Year while she tidied up the displays. True to her experience, Monday mornings were slow, and this snippet of data eased the guilt Kelly felt when she slipped out of the boutique to attend Diana's funeral. Breena assured her she could handle being on her own until Pepper came in or Kelly returned.

Kelly arrived at the church, and it was packed. She was able to squeeze between two elderly women in a pew way in the back of the church. She noticed two men dressed all in black with cameras hoisted on their shoulders. What in the world? She shouldn't have been surprised, but it appalled her. And from the grumbling the two little ladies were doing, she wasn't alone in her assessment.

A somber tune played, and Diana's casket was wheeled to the altar and blessed by the minister. For the next forty minutes, friends, family, and coworkers eulogized Diana. Each one of the cast members of *LIL* had their moment up on the altar—aka spotlight—including Janine. The two old ladies seated behind Kelly were infuriated that Janine had the nerve to speak at the funeral. Their indignation had Kelly squelching a giggle.

The service finally ended, and the mourners were exiting the church in an orderly manner. The *LIL* cast members all had tissues in hand, except for

Janine. Instead, she had her fingers intertwined with Aaron Delacourte's. They somberly passed Kelly's pew. Aaron looked appropriately grief-stricken, while Janine's head was lifted high, and a neutral expression covered her face. Kelly guessed she didn't want to look all blubbery and ruddy for the cameras.

"Look at the hussy. Talk about brazen," the woman muttered behind Kelly.

"She could show some respect," the other lady said. "I don't see Diana's stepdaughter, do you?"

"No. Guess she's too busy partying out in Los Angeles. Did you see the article on Lulu last month and that disgusting photograph of her dancing on top of a table in that short skirt?"

Kelly remembered the photograph. After checking the website for intel on Marvin, she'd searched for the article about Beryl Delacourte. The old lady was right; the skirt was far too short for dancing on a tabletop.

"Can't wait for next season," the older lady said, her tone a little gleeful.

Outside the church, Summer approached Kelly. She'd tucked her blond hair under a floppy black hat and held a sleek black satchel.

"I didn't expect to see you here." Summer dwarfed Kelly, thanks to her four-inch-heeled leather boots.

"I wanted to pay my respects." Kelly shivered at the memory of finding Diana's body out in the snow. She was curious about how long she'd be revisiting the image.

"The fact that Hugh is filming for the show didn't play into your decision to attend the service?" Summer crossed her arms over her chest.

"Absolutely not. I can't believe you'd think it would. I've told you I want no part of the show."

"Hugh says otherwise."

"He's a manipulator. Can't you see that?"

"Humpff."

"Whatever, Summer. I'm freezing."

"Wait, are you going to Aaron's house for the reception?"

The press release stated that the burial was for immediate family only, while the reception was for all who had attended the church service. Kelly debated whether to go. She wasn't friends with Diana, but having found her body, she felt a connection to the dead woman. Even though she'd be a stranger to Aaron, she hoped her words of sympathy would mean something to him. They had meant something to her the day she'd buried her granny.

"I am. Guess I'll see you there." Kelly hurried to her Jeep, waving good-bye to Summer before she huffed and spun around. She marched toward her Mercedes.

Kelly called the boutique to check in with Breena. She said Pepper had just arrived. She looked rested and wasn't coughing. Relieved, Kelly could focus on the lengthy list of ideas Breena rattled off for marketing in the New Year. Her enthusiasm and energy were dizzying, but Kelly appreciated her part-time employee's commitment to the boutique. After disconnecting the call, she traveled along a busy thoroughfare and turned up the volume of the Christmas carol playing on the radio. Despite burning her first batch of gingersnaps, being stalked at the cemetery, and just leaving a funeral, she would rally up a dose of holiday cheer. Her head bopped along with the snappy song, and a smile stretched along her face.

Merry, merry, merry Christmas.

What would make the moment absolutely awesome would be a cup of Holly Jolly coffee from Doug's.

An incoming call interrupted the music and her festive mood. What did Summer want now?

"Hey, Summer, what's up? Are you at the Delacourte house already?"

"No! I can't believe what's happening. The police are here! They have a search warrant."

"Wait. Slow down. The police are where?"

"Wendy's house. After the burial, I followed Wendy back to her house. She didn't want to go to Aaron's house, and I thought I'd stay with her for a little while before going to the reception. When we arrived at the house, the police were here ready to search her home. This is insane. Wendy isn't a killer!"

"Calm down."

"I am calm. It's Wendy who's out of her mind." There was a pause, and when Summer spoke again, her voice was low. "I need help here. Come over. Now."

Things must have been bad for Summer to admit she needed Kelly's help. After a quick check of the time, Kelly decided she could make a quick stop at the Delacourte house and then drive to Wendy's house.

"I'm halfway to the Delacourte house. Let me pay my condolences, and I'll head over to Wendy's house. Text me her address." Before Summer could object, Kelly disconnected the call and turned off the radio. She wasn't certain if Aaron would be back from the cemetery by the time she got to the house. If he wasn't, she wouldn't hang around. Summer needed her.

She switched lanes and continued along the highway. A murder, a stalker, a funeral, a search warrant, and burned cookies. Not exactly how Kelly thought she'd be spending the month of December.

Merry freakin' Christmas.

Kelly entered the palatial foyer of Aaron Delacourte's mansion and stood in line with several fashionably dressed women. Each wore chic black and diamonds. Kelly glanced down at her Ted Baker cashmere-blend, gray wool coat. She'd saved for months to afford the wardrobe staple from Bishop's. Thank goodness, she had her thirty-percent employee discount because, without it, she'd never have been able to buy the coat, even on sale. Over her shoulder, she slung a sleek black quilted purse. The line moved forward as the guests continued farther into the house.

On the drive to the house, her GPS had recalculated twice because she missed turns. While the rerouting added extra time, it still surprised her Aaron had made it back to the house before she arrived. The burial ceremony must have been short.

With the woman ahead of her dramatically expressing her sadness at Aaron's loss, Kelly caught Janine's attention. Janine's lanky body was pressed along the side of her fiancé, and her arm was wrapped around Aaron's arm. Her black dress was far too short to be considered appropriate for a funeral, but Kelly had an inkling Janine hadn't intended to be appropriate.

Drama Lady moved ahead, joining a small cluster of other guests, and together they entered a parlor off of the foyer. Kelly reached out her hand to shake Aaron's. She recalled the wedding photo she saw of him and Diana. He hadn't changed much since his wedding to Diana. His hair was now salt and pepper, he had deep crease lines around his dark blue eyes, and his jawline had softened with age, but he still was handsome and, by the looks of it, still very attractive to younger women.

"I'm very sorry for your loss," Kelly murmured. The words came automatically to her. Maybe it was because they were forever etched in her brain. She'd heard the sentiment countless times during her granny's funeral and for weeks following. She'd accepted the condolences, although no one knew how deep her loss truly was.

"Thank you, Miss . . ." Aaron extended his hand out to Kelly. He towered over her, and his mournful gaze hit her hard, bringing back every minute of her granny's funeral—from dressing to leave for the church to returning to Pepper's house and collapsing in a pile of pillows on the guest bed for a good cry.

"Who invited you?" Janine's sharp voice snapped Kelly out of her thoughts and returned her to the present. Janine had tightened her grip on Aaron and leaned close to his ear. "She's the one I told you about." Aaron pulled back his hand. His demeanor shifted, and he gave Kelly a dark look. "What are you doing here?

"I'm here to offer my condolences." Kelly didn't want a scene, but what should she have expected with Janine present.

Her loud voice had already perked up the ears of some of the guests standing nearby.

"You should since your uncle's wife and her bestie probably killed Diana!" Janine cocked her head sideways and pursed her lips.

Kelly twisted around, looking for a camera crew. There had to be one for Janine to be acting so badly. But there wasn't a crew filming. Her behavior wasn't for an audience. It was just the way she was.

"Summer didn't murder Diana. You should be careful what you say about people." Kelly had firsthand experience with rumors and idle gossip. While Summer wasn't her favorite person, being accused of murder could hurt Summer's reputation and effect Juniper.

"Are you threatening me?" Janine straightened, and her nostrils flared.

"No. I'm telling you that what you say about someone can have a big impact on their lives. Like accusing someone of murder when there's no evidence. But since you've brought up the murder—like you did the day I was in your home by invitation—I'm curious why you had a restraining order against Diana."

Janine huffed a breath. "None of your business, shopgirl."

Wow. Janine's nastiness was apparently boundless. "According to your bio on the show's website, before joining the cast, you worked as a shopgirl too, until your break as a model. And now you're engaged to the widower of a former cast member who has been murdered."

"What are you insinuating?" Janine challenged.

"Nothing. Only stating facts. Like the fact that you met with Diana's former housekeeper the other day. What did you two talk about?"

Aaron looked at his fiancée. "Janine, you met with Nanette? What on earth for?"

"I'll explain, but not in front of her!" Janine whipped around and stormed out of the foyer. Her high heels clicked heavy on the marble floor.

"I must insist you leave. Now." Aaron left no room for discussion. His words and voice were firm.

Kelly turned around and walked out of the house—one more time when all eyes were on her, and not for a good reason. There were murmurs as she passed by the line of guests that reached out to the front walk. She couldn't make out what they were saying, but she was confident it wasn't flattering.

Chapter Nineteen

Back in her Jeep, Kelly called the boutique again and updated Breena on her next stop—Wendy's house. She provided a quick recap of Summer's call earlier and what had happened at the Delacourte house. Being the fangirl she was, Breena ate up all the info, then reassured Kelly she had everything under control.

Kelly disconnected the call, entered Wendy's address into her GPS, and pulled out of her space. By the time she arrived at Wendy's house, the police were in full swing of their search of the premises. Summer dragged Kelly from the entry hall into the two-story living room. Kelly was in awe of the breathtaking views of the dunes through the wall of glass. A deck stretched along the house, invoking images of lazy Sunday mornings with the latest issue of *Vogue* magazine and a cup of coffee.

"Kelly, are you listening to me?" Summer let go of Kelly's arm.

The question snapped Kelly out of her *Lifestyles of the Rich and Famous* daydream. "I'm sorry. What did you say?"

Summer heaved a sigh, and Kelly concluded she'd been hanging around the ladies too much because she was taking on their bad habits. Kelly had secretly binge watched *LIL* to get the lay of the land.

"They're trashing my house! Thank goodness, Hugh doesn't know about this or he'd have a camera crew here taping every moment of this invasion of my privacy." Wendy, carrying a filled wineglass, came from behind the sofa and walked to an upholstered chair. After she plopped down on the chair, she took a long swig of the wine.

Kelly leaned into Summer. "Should she be drinking at a time like this?"

"Probably not. But I'm not going to try to take the glass away from her. Are you?"

"No. No, no, no." One of the life lessons Kelly had learned from her binge watching of the show was never to come between a Long Island lady and her alcohol. Bad things happened to people who tried, and since she wasn't a hundred percent certain Wendy was innocent, she'd play it safe.

Detective Wolman entered the living room carrying an evidence bag in her gloved hand, her badge visible on her pants belt. "What are you doing here?" Her stern look deepened as she looked at Kelly.

"I called her," Summer said. "Wendy is very upset. Can't you see what all of this is doing to her? I needed help since you've offered none. You'd think the least you could do when you search someone's home, going through their private belongings, is to bring along someone who can help Wendy get through this."

Wolman lowered her eyelids for a moment. Kelly guessed the maneuver was to keep from rolling her eyes at the suggestion of providing a therapist to support a murder suspect during a search for evidence.

"Mrs. Blake, we'll take your suggestion under advisement. Now, you, Miss Quinn, can leave. Your presence here isn't needed." Wolman's dismissive tone wasn't offensive to Kelly. She was getting used to it. And, for once, she wouldn't mind being thrown out.

"I want her here." Wendy looked at Wolman over the rim of her glass before she set it on the end table. "Your authority is limited here. This is still my house."

Wolman stepped forward and positioned herself in front of Wendy. "You're right. This is your house. Look what we found in your house." She lifted the evidence bag, and Wendy's face paled.

Kelly and Summer shuffled to get a better view of the bag's contents. A knife. There appeared to be blood on it.

"We found this knife in your car trunk. How did it get there, Mrs. Johnson?" Wolman lowered the bag and waited for an answer.

"It's obvious. The killer, to frame Wendy, planted the knife," Summer said.

"What's obvious is we have a motive for the murder and what appears to be the murder weapon." Wolman sounded confident and pleased with herself.

Wendy leaned to the side, looking past Wolman and directly at Kelly. "What do I do now?"

Wolman turned toward Kelly and stared down at her. The tension in the room had ratcheted up, and the weight pressed on Kelly's shoulders. Why was Wendy asking her?

Wendy's designer-boosted bravado was gone. Her dark eyes were watery and her brows pinched with worry and fear. The police had just found what appeared to be the murder weapon. She should be frightened to her core.

"You shouldn't say anything without a lawyer present." Kelly had gotten that advice from her sister a month earlier when she was considered a person of interest in a murder. It was a solid recommendation, and Wendy needed to follow it.

Wolman lowered the evidence bag and returned her attention to Wendy. She gestured for Wendy to stand up. "You can call one from the police department. Wendy Johnson, you're under arrest for the murder of Diana Delacourte." Exiting the room, Wolman explained Wendy's rights.

Kelly and Summer followed. In the entry hall, Wendy was handcuffed and escorted out of the house.

Summer rushed to the open front door and watched the detective assist Wendy into a police car. "The detective is making a big mistake. I'll have to get Ralph to talk to the chief."

Kelly joined Summer at the doorway in time to see the police car pull out of the driveway, though several officers remained inside the home to continue the search. She guessed they wanted to find more incriminating evidence.

"If she's guilty, then she's probably the person responsible for cutting your brake line and causing the crash. And for leaving the threatening note on my windshield."

"What note? What are you talking about?" Summer stepped aside and closed the door.

"It's a long story. Look, we've both done what we can for Wendy." Kelly wasn't as certain as her aunt about Wendy's innocence. But somehow, she didn't buy that Wendy would be dumb enough to leave the murder weapon in her car. Either she'd dump it in the Long Island Sound or plant it on someone else.

Kelly's bet was on the latter. It seemed like a Long Island Ladies kind of thing to do.

Which one of the cast framed Wendy? Which lady was a murderer?

Kelly was finally able to persuade Summer to leave Wendy's house because there wasn't anything more either of them could do there. Wendy was on her way to the police department, and her husband had been notified. Summer reluctantly agreed and headed home.

Kelly's plan for the night was to disconnect from the world by soaking in a bubble bath with a glass of wine. On the way to her Jeep, her phone chimed. She'd gotten a new text message. She pulled the phone out of her tote bag. The message was from Liv.

Dinner? My place? Takeout?

So much for her bubble bath. However, she had to eat, and Liv had Netflix. They could watch a chick flick or two. Kelly liked the new change of plans.

Sure. Chinese or pizza?

After she unlocked the car door and slid in behind the steering wheel, Liv's reply came.

Thai.

Thai?

Different. But Kelly was good with the choice. She'd have to search for a Thai restaurant on the way back to town. She replied and then started her Jeep after searching on her phone's map for a restaurant. She found one and set her route.

Breena had stayed until closing, and in return, Kelly gave her the next day off. Now, with Wendy arrested for the murder, it appeared Kelly was no longer obligated to clear her. The whole matter was now in the hands of the police and the district attorney's office. There was nothing left for Kelly to do.

Well, there was one thing left for her to do, and that was to finish watching the episodes of *LIL*. She hadn't intended to get hooked, but she was and hated herself for it. Though a gal needed a guilty pleasure, and with her tight budget, reality television was within her means.

* * * *

Kelly parked behind the row of shops just north of her boutique where Liv rented an apartment. It was more economical to rent an apartment above the retail stores for young working women like Kelly and Liv, though what they gave up were views of the beaches, dunes, and marshes. Being young and building a life wasn't for the faint of heart.

Night had laid a thick blanket of darkness over Lucky Cove. As a kid, Kelly had loved the longer nights. She curled up on her bed with a Nancy Drew book and an afghan crocheted by her granny over her lap and read for hours. There was no reading or snuggling under an afghan tonight. Instead, she'd have yummy Thai cuisine and watch a couple of movies with her bestie.

Being young and single was fun . . . sometimes.

With her Jeep shifted into PARK, she climbed out of the driver's seat. Her phone rang. It was Liv's ring tone. Kelly swiped her phone and pressed the SPEAKER button.

"Checking up on me? I'll be up there in a minute." She dashed around to the passenger side to get the bag of food—two orders of pot stickers, pad thai, and steamed mixed veggies should be enough for their dinner. Then again, she didn't know how hungry Liv was.

"What are you talking about? Where are you?" Liv asked.

"Your apartment. I picked up the Thai food. I'll be right up."

The parking lot was a lot like the one behind her boutique—a communal area for shop owners and customers to park, with easy access to all the businesses along Main Street. The one thing the town could improve on was the lighting. The tall lamps seemed not as bright as they needed to be, and on a cold winter's night, with the businesses closed for the day, it felt a little eerie.

"When did you get into Thai food?" Reaching for the handle of the car door, Kelly realized how alone she was in the lot and was grateful she'd be upstairs in Liv's apartment within minutes.

"I'm not. What are you doing there? I'm not home. I'm at the church for the gingerbread house decorating contest."

The annual gingerbread house competition. A flashback swept Kelly to the church's community room the night of her first time entering the contest. Her dream of winning first place with her masterpiece of a gingerbread house crumbled, just like the walls of the elf-sized building, thanks to watery icing. Eve Whitney gloated when she won the first-place ribbon.

"Why did you text me you wanted me to pick up dinner and bring it over to your place?"

Kelly pulled opened the passenger door and bent over the seat. Juggling the phone and key fob while reaching for the bag at an odd angle was too much and something had to fall. The key fob.

Shoot.

The interior was dark, just like the key. She groaned as she patted the floor mat with her free hand, searching for the key.

"Kelly! Are you still there?"

She either needed to turn down the volume on her phone or Liv was upset. Wait, a minute. Why was she upset? She was the one running late.

"Yes. I dropped the car key. How long are you going to be? I'm hungry." Kelly's fingers gripped something. "Ah ha!" She'd found the key fob. Victory was hers.

"I'm going to be here for hours judging. I didn't text you about dinner."

"What?" Kelly rested her other hand on the seat. "I have your message on my phone. You asked for Thai."

"I don't like Thai."

"I know. I figured you were expanding your palette. If you weren't going to be here for dinner, why did you ask me to pick it up?"

"I didn't. Kelly, I have a bad feeling."

Chapter Twenty

The hairs on the back of Kelly's neck prickled. Her heartbeat kicked into overdrive. There had to be a logical explanation. A simple mix up. Liv sent the text by mistake.

A noise from behind her made her heart thump, and she froze.

"Kell, you need to leave and go home."

"Good idea." Kelly stepped back and grabbed the car door. "I'll call you when I get home." She swung the door shut and screamed at the sight of a person—dressed in black from ski mask to shoes—standing there, just feet away from her.

"Kelly! What's going on? Someone call the police! Kelly's in trouble."

Kelly stumbled backward as she stretched out her hand holding the key fob. "Here, take my car. My wallet is inside. Take it!"

The person didn't move.

Kelly swore her heart stopped beating as they held the standoff.

"Kelly! Are you okay? The police are on their way."

Kelly heard Liv's voice. She wanted to reply, but she couldn't speak.

The person reeled around and ran to the lot's exit between Liv's building and the nail salon.

Kelly pried her feet from the pavement and started to chase after the figure. Her arms pumped at her side as she sped up. She wanted to catch the person. What she'd do next was up in the air. She'd figure it out. When she reached the sidewalk, she stopped and looked right, then left.

The person was gone.

"Talk to me, Kelly!"

Kelly lifted the phone up to her face. "I'm okay. He . . . she . . . whoever . . . is gone."

"Thank goodness. You didn't get a look at who it was?"

"No. The person was wearing all black, including sunglasses." Kelly turned and headed back to her car. "Someone wants to scare me."

"Whoever it was certainly scared me."

Kelly reached her car and leaned her back against it. She became light-headed and blamed the adrenaline rush that pumped through her. She exhaled controlled breaths in hopes of keeping herself from fainting.

"It's not going to work. I'm more determined now to find out who killed Diana."

"Oh, boy."

"I know it wasn't Wendy because she's in police custody."

"I heard. Maybe she made bail."

"I don't think it would happen so fast." Police sirens perked up her ears. "You really did call the police?"

"Mama called."

A police vehicle came speeding into the parking lot with its strobe lights flashing and sirens blaring.

"Thank your mom for me. I'll call you later." Kelly ended the call and took a moment to regroup. She'd had the daylights scared out of her by a stranger donned in black who'd lured her to an empty parking lot. Regrouping was necessary.

The officer approached and, after making sure she wasn't hurt, took her statement. He said it sounded like the unidentified person spoofed her cell phone by making her believe Liv was texting her. Uneasiness bubbled in her belly as the officer explained how spoofing worked, and she eyed her phone warily. It was far too easy to be lured into a dangerous situation.

* * * *

The next morning came quickly for Kelly. The events of the past days, including the confrontation with the stranger clad all in black, left her waking with what felt like a hangover—throbbing head, heavy eyelids, and zero energy. All she wanted to do was pull the covers over her face and stay here for a day or two or three. Yet, she didn't have the option, thanks to the ten-pound cat sitting on her chest and meowing in her face.

She forced one eye open and stared at Howard, who stared back with what she perceived as irritation. He was hungry and wanted Kelly to do something about it.

"Fine. I'll get up." Kelly yawned and removed the cat from her chest.

He didn't go far. She guessed he wanted to make sure she didn't change her mind.

"I'm getting up. See." She tossed off the covers and sat up, taking a big stretch with her hands overhead.

Howard looked disinterested, jumped off the bed, and sauntered out of the bedroom.

She was tempted to close the door and climb back into bed, but she resisted. It was her day to work in the boutique. No errands, no questioning murder suspects, no being followed by a killer. As she stood and slipped into her slippers, she conceded it would be a nice change of pace.

In the shower, she welcomed the hot spray of water against her back and lingered there longer than she should have. She had to be at work on time, and she was jonesing for a Holly Jolly coffee from Doug's. The water and the coffee kept her mind from drifting back to the worst-case scenario of last night. She didn't want to go down that path again. Most of the nightmares she'd had overnight were because of all the things that could have happened to her.

Out of the shower and dressed casually in a chunky, nutmeg-colored sweater and skinny jeans, she pulled on her brown suede ankle boots after feeding Howard and was all set to dash across the street for her coffee fix when she heard a knock at her door.

There were only three people who had keys to the building: Breena, Pepper, and Gabe. Breena had the morning off, leaving either Gabe or Pepper as the probable person at the door.

Kelly opened the door and found Pepper standing on the welcome mat, holding a basket covered by a blue-and-white-checked cloth.

"After the night you had, I figured you could use something yummy to start your day." Pepper breezed by Kelly and set the muffins on the dining table. She unzipped her quilted parka, revealing a deep-rose-colored turtleneck sweater over black slim pants. "How are you doing?"

"Me? I'm good. How about you?" Kelly closed the door and followed Pepper to the table. She lifted the cloth; the fragrance of homemade cranberry and walnut muffins wafted in the air, and she smiled. "I love these. Thank you."

"No need to thank me. Martha would want me to look after you." Pepper pulled out a chair and sat. "We need to have a chat."

And there it was—the Pepper glare. She looked over the rim of her glasses and telepathically transmitted her disapproval of what had happened last night.

Kelly was in total agreement with her. She disapproved of being deceived and led to a deserted parking lot by a stranger and scared out of her wits. Maybe that person should have been subjected to the Pepper glare. Trying her best to ignore the look, she plucked out a muffin and sat. She pulled back the muffin paper and sank her teeth into the moist, light muffin and chewed the bigger than normal bite. She hadn't realized how hungry she was.

"From what I heard, you've managed to find yourself in danger again. First, the note left for you on your car."

Kelly's head swung up. "Gabe told you?" He had to have been the one to rat her out.

"I don't reveal my sources."

"You're not a reporter."

"Why didn't you tell me?"

"I didn't want to worry you. You haven't been feeling well."

Pepper shook her head. "I thought we cleared this up. I'm not dying. I had a cold. Besides, you're like a daughter, which means there's no way I'll never not worry about you."

Kelly dipped her head. "You're right. I should have told you."

"Someone is warning you to mind your own business. This is serious, Kelly."

There went her appetite. Kelly set the muffin down. "I know, and I've received the message loud and clear. I was at Wendy's house when she was arrested."

"I wasn't aware." The Pepper glare took on a whole new level of disapproval. Yikes!

"When Summer and I left the house, I was certain I was done with . . . investigating, asking questions, whatever it was I was doing. I was finished."

"Because they arrested Wendy?"

"Exactly. While I had a hard time believing she left the threatening note on my car, it was possible. But last night when someone lured me to a place he or she knew I'd go without question and be alone, I knew it wasn't Wendy. She didn't kill Diana. The person who framed Wendy is the person trying to scare me off."

Pepper leaned forward and clasped her hands together. "I'm sensing you're not scared off."

"I'm not. What happened last night has made me more determined now to find out who the killer is. He or she sent me the text message to pick up Thai food and bring it to Liv's apartment."

"Thai? Liv doesn't like Thai. Remember when we went into the city and made reservations at the Thai restaurant?" Pepper laughed at the memory. The memory flashed in Kelly's mind. It was a couple weeks after Martha's funeral, and Pepper had sensed Kelly needed a pick-me-up. Pepper decided a girl's day out was in order. The three of them took the train into the city, and they'd had a mini shopping spree followed by lunch. Liv had barely eaten anything at the restaurant and ended up buying a pretzel from a street vendor on the way back to Penn Station. How could Kelly have forgotten that?

"I should've sensed something was amiss. I appreciate your concern and promise to be careful. I hope you can understand why I need to see this through."

"It's hard for me to wrap my head around why you insist on putting yourself in danger for someone you barely know."

Kelly reached out and covered Pepper's hands with hers. "Ten years ago, I should have been a better friend to Ariel. A better person." She stopped Pepper's objection. "I failed her. I can't change what happened. I do know I never want to feel like that again, so if someone needs my help, I'm going to help. And if someone is coming after me—well, then, I will take them head on. I won't be scared or intimated."

"Wendy still needs your help?"

"Not now. What she needs is a good attorney. I will be careful. You have my word."

"You better be." Pepper stood and kissed Kelly on the top of the head. "I'll see you downstairs. Oh, and pick me up a Holly Jolly when you go to Doug's."

"How . . . ?"

"I know everything." Pepper smiled and headed for the door.

Kelly grabbed the muffin and finished eating it. It was too good not to eat. After she scarfed down the muffin, she grabbed her coat and tote bag. She hurried down the stairs and dashed across the street to get two coffees and put in a solid day of work at the boutique.

Chapter Twenty-One

Kelly hurried around to the front of her boutique and headed to the curb. Her wristlet was clutched in her hand. The wind gusts had kicked up since last night, and she regretted slipping on her pale blue wool-blend coat. She needed her sub-zero puffer jacket.

"There she is!"

Kelly turned at the sound of Liv's voice. Liv was bustling down the sidewalk with Gabe behind her.

"Thank God you're okay!" When Liv reached Kelly, she pulled her in for a hug. "You could have been killed last night. What were you thinking?"

"I was thinking I was getting us dinner." Kelly wriggled in her friend's tight hold. "I. Can't. Breathe." She survived an ambush by a stranger, possibly a killer, only to be squeezed to death by Liv.

"Liv, she's okay." Gabe put a hand on Liv's shoulder. "Kell, she's right, though. You got lucky."

Kelly was able to break free of Liv's hold. "I know she's right. But if the person wanted to kill me, why did he run away?"

"Why did you chase after him?" Liv asked.

Kelly shrugged.

"Are you saying it was a man? Are you sure?" Gabe let go of Liv's shoulder, and his worried looked morphed into professional cop mode.

"No, I'm not certain. It was too dark, and I wasn't close enough."

"Thank God!" Liv's head swung upward at Gabe. "Her life is in danger. What are you going to do to protect her?"

"The best way to keep her safe is for her to back off of the investigation."

"Not much of a plan. Or a way to make her feel safe." Liv shoved her gloved hands into her coat pockets and frowned.

"He doesn't have to come up with a plan. I'll be fine." Kelly definitely wouldn't be going places based on text messages. No, next time she'd confirm with an old-fashioned phone call. "I appreciate your concern, but I need coffee, and I'm freezing." Her teeth were chattering, and her eyelids were heavy. She needed a jolt of caffeine. An extra-large jolt.

"It's cold, and I have to get back to the bakery." Liv threw her arms around Kelly and hugged her, this time not squeezing the life out of her. "Call me later."

"Yeah. I have to get to work. Talk to you later." Gabe turned and headed down the street, while Liv took off in the opposite direction and Kelly dashed across the street.

Inside the warm store, Kelly found herself at the end of a long line of caffeine-deficient individuals like herself. After a few minutes, the line moved up one person, and Kelly took a step closer to her coffee and bagel. She needed something more substantial to balance out the cakey muffin. A toasted bagel slathered with cream cheese seemed to be a good choice. By the time she'd returned home last night, it was late, and she didn't feel like eating. She'd tossed the takeout food into the refrigerator but now doubted she'd be able to eat it. It came with a bad memory of being lured to her potential death. It was enough to make any food unappetizing.

A woman wearing a pale gray snood over her head approached Kelly. The scarf was tucked into the neckline of her coordinating mid-length coat. Nanette's round-shaped face peeked out of the scarf.

"Good morning, Kelly. It's busy this morning." Nanette glanced around the store.

"It is."

"I have a long day ahead. Movers are coming to take out all the furniture from the house." Nanette's sadness was palpable. She probably was the only person who was truly mourning Diana. "I heard about the incident at the reception. Janine has a nasty streak. Sorry you experienced it."

"I'm getting the feeling most of the women on the show have a very unpleasant side."

"Guess you don't make it onto television these days by being nice."

Kelly couldn't have agreed more. "She got upset when I mentioned that I saw you and her at the café the other day. I asked why you two met. She never answered."

"No? It's not a big deal. She offered me a job. Since Diana is dead, I'm technically out of work. I've worked for Mr. Delacourte before. I joked that Diana got custody of me in the separation."

Kelly gave a little laugh. It was kind of funny. "You'd work for him again?"

"I know I said some not-so-nice things about him. But his money is as good as anyone else's. Besides, the Delacourte house is stunning. I enjoyed living there."

Kelly couldn't argue with Nanette's logic. She needed work, and the house was breathtaking. "Nanette, did anything strange happen right before Diana was murdered?"

A look of pain clouded Nanette's blue eyes. There must've been a nice side to the woman for her to have instilled a deep sadness in Nanette.

"No. I can't think of anything. Wait, there was something. A former member of the crew came to see Diana. She showed up a couple of days before Thanksgiving. Give me a moment to remember her name."

"Patrice?"

She snapped her fingers. "Yes. Her."

Funny how Patrice didn't mention to Kelly that she'd seen Diana days before the murder. "Do you know why she wanted to see Diana?"

Nanette shook her head. "Diana took the meeting privately in her home office. She didn't tell me what Patrice wanted. I need to get going. I have appraisers coming to the house in an hour. I'm sorry I couldn't be more help."

"You did great. Thank you."

The person behind Kelly in line cleared his throat, prompting her to look back at the line she was in. She was up next to order. She placed her order, and a few minutes later she walked out of Doug's with her breakfast and new unanswered questions. Why had Patrice come out to Lucky Cove to see Diana? What was so important that it required a face-to-face meeting? And was it only a coincidence that a few days later Diana was killed?

Those questions percolated in her brain all day long as she rang up sales, tidied merchandise, and vacuumed the boutique. She wasn't sure how, but she felt Patrice was caught up in the murder.

Could she have been the person in black last night in the parking lot?

A chill skittered down her spine. But she wasn't sure if it was the thought of last night's frightening encounter or the boutique's door opening and ushering in a swath of cold air. She finished refolding a V-neck, cable-knit sweater and hesitantly smiled at the man who'd entered her boutique.

Alarm bells went off in her brain, and she crept backward. She wanted to get to the sales counter, where her phone was.

"I'm looking for Kelly Quinn. Have I found her?" The man stopped between two circular racks of blouses and removed his brown leather gloves. Several inches taller than her and dressed in a leather bomber jacket and dark jeans, he didn't look threatening. His thick, dark brown hair was mussed from the wind, and he had the darkest eyes she'd ever seen. They reminded her of coal. "I'm Barlow Childers, grandson of Marvin Childers."

Kelly rested her hand over her heart and let out a relieved breath. "Thank goodness, you're not a . . ." She stopped short of saying *stalker.*

"Have I come at a bad time?"

"No, not at all." She lunged forward with her hand extended and shook Barlow's hand. "I'm Kelly Quinn. How can I help you?"

Barlow's grip was firm but not crushing, and their contact lingered for an extra moment. She slipped her hand from his and then laced her hands together.

"It seems I have an inheritance to collect. This boutique and building, I believe." He smirked.

His words were like a punch to the gut. They knocked the wind out of her, and her knees wobbled.

"Whoa. Slow your roll. You can't just come in here and think you can take my grandmother's business. She left it and this building to me." She hurried back to the sales counter. She needed to grip onto something to steady her shaking body. Who did Barlow Childers think he was to barge in and claim her grandmother's legacy as his?

"Your grandmother was married to my grandfather at the time of her death—"

"That doesn't automatically guarantee him Granny's estate. I think you should go now." She wouldn't hand over the keys to the building without a fight. Her granny had left Kelly the business to bring her back to Lucky Cove and to rebuild her relationships with Caroline and Ariel. Old man Childers and his greedy grandson wouldn't take it away from her. At least not without a fight.

Barlow pulled a business card from his coat's breast pocket and placed it on the counter. "Call me when you're ready to have a rational discussion." He swiveled and swaggered out of the boutique.

Rational? She seethed with anger and frustration as she snatched up the card.

Barlow Childers, VP of Childers Enterprises.

VP. La-di-dah.

She propped her elbows on the counter and rested her head in her hands. This was bad. Really, really bad. She hadn't considered Marvin having any family members who'd jump at the chance to get their hands on a prime piece of real estate in Lucky Cove.

What had she done?

She straightened up and squared her shoulders. She knew what she had to do. She needed legal advice, again.

She grimaced.

Caroline would lecture her about her impulsiveness. About jumping the gun. About leaping before looking. About going to her granny's secret husband and reminding him his estranged wife had valuable property. While Kelly's decision to keep the business left her land rich but money poor, selling the property would make Marvin and his heirs a nice amount of money.

So much for staying at the boutique all day. Barlow Childers's unexpected visit turned Kelly's plan for the day upside down. He thought he was so clever swooping in and blindsiding her with his news. What he didn't know was she had a sister who was a top-notch attorney. Kelly sprinted to the entrance of the law firm. The strong wind gusts earlier in the day had upgraded to hurricane-force strength and bore down relentlessly on Long Island. Mother Nature definitely had her Spanx in a twist. Despite the struggle and her hood being blown off, Kelly made it to the polished oak door.

The law firm was located in a charming Cape Cod–style home in East Hampton and was exactly where Kelly had expected her sister to land after law school. A nice private practice with well-heeled clients who paid a steep price for their legal services. Caroline's life was shaping up to be perfect.

Perfect job. Perfect home. Perfect fiancé.

The one thing that wasn't perfect in her life was her sister.

Kelly had managed to fail to live up to Caroline's expectations time and time again. Kelly would have liked to believe it all started with Ariel's accident, but there were signs that Kelly wasn't the perfect little sister well before that fateful night.

Caroline excelled at school and in sports, and she was a natural at dinner table conversation with family and guests. Kelly, on the other hand, did so-so with grades, sports weren't her thing because they left her sweaty, and the adults in her life back then didn't like talking about fashion or boys. Yeah, Kelly was a disappointment from early on.

Inside the bright and airy reception area, a middle-aged receptionist greeted Kelly. Seated at an organized desk, the dark-haired woman had a few gray roots showing and a pair of readers dangling on a crystal chain around her neck. The zebra-striped blouse she wore had one too many buttons undone for her stage in life. Kelly would have suggested buttoning up at least one more button and adding a chunky necklace for a fashion-forward, ageless vibe.

The receptionist instructed Kelly to have a seat and wait.

Kelly couldn't balk at the receptionist's terseness since she'd showed up without an appointment. Resisting the urge to sigh, she turned and walked to the comfortable seating area. She settled on the sofa and reached for a magazine. There was a spray of home and gardening magazines on the glass-topped coffee table. She opened the glossy publication, and her phone buzzed, alerting her to a new text message. She retrieved the phone from her tote bag and read the text from Liv.

Lulu Loves Long Island. OMG. You're on the front page.

Kelly squeezed her eyes shut. *Not again.* She opened her eyes and swiped away the text message and navigated to the website.

Last night Lucky Cove retail merchant Kelly Quinn reported an attempted assault . . . Ms. Quinn is reportedly vying for a spot on the reality show Long Island Ladies *and has been seen cozying up with the current stars of the show. . . . Can't help wondering if last night's incident was nothing more than a publicity stunt by the consignment shop owner.*

Publicity stunt?

Kelly tossed the phone back into her tote bag and huffed.

The nerve of that woman!

"Ms. Quinn is ready for you now."

Kelly's head turned toward the voice. The receptionist waited by the entry to the hallway, where the offices were located. Kelly grabbed her tote and stood. She followed the receptionist, all the while her stomach somersaulting with worry about Barlow's claim on her inheritance and now the stupid article on the stupid website.

The receptionist pushed open the office door, and Kelly entered.

"Thank you," she said, and the receptionist returned to her desk. "Hey, sis."

Caroline looked up from her leather agenda. There were strong physical similarities between the two sisters. Same height, same eye color, and same hair color, though Caroline's blond hair was cropped short, giving her an edgier look.

"Come on in. Have a seat. What's going on?" Her sister wasn't big on small talk.

Kelly settled on one of the two chairs in front of the desk and set her bag on her lap. "I need legal advice."

"Again?" Caroline's voice had raised, and she offered an apologetic smile. They both had agreed to make an effort to rebuild their relationship, and it appeared she was trying, but Kelly knew old habits were hard to break. She gestured for Kelly to continue with her story.

"I'm afraid so. It's all a mess this time."

"Then what do you call what happened last month? You needed three legal referrals, if I recall correctly."

"I need only one now." Of course, her sister wouldn't see the bright side. "I've been packing up Granny's belongings for storage, and while clearing out the hutch, I found this." She pulled out the folded marriage certificate from her tote and handed it to her sister.

Caroline leaned back and reviewed the document. "Granny remarried? She never said anything. I wonder if Uncle Ralph knows. Who is Marvin Childers?"

"A retired illustrator who lives on Glendale Road. He seems to be a very nice man."

Caroline looked up from the document. "You know him?"

"I met him the other day when I went to his house."

"You what?"

Kelly swallowed. She'd suspected her sister would disapprove of her visit to Marvin. The best thing to do was to keep talking and get it all out. Then brace for the lecture.

"He confirmed he'd gone with Granny on a trip to Las Vegas sponsored by the Senior Center, and they married at a chapel." Kelly pointed to the certificate.

"You've spoken to him about this?"

"Yes. It's why his grandson showed up earlier today at the boutique claiming his grandfather is the rightful heir to Granny's business and house. Caroline, I can't lose the business or my apartment."

Caroline took a deep breath, dropped the certificate on the desk, and took another deep breath. She stood and came around to the front of the desk. She wore a navy blue, tie-front sheath dress with elbow-length sleeves. Her flower-drop earrings added a little sparkle to her attorney-mode dress. She leaned against the desk and braced her hands on its edge.

"Why on earth did you talk to Mr. Childers before consulting me? I would've told you to not talk to him."

"I didn't think."

"This is the problem, Kell. You don't think before you act." Caroline's judgment-filled gaze lowered to the carpeted floor. "I don't like lecturing you."

"Could've fooled me." Kelly's response was quick and stupid, and right away she regretted it. "I'm sorry. I didn't mean it. You know I don't like having to ask others for help or lean on people. I wanted to take care of this on my own."

Caroline lifted her gaze, and she leaned forward and patted her sister on the knee. "It'll all work out. How can the grandson be reached?" She pulled back and returned to her seat.

Kelly dug out Barlow's business card and handed it to her sister. "When I talked to Marvin, he didn't ask about Granny's estate. I think it's his grandson's idea to pursue this."

"Probably. He's looking for a way to bolster his inheritance. Is there anything else I need to know?"

"No. I've told you everything. And you have the marriage certificate."

"What about the incident last night?" Caroline leaned back and rested her hands on her lap. "Lulu Loves Long Island recapped it all. Are you really thinking about appearing on a reality show?"

"No! Never. Wait . . . Do you think it could have been Barlow last night?"

Caroline shrugged. "Killing you would be easier than a legal battle." She smiled. Only a sister could get away with saying that, and she knew it.

"Not funny." Kelly grabbed the handles of her tote and stood. "Not funny at all. I have to get back to the boutique, and you have to get back to work." She'd told Pepper she had to make a quick visit to Caroline and remained vague as to why. To her credit, Pepper hadn't pried and told her to take all the time she needed.

"Wait, Kelly. Are you okay? Someone set you up last night to possibly hurt you, and the other day a threatening note was left for you."

Her sister had a lot of intel on Kelly, and she wondered who'd been sharing it with Caroline. Ariel, of course. She must've heard what happened last night and contacted Caroline. It was like high school all over again. Friends told friends what other friends did.

Yeah, high school.

"I'm fine. I promise. Let me get going back to the boutique. Please make sure I don't lose it."

"I'll do my best. I'm not familiar with marriage licenses in Nevada. When I have news, I'll call you." Caroline pulled herself closer to her desk and returned to her work, while Kelly showed herself out of the office. Caroline had made no promises, but Kelly felt some measure of relief as she made her way to her Jeep. One dragon almost slain. Now, to find the murderer who was stalking her.

Chapter Twenty-Two

Kelly returned from her sister's office with lunch for herself and Pepper. Over their meal, Pepper brought up the article on Lulu Loves Long Island, and without missing a beat, Kelly directed the conversation back to business. She wanted to talk about something positive and fun, like the upcoming Holiday Edit. She'd gotten a peek at the marketing materials Breena designed and encouraged Kelly to move forward. Pepper offered to help get donations for the goody bags. While Kelly appreciated the offer, she didn't want her friend to overexert herself.

When they finished their lunch, Pepper went to package the few items that had sold on the resale website and said she'd drop them off at the post office on her way in the next morning. Kelly stayed in the staff room and completed the plans for the Holiday Edit, then put the finishing touches on the holiday decorations. Displaying a few snowmen and hanging a wreath would make Pepper happy.

By the time the decorating was done, and she'd finished the article for Budget Chic, it was time to close out the register and lock up the boutique.

Upstairs in her apartment, Kelly changed into her comfy lounge pants and a cozy fleece top. Her number-one task for the evening was to finish emptying the hutch.

She'd fallen behind in her schedule of packing up the items she wanted to store away. What was left to clear out were the drawers, and then the monster piece of furniture would be ready to be wrapped securely and moved into the storage unit.

By the time Howard came looking for dinner, Kelly had gone through four drawers. She sorted out the silver-plated flatware, the stash of table linens, and an endless amount of tissue paper. She was thrilled to find the tissue paper because she could use it for the goody bags. A little extra savings made her smile.

She pulled out another drawer and placed it on the floor. She got down on the floor and sat cross-legged to do the sorting. Just one more drawer after this one, she told Howard, who was rubbing up against her.

He was definitely hungry. However, she didn't understand why. He'd slept all day. How could he have worked up an appetite?

This drawer was filled with birthday cards, magazines, and Mass cards. This busy work kept her thoughts from Marvin and his greedy grandson. She tossed the magazines into a pile, one after another, and then she came to an envelope with her granny's name written on it.

She worked her lip, trying to decide what to do. The last time she'd opened an envelope her granny had hidden, she'd uncovered an ugly can of worms. Even if opening the smaller envelope now didn't cause a big to-do, it would feel like invading her granny's privacy. Again. She tossed the envelope onto the floor and continued to go through what remained in the drawer.

Howard meowed loudly after he butted his head against her thigh. She was getting the message. Dinnertime. She uncrossed her legs and stood while the little guy trotted toward the kitchen.

"If only I could teach you how to open your own can of food." She followed her feline companion and emptied a can of tuna casserole Kitty Delight into his dish and refilled his water bowl. While he feasted, she poured a glass of wine and returned to the hutch.

It looked like a tornado had passed through, and she wasn't sure she was making any progress in claiming the space as her own. Her sights zeroed in on the envelope with her granny's name on it. The curiosity was overwhelming. She bent down and picked it up. At the table, she set her wineglass down, opened the blue envelope, and pulled out the floral card.

Opening the card felt like spying on her grandmother, but she pushed through and found a handwritten note.

Our fling was nice while it lasted. You're the best one-day wife I ever had. Marvin.

She closed the card and pressed it to her chest.

One-day?

One-day wife? The marriage certificate wasn't legit?

Her breath caught. If her granny and Marvin weren't married, then he and his grandson didn't have a claim to the estate. She pressed the card against her chest.

"Thank you, thank you, thank you. Wait . . . I have to show Caroline." She grabbed the envelope, her coat, and her tote bag and rushed out of the apartment.

By the time she reached the parking lot, she'd thrown on her coat, slipped the card into her tote, and cursed herself for not changing from her Ugg slippers into boots. Not a good choice when the slippers cost three digits and it was slushy and snowy outside, but it was too late now. She didn't want to turn back.

She was too elated. She wasn't going to lose her inheritance.

"I was coming to see you!" Ralph's voice boomed in the parking lot and zapped the spring out of Kelly's step.

"Is everything okay with Summer and Juniper?" Somehow, over the past couple of weeks, she'd worried about Summer. She chalked it up to the fact that a murderer was still on the loose and both she and Summer had been threatened.

"They're both fine. I wanted to talk to you about Marvin Childers." Kelly huffed. The weasel grandson. "You know?"

"Can't believe my mother never told me she remarried. She probably thought I'd disapprove. Water under the bridge." Ralph attempted to chuckle, but it turned into a coughing fit.

"How very mature of you, Uncle Ralph." She continued toward her Jeep.

"Not much I can do about it now." He followed her. "Like it or not, he's my stepfather. And luckily for me, my stepnephew, Barlow, is a savvy businessman like myself."

Kelly held back the laugh that tickled her throat. "Is that so?"

"I'm confident I can convince Barlow to sell this property. He'd make a nice little profit for his grandfather. Yes. We'll all make out nicely. Well, except for you, kiddo."

Kelly's urge to laugh disappeared. Now she simmered with irritation. Ralph wasn't going to let the fact that his niece would be homeless and out of work interfere with a business deal. No. He didn't care who got hurt as long as he made money.

"Though you'll probably get to keep the cat—what's its name again?"

"His name is Howard. And, yes, I'll be keeping the cat."

And the business and building too. Thank you very much.

She tightened her hold on her tote bag. Inside was her proof Granny wasn't really married to Marvin, but she wasn't going to share the information with her uncle. Let him plan how he was going to finally be rid of his executor duties and make a little profit somewhere in the deal. Then bam! The whole deal would go up in smoke.

"I've gotta go, Uncle Ralph. Let me know what Marvin decides." She turned and rushed around to the driver's side of the vehicle. Backing out of the space, she saw her uncle head back to his Mercedes and slip behind the wheel. She'd known him all her life and didn't doubt for one second that he was counting the dollars he expected to get from Marvin Childers. She laughed. The joke would be on him.

* * * *

"You won't believe what I found." Kelly followed Caroline into the kitchen, where the aroma of something had her nose sniffing. "Oh, boy, I've interrupted your dinner. I'm sorry. I lost track of the time."

"No, no, you haven't. It's about to come out of the oven and needs to set for a few minutes. I made baked shells. Have a seat." Caroline grabbed a pot holder and pointed to the stool at the peninsula. At the wall oven, she pulled out the deep dish of bubbling cheese and took measured steps to the trivet on the counter. "I wasn't expecting you. What's up? Another legal battle on the horizon?"

"No." Kelly wanted to add "smarty pants" to her reply, but since their relationship still wasn't solid, she kept it to herself. "Actually, it looks like there may be no legal battle with Marvin Childers." She pulled the card she'd discovered in the drawer out of her tote and handed it her sister.

Caroline discarded the pot holder and opened the card. She read the note. "Interesting."

"It's more than interesting."

"What might have happened was Granny and Marvin married at the wedding chapel and received the marriage certificate, but it was never officially filed."

"Then the marriage isn't real." Kelly's shoulders relaxed. The tension she'd been carrying around since finding the certificate vanished.

Caroline held up a hand. "We don't know for sure, but from what I've found out so far and what Marvin wrote in this note, it looks like he won't have a claim on Granny's estate."

"You have no idea how much I needed to hear this." Kelly went to stand up, and her sister waved her hand, gesturing for Kelly to stay seated.

"You're here and dinner is ready. Stay and have dinner with us."

Could tonight get any better for Kelly?

"I'd like that." She shrugged out of her coat and handed it to Caroline, who carried it to the hall closet. When Caroline returned, together they made the salad. Working side by side, it felt like old times when they'd helped their mom prepare supper. By the time the salad bowl was set on the table and the stuffed shells were ready to be served, Caroline's fiancé had arrived home, and they ate together as a family.

Chapter Twenty-Three

Bright and early the next morning, Kelly set to work stuffing the goody bags for the Holiday Edit event. As she filled the petite shopping bags, she hummed her favorite carol, "The First Noel." Finding the card from Marvin and having her sister agree that most likely the retired illustrator and his greedy grandson had no claim on the boutique had improved her mood.

Breena entered the staff room from outside and shook off the cold. Temperatures had dipped below twenty degrees overnight and had gone up little since sunrise.

"I can't imagine what it will feel like in the middle of January if this is how December is going." Breena unzipped her coat, hung it on the coatrack, and then pulled off her hat. "You have most of them done." She joined Kelly at the table and peeked inside the little shopping bags. "Too bad we didn't have the budget for customized bags."

"I know. But, hopefully, we will at the next event. RSVPs have been coming in."

Breena's head bobbed up and down. "I saw. This will be off the charts. I completed the menu with Frankie last night, so he's all set. He's making a cranberry cocktail and three appetizers. Do you think that's enough?"

"Absolutely. We want the ladies focused on clothes and buying, not eating. Besides, the budget is tight. Frankie is donating his services, but we have to pay for the food and the beverages."

Having a cousin who was a trained chef was a perk not only because he fed her often but because he kindly worked for free.

"Good point." Breena stood. "I'll open, okay?"

Kelly nodded as she dropped small bags of chocolate into each goody bag. There were a few more items to add, and she'd be done. Her cell phone rang, and Breena grabbed it from the desk and handed it to Kelly on her way out to the sales floor.

Kelly glanced at the caller ID. Patrice. She swiped the phone on. "Good morning, Patrice."

"Hey, Kelly. Hope I'm not catching you too early, but I'm on my way to class and won't have a chance to talk to you later."

"No problem. I've wanted to talk to you."

"I can't believe they arrested Wendy for Diana's murder. I'm positive she didn't do it."

"What is believed to be the murder weapon was found during the search of her home." Kelly pressed the SPEAKER button and set the phone down to finish the goody bags. She could multitask with the best of them.

"If it is the murder weapon, then someone is setting Wendy up. I think it's Yvonne."

"Why?"

There was silence on the line.

"Patrice, are you still there?"

"Yeah, I'm ashamed to say why. I was stupid. Really stupid."

Kelly slid a glance at the phone. She wasn't a stranger to doing stupid things she was embarrassed about. "How stupid?"

"I had an affair. It was brief, with Yvonne's husband."

Kelly dropped the bag of chocolate and lunged for the phone, taking it off speakerphone. She held it up to her face.

"What?" She cringed. Her question came out louder and more shocking than she'd expected.

"I think it was Yvonne who set me up at the airport, and I think Diana figured it out. If Diana threatened to reveal that, I'm certain Yvonne would have not only been tossed from the show but probably would have been arrested."

"She most likely would have been arrested." Kelly fell back into the chair. She had a hard time imagining the prim and proper socialite planting cocaine on the production assistant. Did she drive up in her Rolls-Royce and buy a bag from the local drug dealer? Kelly shook her head. In the world Yvonne lived in—television, extreme wealth, and privilege—drugs were easy to come by. No distasteful trips to back alleys needed.

"Did Hugh know about you and Yvonne's husband?"

"No. It was brief. I think Yvonne's husband got worried she'd found out about us. He ended the relationship. Besides, Hugh's too busy with his own girlfriend of the month to notice much else."

"What are you talking about?"

Patrice gave a throaty laugh. "He practically has a new girlfriend every month. He gets bored easily. I'd put money on him having one right now. Between producing the show and sneaking around with his mistress, he doesn't have time for anything else."

"What about his wife?"

"What about her? All she cares about is ratings. So far, Hugh has gotten awesome ratings for the show. Look, I have to get going."

"Wait. I need you to answer a question. Why didn't you tell me you went to Diana's house just days before her murder? What did you two talk about?"

"Does it matter now?"

"Yes. It does."

"You know I got probation, and that was all thanks to Diana. If she hadn't intervened, I'd probably still be in a Florida prison. While I'm grateful I didn't go to prison, I'm determined to clear my name. I wanted Diana to help me. I know she knew more about the incident than she let on."

"Did she?"

"She refused to help me."

The swinging door opened, and Breena poked her head in and cleared her throat, catching Kelly's attention. "We're getting busy."

Kelly nodded and silently mouthed, "Okay".

Breena smiled then disappeared.

"I have to go, Patrice. Thanks for calling. I'll be in touch." She disconnected the call.

Was it possible Yvonne was responsible for Patrice's legal problems and Diana had discovered the nasty deed? Yvonne had lied about when she last saw Diana. People typically lied when they were trying to hide something. Was Yvonne trying to hide the fact that she murdered Diana?

She stood and swiped up her phone. She'd already told the police about Yvonne's visit to Diana's house the night of the murder. Should she tell them about Patrice and her suspicions? Maybe it would be better for Patrice to contact Wolman directly. She pushed open the swinging door and was struck with the chatter she heard. And as she made her way to the sales floor, she was pleased to see so many customers.

Breena came up to her with an armful of clothing. "They're on fire. Look at them."

"Where did everyone come from?"

Breena shrugged. "Don't know. But a lot of them have asked about the Holiday Edit. Guess our marketing is working. I have to hang these in a changing room for Mrs. Bancroft. Oh, there's someone at the register."

"I've got it." Kelly broke away while Breena continued to the changing room. For the next several hours, there was a steady stream of customers, all in good spirits and many sharing holiday memories of Kelly's granny. She found the stories heartwarming and comforting. Her granny was beloved by many people in Lucky Cove.

"Martha and I went way back." Mildred Fisher pulled out her wallet from her sturdy brown leather shoulder bag. "We grew up next door to each other. Oh, your great-grandmother could cook like no one else. My mother was so envious."

"Is that where Granny got her cooking gene from?"

"Gene? Oh, I'm doubtful Martha inherited any cooking genes. There was one Christmas when we were teenagers and home alone on a Saturday. Martha got it into her head we'd bake." Mrs. Fisher handed her credit card to Kelly. "Not only did we make a big mess of the kitchen, but there was smoke everywhere. Your great-grandmother was furious with us. Martha had burned a sheet of cookies." The older woman laughed at the memory.

Kelly hadn't laughed at the incident in her own kitchen the other night, but hearing the story of how her granny also failed at an early attempt at baking made her feel better. "I never heard that story." Kelly handed the card back to her customer.

"I'm not surprised. Martha wouldn't ever tell the story." Mrs. Fisher leaned forward. "I have more stories. You let me know when you're ready to hear them. Merry Christmas." She took the shopping bag from Kelly and left the store.

Kelly made a mental note to follow up with Mrs. Fisher. She wanted to know as much as possible about her grandmother's life. It seemed they had a lot in common.

* * * *

The day progressed with a steady flow of customers, and by closing time, Kelly and Breena were both exhausted. Kelly closed out the register while Breena did a quick tidy-up of the boutique before leaving. With the end-of-day bookkeeping tasks completed, Kelly climbed the stairs to her apartment.

Her thoughts were still working on the information Patrice had shared with her. All day long, snippets of their conversation rolled around in Kelly's mind. The most intriguing part was Patrice's admission that she went to ask Diana for help and Diana refused. What was at stake for Patrice was significant—being cleared of a drug crime. Patrice could have returned, determined to force Diana to help her; one thing might have led to another, and with emotions running high, Patrice may have killed her.

But where did the knife come from?

Kelly had gotten a quick glimpse of it, and it didn't look like a kitchen knife. But it didn't look like a pocket knife either.

At the kitchen counter, she opened a can of soup, and while it heated in the microwave, she tossed together a salad. Patrice could have brought the knife with her. She was a single woman living in the city, and it wasn't unreasonable to think that she carried some kind of personal protection.

After Kelly finished eating her dinner, she fed Howard and then curled up on the sofa with her favorite reading material, fashion magazines. There were plenty of things she could have been doing, but she needed downtime. She hoped the glossy pages would suck her in and not let her think about the murder or her stalker or what a dog Hugh was.

It sort of worked. The magazines engrossed her for over an hour, and rarely did her mind stray beyond the pages of outrageously expensive clothes featured in the extravagant, over-the-top editorial layouts. When she couldn't stop yawning, she knew it was time to go to bed. She closed the January issue of *Marie Claire* and stood. As she stretched, she looked for Howard. He was nowhere in sight, so he must've been on the bed already.

Sure enough, the orange cat was curled up on a corner of her bed.

She set the alarm on her phone, kicked off her slippers, and slipped into bed, pulling the covers over her. She might have tugged on the covers a little too hard because Howard lifted his head and meowed at her.

"Sorry." She dropped her head on her two down pillows. When she'd moved back to Lucky Cove, she didn't have money to rent a moving truck, so she was limited in what she could bring with her. Luckily, all of her clothes and accessories and a few family mementos fit into the Jeep Pepper had loaned her, and there was enough room for her cloud-soft pillows. She left everything else. Priorities, you know.

She closed her eyelids and willed herself to fall asleep. Too bad her mind had other ideas, playing a loop of conversations she'd had with Hugh, Wendy, Yvonne, Janine, and Wolman. Every now and again, there was a break in the loop. Recalling the figure in black, the threatening note, and the screeching smoke alarm made for a restless night.

Kelly didn't know what woke her in the morning. A noise from a passing truck on Main Street? Was someone breaking into her apartment? Her heart seized. Was someone in the apartment? She bolted upright and listened. Nothing.

An intruder could be lying in wait. Or she could be overreacting, and considering the past few days, she had reason to overreact.

She grabbed her phone from the nightstand and pushed off the covers. The morning chill sent a shiver down her body. Standing, she looked around for Howard. He was nowhere in sight. She tiptoed out of the bedroom. The hardwood floor was cold. She should have put on her slippers, but the adrenaline was pumping through her, and she couldn't think of anything but the intruder.

She should have grabbed something to use as a weapon. On second thought, there wasn't much available to use.

She peered around the corner to the living room.

No one.

She exhaled a relieved breath. There was no one in her apartment except for her jerk of a cat.

He was doing what reminded Kelly of a yoga cobra stretch on top of the dining table. Her gaze lowered, and she spotted, on the floor, the container of spray cleaner she'd been using on the hutch.

"You couldn't resist, could you?" She marched to the dining area and swiped up the cleaner, setting it back on the table.

"Now that I'm up, I guess you're expecting breakfast."

Howard meowed, leaped off the table, and trotted to the kitchen.

"Maybe I'll get you one of those cat food-dispensing thingies for Christmas." Following him into the kitchen, she glanced at the wall clock. She was up thirty minutes earlier than she'd set her alarm for. The option to go back to bed seemed silly. She was wide awake, and it was doubtful she'd fall back to sleep.

She filled Howard's bowl and then poured herself a glass of orange juice. The mindless tasks allowed her brain to replay yet again her conversation with Patrice. She hoped Patrice would go to the police and tell them her suspicions, even though she had no evidence. She guessed the police wouldn't take her suspicions seriously. No, they'd probably view what she said as conjecture and sour grapes since her married boyfriend had dumped and then fired her after she was arrested.

The police wanted proof. Evidence. Something they could take into court and use to say, without a hint of doubt, that the accused was guilty.

Like the blood-speckled knife found in Wendy's car.

Talk about a piece of evidence. Wolman was probably giddy with excitement when it was discovered. She had her evidence, motive, and suspect. All nice and tidy.

Nice and tidy.

Except for Patrice and her suspicion that Yvonne had planted the drugs in her luggage.

Patrice wasn't the only cast member at the airport. All of the ladies were, and so were other *LIL* crew members. It was possible Yvonne wasn't involved.

Kelly drained the last of her orange juice and set the glass in the sink, while Howard brushed by her on his way into the living room. With his tummy full, he'd settle down for a nap on the sofa for a few hours. Oh, the life of a cat.

While her little buddy dozed off, she padded into the bathroom for a shower. After toweling off, she dressed in something practical and warm, yet cute. After ten minutes of staring at her clothes, Kelly selected a pair of black leggings, a tunic-length, seed-stitch gray sweater, and a pair of tall, flat boots.

Downstairs, she unlocked the front door of the boutique and opened the cash register. Footsteps approached from the staff room. She looked up from the register drawer.

"Good morning, Kelly." Pepper looked well-rested and healthier than she had in days. Her hair was blown out, and she'd added color to her face and donned her newest obsession—flat, thigh-high suede boots.

Kelly closed the register drawer and tucked the bank bag away. "Before customers arrive, I want to run something by you. I've made a lot of changes to the business since I took over, and there's one more I'd like to make."

"Oh?" Pepper approached the sales counter with apprehension. "What do you want to change now?"

"Being open on Sundays. I think after Christmas we should close on Sundays at least until April or May. Seven days a week is a lot, and I don't expect there'll be much traffic on Sundays during the cold, wintry months. Do you?" Retail ebbed and flowed, especially businesses that relied heavily on seasonal traffic. Lucky Cove's population swelled in the warm weather months.

Pepper didn't reply right away. She seemed to consider her answer. She'd had more experience in the boutique and knew better than anyone if it was really worth being open seven days a week. "No, I suppose not." "Great." Kelly was relieved Pepper was on board. They'd all been working so hard, and being open seven days a week was a strain for her and her two part-time employees. She was also still concerned with Pepper's health. She felt responsible for Pepper's recent bout with a nasty cold because she'd relied too much on the older woman. Sundays off would be a good thing for all of them. When spring arrived, maybe she could afford to hire a teenager for a few hours a week.

Kelly might have to consider being closed one day during the weekday if business slowed down any more after the holidays.

"It'll be nice to stay snuggled inside on a Sunday." Pepper patted Kelly's hand. "I'm going to get a cup of coffee."

The boutique was quiet for the first part of the morning, allowing Kelly to submit her article to Budget Chic and Pepper to continue decorating. A handful of customers came in, and they did some serious shopping. Each one of the ladies appeared to be on a mission. Kelly assisted them while she let Pepper continue to focus on adding holiday cheer to the shop.

"Thank you, and have a great day." Kelly handed a shopping bag to a customer, who smiled and then walked away. Kelly's cell phone rang. She picked it up from the counter and swiped it on. "Hi, Patrice."

"I've decided to confront Yvonne. The more I think about it, the more certain I am she framed me."

"Whoa! Slow down. You were supposed to go to the police."

"I will. After she tells me the truth."

"That's not a good idea." Kelly moved out from behind the counter.

Patrice getting into Yvonne's face with accusations wasn't a good idea if Yvonne was indeed responsible for setting Patrice up and killing Diana.

"Where are you? Let's meet and discuss this."

"I've added more greenery to the mantels." Pepper entered the room but stopped and gave Kelly a questioning look.

"No time to meet. I'm almost at Yvonne's house. I'll call you later."

"No, no, no."

The line went silent.

"Shoot." She swiped the phone off. "Pepper, can you cover for me?" She didn't wait for a reply as she raced to the staff room. She heard Pepper call out, but there was no time to explain. She had a terrible feeling about Patrice going one-on-one with Yvonne. Passing through the staff room, she grabbed her coat and tote bag.

Chapter Twenty-Four

Kelly struggled to maintain the speed limit over to Yvonne's house. She didn't want to be stopped for speeding, nor did she want to get into an accident, but when she arrived at her destination, she pressed her foot hard on the gas pedal and sped into the driveway.

She spotted a black Mercedes and a late-model sedan. She shut off the ignition, but before stepping out of her Jeep, she left a voice mail for Gabe, a quick summary of what was going on.

Kelly made her way to the front door and pressed the bell. She waited for the housekeeper and was surprised to see Hugh open the door.

"This is an unexpected pleasure," he smiled.

"What are you doing here?" She did a quick glance over her shoulder. The Mercedes was his. She remembered seeing it pull away from her boutique when he'd stopped in the other day.

"Yvonne and I are having a working lunch." He opened the door wider. "Come on in. We have plenty."

Kelly entered the foyer. "Thanks, but I'm not hungry. I'd like to speak with Yvonne. It's important. Is Patrice here?" If the Mercedes belonged to Hugh, then the other car must be Patrice's.

"Follow me." Hugh led her to the dining room but didn't answer her question.

As spacious as the living room, the dining room had a long, formal table set for two beneath a breathtaking chandelier. On the wall opposite the entry stood a massive hutch that made her granny's look as if it belonged in a dollhouse.

"We're making do with paper plates. Yvonne is leaving for California tonight, so her staff is off."

Yvonne looked up from the file folder open next to her plate and water glass. "Another unexpected visit?"

"I apologize for showing up uninvited. Is Patrice here? She called me to tell me she was on her way over here. She's upset." Kelly took a moment and allowed herself to be awestruck by the grandness around them, from the chandelier to the drapery to the crystal glass Yvonne took a sip from.

"Why on earth would Patrice be upset?" Hugh hadn't returned to his place setting at the table. He stood beside Kelly.

"Yvonne, can I talk to you in private?" Kelly asked. Maybe the other car outside wasn't Patrice's.

"Whatever you have to say, you can say it in front of Hugh. Go on, say it." Yvonne set her glass down.

Kelly glanced at Hugh and then back at Yvonne. "Awkward" would be an understatement. But Yvonne had insisted. "Did you set up Patrice to be arrested for drug possession because she was having an affair with your husband?"

"How dare you!" The well-bred socialite's face reddened, and her nostrils flared. She leaned forward and bared her teeth at Kelly. "Get out!" She raised her hand and pointed for emphasis.

Kelly stood her ground. "Patrice believes you framed her, and somehow Diana found out about it."

"This is insane. You and Patrice!" Yvonne leaped to her feet. "Get out of my house!"

"Patrice will tell the police everything."

Yvonne dropped back into the chair. She rested an elbow on the chair's arm and held her head. "I can't believe this is happening to me." She lifted her head. Her green eyes were blank with emotion, like her voice. "The little tart was seeing my husband. There was no way I would let her destroy my marriage. I would not end up like Diana, pitiful and broke."

Kelly stepped forward. "Because of what you did, Patrice was arrested. She has a criminal conviction on her record. You ruined her life."

"What do you think she was doing to me? Besides, it was her first offense. And the amount of cocaine wasn't a lot. I made sure so she wouldn't get jail time."

"Diana found out?" Hugh had taken a step forward, which kept him beside Kelly.

Yvonne nodded. "Yes, she did. Somehow, she put it all together and rallied for Patrice. Got her a lawyer and into drug counseling to appease the judge. It wasn't long before she let me know she knew. She wanted me to get her back on the show."

"Why did you go to her house the night she was killed?" Hugh asked.

"To tell her she was wrecking her chances of getting back on the show. Diana was alive when I left. Now I think you should go, Miss Quinn. And don't think for one minute you can go to the police. I'll deny everything I've said," Yvonne said.

Kelly glanced at Hugh.

"Don't expect him to back you up, Miss Quinn." Yvonne's voice was confident.

"Fine, I'll leave, but I want to know why you tampered with Summer's brake lines." Kelly would figure out a way to get Detective Wolman to believe her when she recounted her conversation with Yvonne. She might have to ask her uncle for help since he was buddy-buddy with the police chief.

"I didn't. Do you really think I'm mechanical?" Yvonne asked.

Kelly thought about it for a moment. Yvonne wasn't mechanical, and she guessed the socialite wasn't tech savvy enough to spoof a text message either, but she could have hired someone to do those things. Kelly's gaze dropped from Yvonne to the table. Chicken noodle stir fry?

"Is that Thai?"

Yvonne scoffed. "What? Are you hungry?"

"No. Not at all. You like Thai, Yvonne?"

"Not particularly. Hugh picked up lunch on his way over."

"Our meal isn't important." Hugh ran his fingers through his hair.

Kelly's spidey senses tingled. "I think it is. You like spicy food. The night of my uncle's party, you wanted a certain appetizer. It was spicy."

"There's no law against liking spicy food. Look, Kelly, I get that you don't want to be on the show." Hugh's gaze darted from her to Yvonne and back to her. "I had no idea you'd become obsessed with the show or us."

"When I got the text from Liv to pick up dinner, I should have known it wasn't from her because she doesn't like Thai food. She's never liked spicy food. But you do. I bet you know how to spoof a text message."

"Hugh, what is she talking about?" Yvonne asked.

"Nothing I can't handle." A slow grin crept onto Hugh's face, and it made Kelly's stomach roll.

"It was you!" Kelly pointed at Hugh. "You caused Summer's accident, left the threatening note for me, and then lured me to a dark parking lot."

"Talk about an early Christmas present." He grinned before turning his attention back to Yvonne. He stalked toward Yvonne. "Who knew you had it in you to be so ruthless? I have a whole new level of appreciation for you, Yvonne. I promise, after you're gone, I'll still appreciate you."

Yvonne's eyes widened with confusion. "Gone? What are you talking about?"

"He's going to kill us." Kelly's pulse raced, and her temples throbbed. All along, it had been Hugh. Had he used the ruse of wanting her on the show because he wanted to keep tabs on her? Had he been worried she'd figure out he was the one who killed Diana and tried to kill Summer? "You killed Diana and framed Wendy."

"Hugh, tell her she's wrong. You couldn't have killed Diana. Tell her." Yvonne's voice cracked, her confidence gone, as Hugh loomed over her.

"I didn't have a choice. Like you, she knew one of my secrets, and if she told my wife, everything I've worked for would be gone. In an instant." He snapped his fingers, and Yvonne flinched. "You, of all people, should understand how it feels to have your whole life hanging by a thread."

"What did Diana have on you?" Kelly asked.

Hugh tilted his head to look at Kelly. "Diana knew about my affair with Beryl."

"Diana's stepdaughter?" Kelly shouldn't have been, but she was more than sickened by the man. He had no morals, no scruples, and no conscience.

"Diana was bleeding me dry. Then Tracy was tightening the purse strings like I'm a child, and Diana wanted more money. More! I had to stop the blackmailing."

"You killed her over an affair?" Yvonne asked.

"You know what Tracy's like!" He pulled back from Yvonne's chair. "If she found out I was sleeping with a cast member or even a stupid stepdaughter, she'd kick me out. For someone who makes her living from reality television, she has morals. Besides, the murder and Summer's accident raised the profile of the show. We're heading into the new season with a guaranteed ratings bonanza."

Yvonne shot up from her chair. "Hugh! Do you hear yourself? How pathetic are you?"

Hugh's face darkened, and his hand came up; he slapped Yvonne. Hard. Her body crumpled and landed on the floor.

Kelly screamed and turned to run out of the room, but Hugh lunged forward and grabbed her tote bag, yanking it toward him.

She yelped as the straps slid down her arm and her bag fell away. She bolted out of the dining room and ran across the marble floor toward the door. She reached out for the knob and grasped it. Her fingers twisted the knob, but before she could open the door, Hugh grabbed her from behind and spun her around fast. He seemed to have stretched to over seven feet tall, the way he towered over her now, and his angry gaze bore into her.

"Don't fight. You're gonna lose."

"We'll see about that." She lifted a knee and shoved it into Hugh's groin. He folded forward, sucking in a deep breath, and his grip loosened on her, giving her a chance to break free.

She started around him. Where she was going she didn't know. Where was the kitchen? The back door? There were patio doors in the living room. Making a split-second decision to set off running for the living room, she started off, but Hugh grabbed her by the hair and pulled her back against his chest.

His arm wrapped around her throat and pressed hard, forcing her to gasp for air. Her eyes watered, her vision blurred, and air was in short supply. Her eyelids closed, and her body went limp as everything went dark.

Chapter Twenty-Five

Kelly's eyes opened with a start. Where was she? Wherever she was, she was cold. She shivered. Her gaze darted to the right and then to the left. All she saw was snow and a white railing. Upward was a gloomy sky. Another violent shiver zapped through her body.

Where am I?

Yvonne's house. She was talking to Yvonne and Hugh . . .

Hugh!

Kelly bolted upright. There he was, dropping Yvonne onto the deck. *The deck. The railing.*

They were on the widow's walk.

"Wha . . . Wha . . ." The words were difficult to get out. Her throat and neck hurt. Then the memory seized her. Hugh had had her in a choke hold and squeezed her neck until she was unconscious. Instinctively, her hand lifted to her neck. Her fingers were frozen, almost numb. "What are you doing?"

Hugh shot her an irritated glance as he straightened up. "What do you think?"

"Let us go. It'll be easier for you." Her clothing was soaked through, and her body was chilled to its core. Goose bumps covered her arms, and her vision was blurry. Sometimes it looked like Hugh had a twin.

Hugh barked a laugh. "This is easier for me. You confronted Yvonne about Diana's murder because you'd uncovered Yvonne's secret. The two of you got into a struggle. You tried to escape but made the dumb move to run upstairs. Tsk tsk. She cornered you. Another struggle ensued, and you both fell from the widow's walk. It's all so tragic."

"No one will believe that." Kelly scrambled to her feet, but she kept slipping. She wanted to check on Yvonne. Her body looked lifeless. Was it too late to save her?

"Most of it's true, isn't it? It's a shame. You would have made such a great addition to the show with your spunk and determination. Too bad the only show you'll be appearing on is the news when they cover your death."

Kelly gulped. "It'll be your arrest the news covers." She finally found her footing and stood. She wrapped her arms around her body and hugged herself. There was no way she was going to die up there. And neither was Yvonne.

Steadying herself on her feet was harder than struggling to stand up. Her body swayed in the blast of wind whipping across the roof. Along with the wind came a pelting of sleet. The frigid pellets of ice assaulted her face, and she winced. She wanted to cry, but she wouldn't give him the satisfaction. The narrow deck and the murderer standing so close to her had fear pulsating through her veins, yet she also felt a reaffirmed determination to get off the roof alive.

"God, you would've killed in the ratings." His malicious smile had Kelly wanting to vomit as her heart squeezed with fear that she would not be able to escape. He stepped forward as a sweep of frigid wind passed over them, and Kelly cursed. Her hands were stiff from exposure, and she could barely feel them. But Hugh's hands, covered in black gloves, were all nice and warm. He extended his hands as he continued to close the space between them.

She backed up, slipping on the snow, but she stretched out her arm, and her hand reached the exterior of the house. She pressed her palm to the white clapboard for stability.

"It's a shame, really. You could've been a star." Hugh lunged and grabbed her by the shoulders. He dragged her to him and spun her around so her back was pressed against his chest.

She flailed her arms and legs and screamed.

"Nobody can hear you," he whispered. His hot breath on her ears had her skin crawling.

He was right. No one could hear her. Her eyelids started to close. They were heavy. She forced them open.

No.

She would not die there.

He dragged her along to the center of the widow's walk, and she looked down. Panic surged, and she forced herself to fight, but her limbs were cold, almost numb, and she was exhausted.

Early signs of hypothermia.

From the far recesses of her mind, she recalled an article she'd read about hypothermia that had cemented her decision never to go out cross-country skiing because you never knew what could happen.

Add to the list: never go to a house with a third-floor widow's walk.

"Too bad it has to end like this." The cockiness in his voice grated against Kelly.

Her body went rigid as it fought back against the pressure Hugh's hands asserted across her back to force her over the railing.

"Stubborn . . . girl." He wrapped his arms around her body, ready to lift her up and toss over the railing, when his body suddenly stiffened, and he yelped in pain and released his hold on her. His body crumpled to the floor.

Kelly grabbed hold of the railing and said a silent "Thank you, God" before looking over her shoulder at Hugh. His eyes were closed, and blood seeped from the back of his head.

What the heck had happened?

Sirens broke the silence, and she looked over the railing. Police cruisers sped into the driveway.

"Are you okay?"

Startled, Kelly looked behind her. Patrice. "I think so."

"I wasn't sure if this would knock him out." Patrice looked at the stone elephant statue in her hands. "It was on the dresser. There wasn't anything else to use as a weapon. It's solid and heavy."

"It looks like it worked." While Kelly had a bunch of questions for Patrice, she was worried about Yvonne. She moved as fast as she could across the area. "Please don't be dead; please, please don't be dead."

Patrice hurried to join Kelly, and she checked the unconscious woman's pulse. "She's alive. I called the police. Sounds like they're here." Patrice dashed inside to what looked like a bedroom from where Kelly was. A moment later, Patrice emerged with a throw and draped it over Yvonne's body.

With Patrice tending to Yvonne, Kelly turned her attention back to the railing. She waved. "Up here! We need medical help!"

An officer tipped his head upward. Gabe. Her heart gave a happy thump.

"He was going to kill you, wasn't he?" Patrice stood and joined Kelly at the railing.

"He was. You saved my life. Our lives." Kelly threw her arms around Patrice and pulled her in for a tight hug. She squeezed her eyes shut and said a silent prayer of thanks.

"You didn't answer my question. Are you okay?"

"Sort of. I'll be a lot better once I get out of this house."

Voices drifted from inside the house, and Kelly released her hold on Patrice.

The police and paramedics had arrived on the third floor of the house. Yvonne and Hugh were transported to the local hospital, while Kelly and Patrice gave their statements to Wolman. A paramedic had examined Kelly and wrapped her in a thermal blanket to help raise her body temperature; she'd be going to the emergency room after her interview. Because she'd been assaulted and exposed to the frigid air, Wolman kept her questioning short and told Kelly she'd follow up with her in the emergency room.

Kelly didn't want to go to the hospital, but with Gabe there, she knew it would be a losing battle to argue. However, she drew the line at being carried out on a gurney. She insisted she could walk on her own. Gabe tried to argue, but she held her ground—well, as much as she could, since she could barely feel her feet. Gabe reluctantly agreed and told her he'd be right by her side. Holding her arm, he led her out of the house to the waiting ambulance.

"I can't believe you did it again. You almost got yourself killed."

"But we now know who killed Diana. It wasn't Wendy. I can't believe Hugh is such a monster." Kelly's teeth were still chattering, and she shivered. Would she ever warm up? She tugged the blanket tighter around her.

Gabe must've noticed because he swung his arm around her and pulled her toward him. His body warmth felt good. "You shouldn't have come here and confronted Yvonne and Hugh."

"Is Yvonne going to be okay? When I saw her, I really thought she was dead."

"She's not dead, but I don't know the extent of her injuries."

They reached the ambulance, and a waiting paramedic reached out his hand for Kelly. She didn't have much energy to resist any longer. Gabe helped steady her, and she climbed up. She lay down on the gurney, where she got strapped in.

"I'll call my mom and Caroline." Gabe closed the ambulance doors.

"Oh, boy. Do you think you could take me to a hospital far, far away?" Kelly asked the paramedic.

Chapter Twenty-Six

"Canceled?" Kelly pulled her legs closer to her body and wrapped her arms around them. Liv had settled her on the sofa after she emerged from a hot shower and slipped on her festive pj's and fuzzy socks. Liv had been mothering her since they arrived home from the hospital earlier in the day. She'd been admitted for observation overnight because of her head injury and exposure to the cold. Even after a warm shower and being dressed in flannel, she was still chilled.

"According to the network's website, *Long Island Ladies* won't see another season. They've wasted no time distancing themselves from the train wreck." Liv handed Kelly a large mug of hot tea.

"How's Summer taking it?" Kelly whispered.

Liv rolled her eyes and then looked over her shoulder as Summer entered the living room with a mug of tea. She was dressed in black leather leggings and an oatmeal-colored cashmere tunic, and her blond tresses were casually curled and bouncy. However, she looked far from happy.

"It's a hasty decision. I'm sure the network will realize their error and bring the show back for another season." Summer dropped onto the armchair and crossed her legs. Beside the chair, she set her exquisite Fendi Peekaboo purse.

Kelly couldn't help thinking it would make an awesome get-well gift.

"They have to. I was meant to be on the show."

"Summer, they were all horrible people. Liars, cheats, and murderers." Kelly took a drink of her tea.

Before Kelly was discharged from the hospital, Wolman had told her that Hugh was still hospitalized but under arrest for murder and three murder attempts. He was looking at a lot of jail time, which he so rightly deserved.

Summer waved her hand. "I was so close."

Kelly looked to Liv for help, but none was forthcoming from her friend.

"I'll get the cookies."

"You baked? When?" Kelly perked up. She could use a cookie or two or three.

"Last night. Frankie gave me the recipe for your granny's gingersnaps. I thought you could use a treat after everything you've been through." Liv dashed out of the room and returned with a plate piled high with perfectly round cookies glistening with sugar. She held the plate in front of Kelly.

Kelly's nose wriggled at the fragrance of ginger and cinnamon. She reached for a cookie. "They look just like Granny's." She took a bite. "Hmmm . . . So good. They taste just like Granny's." She finished the cookie. "Thank you."

"You're welcome. When you're feeling up to it, I'll give you a baking lesson." Liv took the plate over to Summer, and to Kelly's surprise, Summer reached for a cookie and ate it.

Kelly and Liv shared a shocked look, and when Liv went to set the plate on the coffee table, Summer reached for another cookie. Kelly was now officially worried about her aunt.

"Summer, you have so much already. Do you think you would have had time for the show?" For some unknown reason, Kelly felt obligated to make Summer feel better. "Juniper needs you, and your Pilates studio is growing. Didn't you add a couple of classes during the week?"

Summer nodded as she chewed. "I did. I'm also adding barre classes."

"You don't need a silly show to expand your business. You just need to continue doing what you're doing. Right, Kell?" Liv grabbed a cookie and plopped onto the sofa next to Kelly.

Summer tilted her head sideways and stared at both women. "You're right. I can open new studios without appearing on a reality show. The show probably would have been a time drain, anyway. You're right. I can do it on my own." Her lips stretched into a smile, but her eyes widened in horror at the cookie in her hand. She reached forward and dropped it onto the plate as though it was a knock-off Louis Vuitton.

Kelly let out a relieved breath. The Summer she knew and had gotten used to tolerating was back.

"Besides, Ralphie needs a little extra attention these days." Summer leaned back. "Tracy isn't moving her production company out here to the island. He got the call yesterday morning before you almost got yourself killed. She's keeping the business in the city."

"There'll be another property for him to develop." Kelly took another drink of her tea. It was hard for her to muster up sympathy for her uncle. Clearly, Summer saw a whole other side of him that Kelly hadn't. Which was a good thing because he'd be dealing with another blow in a matter of days, and he'd need some consoling.

Before Kelly was discharged, Caroline had visited the hospital for two things. She continued to lecture Kelly about putting herself in danger yet again. Then she told Kelly their granny and Marvin Childers were never legally married. Caroline had been right when she suggested the marriage hadn't been officially filed. This meant he and his weasel of a grandson had no claim on the business or the building. They belonged to Kelly. Talk about a weight being lifted off her shoulders.

While the news about her inheritance was a welcome relief and she was thrilled to be alive, she was worried about Yvonne. She was in a coma. Kelly had watched Yvonne take the hard blow from Hugh that sent her body crumpling to the floor. The blow kept flashing in Kelly's head like a motel's neon sign.

"Hey, you okay?" Liv patted Kelly on the knee. "You look kinda far away."

"I'm good." Kelly twisted around and set her mug on the end table just in time for Howard to stroll into the living room, jump on the sofa, and curl up next to Kelly. Her heart welled up with love, and she stroked the cat's head.

"You are good," Liv said.

"I have to get going. Juniper should be getting up from her nap." Summer lifted her purse and stood.

"Give her a kiss for me," Kelly said.

Summer nodded. "I will. Kelly, I'm glad you weren't seriously hurt yesterday."

Kelly was once again shocked by Summer. Maybe there was hope for a true friendship between them.

"However, I wish you'd find another hobby than tracking down killers. It's not an appropriate thing to be doing. Our family does have a reputation to maintain." She spun around and sashayed to the door in her stiletto-heeled ankle boots. She took her faux fur leopard coat off of the coatrack and shrugged it on. She gave a final wave and left.

When the door clicked shut, Kelly and Liv looked at each other and burst into laughter.

"I think my relationship with Summer is improving." Kelly reached for another cookie. She wanted to be good, but after what she'd been through, a couple of cookies wouldn't be so bad. Besides, her leggings all had elastic waistbands.

"You should get credit for not getting arrested this time around," Liv said between laughs.

"Right?"

"Have you heard from Mark?"

Kelly nodded and smiled. "He called earlier."

"And?"

Kelly giggled.

"Come on, spill."

"He asked me to be his New Year's Eve date."

Liv squealed. "I'm so happy for you!"

"It's only a date." However, since he'd asked her, she'd been thinking about what she'd wear. Before she emerged from her bedroom, she'd checked out MineNowYours.com and found a stunning velvet-wrap minidress in a deep purple color. Paired with high-heeled ankle boots and a faux fur vest, it would be perfect for the evening. The more she thought about it, the more she had to order the dress.

"What about Christmas?"

"His parents have a house upstate, and the whole family gets together for the holiday." She'd hoped to see him at least on Christmas Eve, but he'd be gone by then. Maybe it was for the best to take things slow, especially since his sister wasn't fond of their fledgling relationship.

Liv glanced at her watch. "I should go too. I told Pepper I'd help in the boutique this afternoon so Breena can finish up the prep for the Holiday Edit."

"The Edit!" Kelly made a move to get up and jostled Howard, who gave her a disapproving look, but Liv pushed her back. "I have to go downstairs and help."

"No, you don't." Liv propped her hands on her hips. "We have it all under control."

"But you have to work at the bakery. It's the busiest time of the year."

"I've got it all covered. I worked this morning and made a gazillion sugar cookies. Now I'll work in the boutique until closing. It's not a big deal. And Breena is doing a fabulous job. You just rest." Liv stood. "If you need anything, text me, but do not, under any circumstances, come downstairs. Your job is to make a full recovery so you can be at the Edit. Got it?"

Kelly didn't like being fussed over or told what to do, but the serious look on her best friend's face made it clear she wasn't to challenge the orders. Maybe taking another day to rest was a good idea. Her head still throbbed, and her neck was sore where Hugh had grabbed her. A flash of gasping for air flitted in her mind's eye, and she shook the image away. "Got it." Kelly saluted, and Liv chuckled.

Before leaving, Liv refilled Kelly's mug and placed the laptop on the coffee table, along with the remote control for the television, before she left to go down to the boutique. Kelly shifted to get comfortable, keeping Howard by her side.

She opened her laptop and checked her e-mails. She found one from the editor of Budget Chic with a new assignment offer. Grateful for the distraction, Kelly immediately replied and got to work on her new article—Ten Budget-Friendly Looks for New Year's Eve.

* * * *

Kelly adjusted the pair of black and nude spectator pumps on the display cube set in the center of the accessories department, aka the ugly addition. Now the square footage was less unattractive thanks to a discounted visual merchandising website. She had acquired several displays for the space, including a small collection of display cubes at various heights and widths that gave the space visual *oomph* when customers walked through the doorway.

She'd added a mixed-media Coach shoulder bag to replace a pair of black pumps she'd sold earlier. She set the leather and coated-canvas bag on the cube and draped the leather chain strap over the top of the bag before moving to the pair of nutmeg-colored ankle boots. She glanced at her watch. There were a mere few minutes before she closed for the holiday.

A week had passed since the incident at Yvonne's house. Referring to it as an incident sounded better than saying "her attempted murder." Hugh was being held without bail, Yvonne had woken from her coma but was still in critical condition, and Patrice was clearing her name. A few days ago, Wendy stopped by the boutique to thank Kelly, and she said that after the New Year, she'd keep her promise of getting her friends to consign at the boutique. Things had turned out well for everyone except for Diana. Then again, if she hadn't blackmailed people, maybe she'd be alive.

Diana's story was another reminder of how the choices a person made could impact her life.

"Kelly, are you done back there?" Pepper's voice interrupted Kelly's thoughts. She gave one final look at the display before turning and rushing through the short hallway that connected the addition to the main rooms of the boutique.

Pepper was at the sales counter closing the register, and Breena was vacuuming.

"It's snowing." Kelly stopped and looked out the front window. The weather channel had forecasted a white Christmas Eve, and Mother Nature was delivering.

"Tori will be thrilled. She can make snow angels on Christmas morning." Breena dragged the vacuum into the main sales area. "I've finished up with the vacuuming, and I wiped down the mirrors in the changing room. I'm going to put this away and head out. Okay?"

"Absolutely." Kelly hugged Breena. "Thank you for everything you've done. The Edit was a tremendous success." A few days ago, the boutique had closed early, and seventeen women came for the private shopping experience. Kelly had had no idea how the event would go; after all, she owned a consignment shop, not a specialty boutique on Madison Avenue. But she was pleasantly surprised.

Each woman made a purchase and enjoyed the feeling of being special with the exclusivity, the appetizers, and a cocktail. The sales Kelly made put a dent in the financial hole she was trying to scrape out of. She'd have to brainstorm more ideas with Breena, come the new year.

Breena's head bobbed up and down. "It sure was."

"Don't forget the bag for Tori when you leave." Kelly let go of Breena. She'd done a little shopping for the sweet little girl and went a tad overboard, but everything was so cute, and she couldn't resist.

"You're spoiling her. And you too." Breena looked at Pepper.

"She's too adorable not to spoil." Pepper came out from behind the counter and hugged Breena. "Merry Christmas. Don't forget those muffins I baked."

"I won't." Breena started to walk back to the staff room with the vacuum but stopped and looked over her shoulder. "You two are the best presents I've received since having Tori. Thank you." Before they all started crying, Breena hurried away.

"That kid!" Pepper wiped a tear and then returned to the cash register. "The deposit is almost done."

The bell of the front door jingled, and Kelly and Pepper looked toward the entrance.

Marvin Childers entered, wearing a dark wool coat and a fedora and carrying a bouquet of white roses.

"Mr. Childers, what brings you by?" Kelly stepped away from Pepper and approached the dapper-looking gentleman.

"Merry Christmas, Kelly." He smiled and then looked toward Pepper. "Hello."

"Oh, Mr. Childers, this is Pepper Donovan. Pepper, this is Marvin Childers, a friend of Granny's."

Pepper lifted her chin and gave him a once-over before smiling and welcoming him to the boutique.

"I realize you're closing for the holiday, but I wanted to come by and give you these." He handed the bouquet to Kelly. "Your grandmother's favorite flowers were daisies, but she loved white roses too."

Kelly inhaled the fragrant scent of the flowers. "Thank you. You shouldn't have, but they are beautiful."

"It's the least I could do, considering what my grandson did. Be certain, I've had a talk with him."

"Grandson? What happened?" Pepper had come up behind Kelly.

Kelly looked over her shoulder. "It's a long story. I'll fill you in tonight over dinner."

"I'll make sure of it. It was nice to meet you, Mr. Childers. Kelly, I'm going to head home to prepare dinner. I'll see you later. Don't be late." Pepper returned to the sales counter and grabbed the cash bag before walking out of the sales area.

Marvin cleared his throat, getting Kelly's attention back.

"Even if I stood to inherit Martha's estate, I would have never taken this shop away from you. It was her intention to make sure it was yours. Martha would be very proud of you."

Tears welled up in Kelly's eyes. The past few weeks had been a roller coaster. Nothing—not even facing a murderer—compared to the fear she felt when she thought she could lose her granny's legacy.

"Thank you for saying that. It means a lot to me. Would you like to join me for dinner this evening? I'm going to Pepper's house, and she always has so much food. She'd be happy if you joined us."

Marvin patted Kelly's hand. "Thank you for the invitation, but I'm on my way to Barlow's place for dinner. Have a wonderful Christmas, dear." He walked to the door. "You know, it would be nice for us to have tea every now and again."

"Yes, it would."

He nodded and walked out of the boutique.

She followed him and locked the door. She turned over the OPEN sign to CLOSED and turned around to take a full, sweeping glance of the boutique. It was now officially her first Christmas as a shop owner.

* * * *

Kelly woke Christmas morning and, for the first time since Thanksgiving, felt rested and refreshed. She climbed out of bed and slipped on her cashmere robe, an indulgent treat from her time at Bishop's, and stepped into her Uggs slippers. She scooped Howard up and carried him to the three-foot tree she'd purchased after her near-death experience. It wasn't as big as the tree her granny used to decorate, but it was a start. Standing at the tree, she scratched Howard's sleepy head.

"Merry Christmas, little guy."

Beside the tabletop tree was Ariel's gift. They'd exchanged presents before Kelly went to Pepper's house for dinner. Ariel had given her a pressure cooker for Christmas.

"Guess since I'm alive and home for good, I should learn to cook." She eyed the box apprehensively. "What can go wrong?"

Printed in the United States
by Baker & Taylor Publisher Services